"Coach Hewitt!" Brock hollered, and the head coach stopped and looked back.

Brock was fifty yards from the coach. He took a step and rifled the football. It arced up into the air, spinning in a tight and perfect spiral. Coach Hewitt's hands shot up in front of his face and he caught the ball. Brock smiled to himself, turned, and walked toward his father without saying anything else.

FIRST TEAM

TIM GREEN

HARPER

An Imprint of HarperCollinsPublishers

First Team

Copyright © 2014 by Tim Green

All rights reserved. Printed in the United States of America.

No part of this book may be used or reproduced in any manner whatsoever without written permission except in the case of brief quotations embodied in critical articles and reviews. For information address HarperCollins Children's Books, a division of HarperCollins Publishers, 195 Broadway, New York, NY 10007.

www.harpercollinschildrens.com

Green, Tim, date.

    First team : a New kid novel / by Tim Green. — First edition.

        pages   cm

    Summary: "The companion novel to *New Kid*, where Brock is in another new town after being on the run with his dad again, and this time, he joins the football team"—Provided by publisher.

    ISBN 978-0-06-220876-7 (pbk.)

    [1. Moving, Household—Fiction.   2. Fathers and sons—Fiction.   3. Interpersonal relations—Fiction.   4. Football—Fiction.   5. Schools—Fiction.]   I. Title.

PZ7.G826357Fir   2014   2014001886

[Fic]—dc23   CIP

                                                    AC

Typography by Megan Stitt

15 16 17 18 19 OPM 10 9 8 7 6 5 4 3 2 1

❖

First paperback edition, 2015

*For Ron Osinski, my first writing teacher, football coach,
life mentor, and the best friend anyone could ever ask for!*

Brock was used to running. It's just what he and his dad did.

He could hear the thump of his own pounding heart. He looked out the window. The darkness outside their racing car was complete. Clouds covered the moon and a light drizzle rushed by in a mist. Up ahead, the headlights from another vehicle pulled out onto the road, blocking their path. Brock twisted around fast enough to make himself dizzy and saw headlights from the car chasing them. It sped at them like a burning rocket.

"Dad!" Brock cried as his father spun the wheel. Tires shrieked. The car slid sideways off the road. Everything scrambled. Brock's head boomed against the passenger window. He saw a flash of light, and the car shuddered to a stop.

"You okay?" Brock's father laid a strong hand on his shoulder, clenching it and turning Brock to look at his face.

Brock nodded and bit the inside of his lip, forcing back tears.

Brock's father flung open his door. "Let's go!"

He dragged Brock by the arm out into the wet night.

Brock's batting glove got left behind, but his baseball cleats helped him keep his footing as they sprinted across an open field toward a shadowy wall of trees. They were halfway to the woods when the vehicle that had been chasing them reached their car, pulled off the road, and shone its headlights on them. Shadows leaped from their feet, stretching like circus stilt walkers toward the woods. Brock heard a zip like an angry insect and then the nearly instant explosion of gunfire.

"Get down!" Brock's father screamed as he lowered his own head and Brock's by forcing his arm toward the dirt.

Brock stumbled and fell, but his father didn't slow down. Brock had to scramble to get his feet underneath him as his father dragged him toward the safety of the woods. Another bullet zipped by, and another gunshot echoed off the low hills like a fading song. When they hit the tree line, Brock's dad hauled him another twenty feet before stopping and crouching before him.

"Are you okay?"

Brock couldn't even answer, but he nodded his head and grunted.

"Come on." His father darted forward again, not running, but slipping through the trees slick as their own shadows, which were now lost in the inky web of branches. They stopped suddenly again.

"Shh." His father tilted his head like a dog hearing a silent whistle. From the direction of the shots came the faint barking of men's voices. Brock's dad cupped a hand around his phone to keep the light from bleeding into the woods and brought up a map application. He got his bearings, clicked off the phone, and whispered again.

"Let's go. This way."

Brock followed, straining his ears for a sound of the men following them. Above, the drizzling sky was only a bit brighter than the tar-colored twist of branches, a true midnight blue. They trudged for what felt like fifteen minutes through the trees before they came to an abrupt end of the woods. Before them, even in the darkness, Brock could see the very long straight opening with what looked like an abnormally wide road.

"What is that?" Brock whispered. "Where are we going?"

His father scanned up and down the long open space.

"It's a runway," he replied, keeping his voice low. "An airport. We have to get out of here."

"Can't we hide?" Brock looked back into the total night of the woods.

His father shook his head, still studying the runway. "They may have night vision. Heat detectors."

"Dad, who are *they*?"

"I think Russians."

"Russians?"

"Organized crime. But maybe the agency. It doesn't matter. Come on."

"Dad, what are you—" Brock's father dashed out of the woods, crossing the runway, then hugging the opposite tree line as they moved back in the direction of their abandoned car, which didn't make sense to Brock. He guessed the agency his father was talking about was the National Security Agency. He had learned only that night that both his mom and dad had worked for the government many years ago, before his mother had been killed.

The pale shape of a large metal building rose up before them. The curve of the rounded roof let Brock know it was an airplane hangar. His father circled the building until they came to a smaller building, with an office and a side door. Brock's dad picked up a rock and smashed the window. The crash of glass startled Brock, but the hissing rain seemed to swallow the sound. His father reached through the hole and opened the door from the inside so they could enter. They hurried through the office and into the enormous hangar. His father used the flashlight on his phone to locate a workbench, where he rattled through a toolbox before grabbing Brock's arm again.

"Come on."

Back outside they went. Brock had barely noticed the two planes crouching beside the hangar just beyond a fuel tank that looked like a huge, round vitamin pill. They stopped at the door of the bigger plane. Brock's dad let go of his arm. He pulled the triangular blocks out from under the landing wheels, then used the claw of the hammer he had to break open the airplane's door. Brock's dad climbed up inside, then turned and held out a hand for Brock. He took it and his father hauled him up and in.

"Hold this so I can see." His dad handed him the phone and lay down on the floor so he could look up under the instrument panel. "Move it down here."

Brock held the light down by his father's head, shining it underneath the panel. His father removed a pair of wire cutters from his pocket and snipped away, grunting as he worked. Brock jumped when the engine rumbled to life. His father wormed his way out from under the panel and into the pilot's seat.

"Dad, you know how to fly?"

Brock realized it was a silly question. His father didn't even look up from the control panel or the switches and levers he was flipping and adjusting. The engine's growl became a whine and they started to move. Brock's dad never slowed. They rolled right out onto the runway, gaining speed. They were halfway down the runway when a vehicle pulled onto the far end. The high beams of its headlights flicked up and down as it sped directly toward them.

"Dad!" Brock yelled. It was as if his father didn't see the oncoming car. They were headed straight for each other in an insane game of chicken.

The plane's engine screamed.

His father's face was grim as he gripped the controls with white fingers. His growl became an angry roar as they rocketed forward, right into the blinding headlights.

Brock shut his eyes and braced himself for the crash.

His stomach dropped to the seat of his pants. He was floating.

They were floating.

The plane skimmed just over the top of the speeding car and continued to rise. His father's angry roar morphed into a crazy belly laugh. Brock laughed too.

He and his father turned toward each other, their faces red, and lips peeled back from their teeth with relief and joy.

Brock turned away to look back toward the ground. The dark strip of the runway twinkled with little orange lights like fireflies.

"Wow. What is that?" Brock pointed down.

"What is what?" His father looked over Brock's shoulder out the window. "They're shooting!"

His father banked the plane, sharp. Brock's seat belt kept him from flying across his father's lap. They swerved back the other way, and he banged against the glass window just as he'd done in the car when they'd spun off the road.

"Dad!"

The plane lurched sideways and dipped. Brock screamed as the plane rattled and shook. His father fought with the controls.

BANG!

There was a flash outside Brock's window. Flames from the right-wing engine licked the night air.

"Dad! It's burning!" Brock shouted.

"Ahhh!" His father's arms shuddered, veins popping, muscles tightly cramped from the battle.

They were losing altitude. Beyond the airstrip, Brock saw the lake, dark as death, moving up at them fast. Suddenly, he felt calm. The roar of the engine and his father were like a soft ocean surf against the sand. He saw his mom from when he was just a toddler and she held out a square red block for him to hold. He saw Coach Hudgens and Bella. She smiled at him, so peacefully. Brock felt calm and relaxed and ready. He knew from stories he'd heard that this was what it was like when you were about to die.

The plane banked again. Brock thought for certain the wingtip would catch the water and send them tumbling end over end until the fuel tank exploded and they ended up as fish food on the bottom of the lake.

But it didn't catch. The wings leveled. The plane sputtered and groaned, but they were no longer leaning and they were beginning—very slowly—to climb. It took them several miles of flying just above the lake to gain enough height to clear the trees onshore. Up and up they went, until finally the earth below disappeared in the misty rain.

"We did it?" Brock was afraid of the answer. His arms were locked against the dash.

"Looks that way. They shot out the right engine, but we can fly on the left one alone." His dad shook his head. "Stupid.

I gave them an easy target. Didn't even think about the lights on the plane."

"We can fly with one engine?"

"For now anyway."

"Where are we going? How can you see?"

"I can't." His father pointed to the dials glowing in front of him. "The instruments tell me a lot. I'm heading south. Getting away from this cold front."

"I didn't even know you knew how to fly." There was so much Brock didn't know about his father, and, true to form, his father simply nodded his head and clamped his lips shut tight. A sob escaped Brock's throat. He tried to swallow it back as best he could. His whole body began to shiver. His father reached over and gripped his shoulder.

"Are you okay?"

"Dad, they tried to kill us." Brock looked over at his dad through a kaleidoscope of tears.

"It's okay." His father gently shook his shoulder. "Not you, just me."

"Why?"

"Let me focus on getting away from here. We can talk more later."

Brock nodded and leaned against the small window beside him. He was suddenly exhausted, but that was no surprise. His day began in Princeton, New Jersey, at a baseball tournament, where he'd pitched a stellar game and knocked in the winning home run before his father whisked him away—yet again—to retrieve some things from their home and get away fast. The only real surprise had been his father's offer to let him stay. Brock didn't try and hide the fact that he was tired of running, moving all the time, changing names, always being the new kid. His emotions blended with the vibration of the plane and were like a powerful drug, and he dropped off to sleep before he could think any more.

Brock walked through the doorway of an empty room. He looked behind him, and when he turned back, there was his mother. She didn't speak, but her look told him she'd been waiting. And next to her, there was Coach Hudgens's wife offering them cookies. Brock told her no thank you. The shadowy shapes of his poorly chosen friend, Nagel, and Nagel's older brother rushed in, dumping the cookies to the floor with wild hoots of anger. Nagel and his brother turned and began bumping into Brock, banging him around, knocking him backward into the wall. Brock wondered where his father was, and he took a deep breath to cry out for help, but Nagel stuffed a fist in his mouth, choking him, while the older brother began to shake him, hard.

"Ahhh!" Brock's scream woke him up. He was shaking, and after a moment realized that the whole plane was shaking. "Dad!"

His father fought with the controls, head and limbs bouncing like a bobble-head toy. "We're losing the left engine! I'm taking us down! Buckle up tight!"

The plane trembled and bucked and Brock tried to see the ground below. The low clouds were gone. He could see the horizon lit by the stars and a slice of moon. An endless blanket of trees covered the rounded mountains below. Brock opened his mouth to ask what his father was doing, but he stopped when he saw a naked strip of land running up the side of a mountain ahead. They veered toward it, a perfect swatch of earth that cut through woods high and low. Brock could only think of a power line or a pipeline.

"Can we land?" His voice broke into a squeak.

"Hang on!" The earth came up at them fast, faster than the water, more certain, more solid.

The plane tilted this way and that, and Brock knew this time they *would* crash. When they hit, they bounced, then hit something that spun them toward the trees. The dark trunks and branches swallowed them whole. They crashed through, wood snapping, metal groaning and roaring, glass shattering.

They struck something solid and Brock thought the muscles would be torn from his bones. His head smashed into something hard. He saw a brilliant flash of orange light, then lost all consciousness.

The smell of flowers, thick and sweet like syrup, wafted in the air.

Brock's eyes fluttered open. The scent filled his nose.

A vase of white flowers spotted with crimson dots bloomed from the table beside his bed. The man looking down on him wore a mask that covered his nose and cheeks, like a band of toilet paper wrapped around the middle of his face. A fresh purple scar ran along the underside of his chin. The skin around it was dark with old bruising.

The eyes, however, belonged to Brock's father.

Brock sensed the bandages on his own face and the stuffiness in his nose. He tried to sit up, but his arms were strapped down to his sides. "I . . ."

"Shh." His father held a finger to his mouth. It could have been pointing to the bandage across his face, Brock wasn't sure. "Brandon. It's okay."

Brock's mind turned the name over the way he would a smooth pebble from a creek bed. He caressed it, then clutched it tight and put it into the pocket of his mind, making it his. He understood the game. There were many names before this one, and there would likely be many more to come.

He sighed.

He liked that Brandon sounded similar to Brock, but wondered if that would make it harder or easier for him when some new classmate or teacher called him by name.

"Where are we?" His throat was dry and his voice croaked.

"Kane, Pennsylvania. The hospital. You've been out for three weeks, Brandon."

"Are *you* okay?" Brock asked.

His father ran his fingers across the bandages. As he opened his mouth to speak, the door behind him opened and a young doctor with a very black mustache came in, rubbing his hands together.

"He wakes." The doctor removed a light from the pocket of his white coat and started flickering it into Brock's eyes. The doctor took Brock's pulse, then hit his knees and elbows with a rubber hammer. After that, the doctor tickled and pricked Brock's hands and feet to make sure everything was working. "Good. Very good."

"How long before he can go home?" Brock's dad asked.

The doctor's dark caterpillar eyebrows knitted together and he turned to Brock's dad. "I still want three more days at a minimum. I've said that all along. He's been through a lot."

"As a precaution . . . ," Brock's dad said.

"Yes."

"But we're beyond the worst?"

"We are." The doctor sat on the edge of Brock's bed and gently unwrapped the bandages on his face. The doctor scowled and tilted his head, studying Brock's nose. "Okay. Good. I'm going to leave these off. I think you'll be more comfortable, and you don't have to go anywhere anyway, so . . ."

The fresh cool air felt good on Brock's cheeks, even though his skin seemed tight and he just couldn't get enough air through his nose. Brock tried to move, but the straps held him down.

"Here, we can get rid of these." The doctor undid the thick Velcro straps. "But I don't want you touching your face."

"What's wrong with it?" Brock croaked.

"Drink?" The doctor took a cup with a straw from beside the flowers and brought it close to his face.

Brock nodded and sucked in some cranberry juice.

"Compared to when you came in, you look super. Your face was . . . a mess. Broken nose. Both cheekbones. Some nasty gashes, but the trauma to your brain was what had us worried. Whenever we get automobile accidents that's our biggest concern."

"But we weren't—"

"Doctor!" Brock's dad burst out. "Let's let him rest. Shouldn't we?"

The startled doctor studied Brock's dad, then shrugged. "Well, he checks out fine. As I said, let's watch him for three days and then back to . . . where? Palm Beach, right?"

"West Palm," Brock's dad said.

"Wish I could get my wife to move south. It's nice now, but the winters here just kill me." The doctor patted Brock's dad on the shoulder and left the room.

"Automobile?" Brock asked.

"Shh."

"But how could they not know?" Brock kept his voice to a whisper.

His father sat on the edge of his bed and leaned close. "We went down in the Allegheny National Forest. I carried you out. It was a long ways. I told them our car went off the road, but I didn't remember where. I played dumb, but you've really been out. You remember?"

"The plane?" Brock's heart clenched with renewed fear. "Yeah, and those people. They shot at us."

"We're fine now." His dad squeezed Brock's shoulder. "I've got half a dozen IDs in my bag. We're Richard and Brandon Scroggins until we get out of here."

"Then who are we?" Brock asked.

His father shrugged. "You're not going to be able to pick like last time. We'll have to choose from what I've already got. Things are different this time."

"Why?" Brock asked.

"Because of this." His dad raised his chin and pointed to a long, thin half-circle scar, then the bandages around his nose. "And this. You too. Both of us. Sometimes life gives you a chance you never even thought of."

"What are you talking about, Dad?"

"Neither of us looks the same. Your face, mine, they're *different*, not entirely, but enough to beat the scanners."

"Scanners?"

"Every time you go through a public place, an airport or a government building, heck, sometimes just down the street. There are video cameras that feed into super computers. The government likes to know where people are. Every face gets scanned. Every person has a unique set of facial points with different ratios: distance between eyes, width of mouth, length of nose, all that kind of thing. But you can beat that now."

"Because of the swelling?"

His dad shook his head. He got up, went over to the dresser, and returned with a hand mirror. "More than swelling. Look."

Brock stared into the mirror and tried not to scream.

Brock hated tears.

His father was like an ice sculpture. Tears weren't part of his deal. He was cold and hard, even though Brock knew his father loved him all the same.

So, Brock struggled to keep the tears from streaming down his cheeks. He sniffled and bucked up, raising his chin.

"Okay." Brock nodded his head and the person in the mirror nodded back.

He wanted to look away, but he couldn't. It wasn't the fading black circles under his eyes, or even the purple gash running from the outside corner of one eye down to his upper lip. It was his *nose*. It had been narrow before, but not like this crease of paper, and . . . the end of it was entirely different. His old nose had turned up at the end like a jump you'd build out of snow for sledding. This, this was like a chip of wood, narrow and pointy and small. Maybe "elfin" was the word, and it didn't fit his face. Maybe alien was a better description. It wasn't *him*.

"You'll get used to it. It's what all the Hollywood people do. Look." Brock's father undid his own bandage. His nose was much the same, also narrow and pointed at the end. He also realized now that something was different about his father's chin. It was . . . bigger, wider. "They had to work on us both anyway. A tree limb smashed right through the windshield. I told the surgeon to do a little extra on me. They love that, those plastic surgeons."

Brock shook his head. It was still his dad, but a bizarre version.

He shrugged and wiggled his legs. "Why do they have these straps on me?"

"They didn't want you coming to and thrashing around," his dad said. "He forgot your legs. Here, let me get you loose."

Brock's dad tore free the Velcro band that had been holding down Brock's legs. Brock let his dad swing his legs over the side of the bed. His legs trembled and his feet felt like blocks of concrete as he stepped onto the cold floor. His dad put an arm around him and walked him around the room before helping him back into the hospital bed.

His father leaned close and spoke low. "I have some things to take care of, but I'll be back and then we'll go. I wanted to make sure you could walk a little first."

"But didn't the doctor say three days?" Brock gently ran a finger down along the thin ridgeline of scar tissue on his face, then touched his new nose.

His father shook his head. "The plane is buried in the

woods, so I don't think they can find it, even with their satellites, but we've been around here longer than I like. With these faces . . . I want us to be someplace new, where no one knows that we changed how we look."

Brock took a deep breath and let it out in a huff.

"Don't look so glum," his dad said.

"I'm not." Brock did his best to sound truthful.

"You haven't heard the best part yet."

"What's the best part?" Brock tried to sound eager.

"You know how you say you always hate being the new kid?" His father's eyes seemed to sparkle back at him.

Brock hesitated while he tried to figure out where this was going. "Yeah."

"So, the next place we go to . . . with these new faces? We stay."

"But I thought we couldn't," Brock said.

"We couldn't before, because they were after me and watching. I kept hoping I'd find a safe way to cash out of all the bank accounts I set up over the years. If I could get to them without someone catching me, we'd live like kings for the rest of our lives."

"So you figured out how?" Brock studied his father's face.

"No." His father smiled warmly at him. "Forget the money. When I was walking out of those woods and I didn't know if you were alive or dead, I realized we don't need that money. I only need you, and I don't need to be running off all the time. I'm done with all that."

"So what will you do?"

His dad shrugged. "No idea. Nothing very exciting I'd

guess, but I'll be around for your games and parent-teacher conferences and all that other stuff I never did."

"We won't have to move away?" Joy bubbled inside Brock.

"Not unless you want to," his dad said.

"I don't. I don't want to move again. Ever," Brock said. "But . . . where are we going? Where will we live?"

"Calhoun, Ohio."

"Calhoun?" Brock wrinkled his brow. "What's it near?"

His father smiled. "It's not near anything. Oh, I guess if you had to say, maybe Charleston."

"Ohio?"

"No, West Virginia. Closest place in Ohio is probably Columbus. I'm not totally sure. It's pretty remote. That's why we're going there."

"Do they have a baseball team?"

"Everyone has baseball." His dad stood. "You get some rest. I'll be back in a while and then we'll go."

Brock's dad waved from the door, then closed it behind him. A nurse came in a few minutes later and asked him what he'd like for dinner. He told her he'd have the chicken and some mashed potatoes with gravy.

"Any vegetables?" she asked.

"Nah."

"I'll bring you some green beans." She made a note, then smiled, nodded, and left him alone.

Brock wondered why adults would sometimes do that, ask you something, then ignore your answer completely. Why ask? He shook his head and laid it back deep into the pillow to think about Calhoun, Ohio. It sounded like a good place.

Brock closed his eyes and when he woke, he could see that it was already dark outside. His dinner sat untouched on a tray beside his bed. His father stood above him wearing dark-blue jeans and a black sweater.

"Shh."

Brock nodded and let his father help him up out of the bed to get dressed. Together, they slipped out of the hospital and into his father's waiting car. Brock tried to move the seat back, but it was stuck.

"Sorry," his father said. "It's a piece of junk, but I had to pay cash and we're going to dump it soon anyway."

They started to drive, but the signs said Route 66 South.

"I thought we were going to Ohio?" Brock said. "That's west."

"We are." His father kept his eyes on the road and his face looked even more strange with its new nose and wider chin in the shadowy light of the passing streetlamps. "I have one last thing I have to do . . . before I leave my old life for good."

"What?"

"A favor. We have to go to Washington, DC."

"A favor for who?" Brock asked.

22

His father glanced over at him, his face heavy with sadness. "Your mother."

"I don't understand." Brock didn't have to remind his father that she was dead.

His father took a deep breath. "I'll try to explain."

7

Their car tires thumped over the gaps in the road with a steady rhythm that filled the silence while Brock waited for the answer.

He had only the ghost of a memory of his mother. Sometimes she appeared to him in his dreams, but he suspected that vision came directly from the old photo his father kept in a private wooden box Brock had discovered years ago. In that same box was a brittle scrap of newspaper with an article about a woman, brutally murdered and left floating in the East River in New York City. Brock didn't remember any of that. He'd been just two years old.

"Your mother and I . . ." His father cleared his throat and glanced out his side window toward a hillside cloaked in dark silent trees before refocusing on the road. "We promised each other that if anything ever happened to the other, and we left the life of . . . well, whatever you call what we were doing."

"Spies?" Brock suggested.

"The intelligence community." His father glanced over at him. "If we left it for good, we have documents that we agreed to release to the *Washington Post*. Kind of a doomsday device."

"Doomsday?" Brock thought that was like an atomic bomb.

"It will reveal secret information and wreak havoc on certain people and certain agencies. Not something you'd want to do if you ever had any notion of sticking around." His father brightened. "But we're not sticking around. This is it. Gone for good. A new life. Just you and me."

"So why do we have to go to Washington?" Brock asked.

"There's a flash drive. In a bank vault. There's some money there too. We could use a little of that. I want to spend some time at the beach, let the summer go by and let things cool down. You and I can get to looking a little more normal, then we'll get a place and get you registered for school. What do you think about a couple months at the beach?"

"Just us?"

"Who else is there?" his father asked.

"And you don't have to go anywhere?" Brock asked.

"Son, I have the feeling you're going to get a little sick of me." Brock's dad grinned at him and Brock grinned right back.

They spent the next two months at the beach in Maryland, not far from DC. His father was gone only occasionally, traveling into the capital on business he didn't discuss, but most of the time it was the two of them together. It would have been perfect, if only Brock's mom had been there.

Something about the ocean and the sand, the wind and the dunes, left his father frowning often into the distant sky. He'd start to talk about the past. "Gosh, I remember . . . ," he'd say, but never finish the thought. Maybe it had something to do with the old photo of his father and mother, the one in the secret box, that was taken on a beach somewhere. Brock didn't ask.

Despite his father's occasional dark and silent moods, Brock loved the time they got to spend together, especially walking on the beach, searching for seashells and shark teeth. Sometimes they'd build a fire in the dunes and roast marshmallows. Sometimes they'd just sit on the deck overlooking the surf, reading books and munching on roasted almonds, his father's favorite. Brock got used to the way he looked, mostly because he didn't spend much time looking at himself anyway. His dad grew a close-cut black beard and Brock got used to that too.

One day, Brock's dad brought home a newspaper along with their groceries. His dad left the groceries in their plastic bags and took the paper out onto the deck. Brock snuck a peek at him through the curtains and scowled at the intense look on his father's face as he stroked his new beard and scoured the inside of the front page. It was a look Brock had grown used to over the years, and now he realized that he'd gotten used to a different kind of dad. His father not only had a new face, but during their time at the beach, he'd grown warmer and sometimes showed flashes of being gentle.

The look his father wore now would scare a young child. It was intense, and hard.

Brock took a deep breath, opened the door, and stepped out onto the deck. "What's wrong?"

"Huh?" His father flashed an angry face that he quickly tried to change. "What? Oh, nothing."

Brock just stared at him.

His father took a deep breath and nodded his head. "Okay, not nothing. Here, look at this."

His father held up a copy of the *Washington Post*, open to page 2. Brock read the headline: RUSSIAN DIPLOMATS EXPELLED.

Brock took the paper from him and read. The story was all about some Russian diplomats who were kicked out of the country because of their links to organized crime in New York City, run by a man named Dmitri Boudantsev who'd suddenly gone missing. Brock studied the picture of Boudantsev's face. The criminal's thick black eyebrows, round flattened nose, and evil stare oozed danger.

Brock's heart pounded against his ribs as he finished reading. "And this is connected to us?"

His father bit his lower lip and nodded. "Yes. I made all this happen. . . ." He pointed to the article. "But Boudantsev got away. How, I have no idea. I'm letting you see this because . . ."

His father gave his head a violent shake. "I really can't believe he could ever find us. I can't think how it's possible, but . . . I've seen other impossible things happen. Anyway, let's not talk about this again. It's from the past, and that's where it will stay. You really don't have to worry, Brock."

"But, what *if*?" Brock had to ask.

His father looked at him. "If you ever did see this man, you need to run. You need to run for your life."

They didn't talk about it anymore, and Brock convinced himself that they were safe. They had to be.

Their faces healed. The thin white scars faded into their tan skin, and Brock even got used to his new nose.

He wasn't Brock Nickerson anymore though. His father had him choose from three possible identities: Thomas Givens, Robert Barrette, and Ian Bodett. Brock chose Robert Barrette.

"Can you . . . call me Brock?"

His father had bitten into his lower lip and remained quiet while he thought. Finally, he'd said, "Okay. I guess your papers can say Robert and we call you Brock. I've seen crazier things and no one's going to find us anyway."

Brock was thrilled. He enjoyed their last few days of summer even more and was sad when they packed up the car and drove away from the small beach house with its deck overlooking the dunes and the ocean.

"You think we can come back?" Brock asked, passing by Pete's Crab Shack, his favorite place for a milk shake.

His father reached out and patted Brock's knee. "This was great, right?"

"I loved it here." They passed the huge parking lot for the national seashore. Lucky people were unloading coolers, umbrellas, and towels, ready for a day of sun.

His father turned onto the main road heading inland. "Things close down, though, once the season ends. Calhoun has a really good school."

"So, can we come back here?"

His father bit his lower lip. "Well, we'll see. This is going to be a new way of life for us. The money is going to run out, and I'm going to have to get a job that's probably not going to leave a lot left over for beach houses. Certainly not for two months."

"Maybe a week, though?"

"Maybe." His father scowled at the road. "The best part of this for me was just being with you. This is like a jumping off point for us."

"To a normal life, right?"

"As normal as I can make it." His father looked over at him and smiled.

They rode for a time before Brock spoke again. "Dad? Did you ever think about . . . I don't know, like . . . dating?"

"For you or me?" His father gave him a serious look and they both burst out laughing.

"You, Dad."

His father took a deep breath and let it out. "I don't know, buddy. It'd take a pretty amazing woman for me to be able to forget about your mom."

"People do it, though, right?"

His dad nodded. "People do, but I don't have to have a wife and you don't have to have a mom for a normal life. One parent happens all the time."

"I know." Brock looked out the window.

He decided not to talk about his dad finding someone else anymore, but he couldn't help wishing for it. His dad was right, a lot of kids only had one parent, but there was something about a *mom*. Brock barely remembered his real mom, and he thought having a second mom would be really nice, not just for him, but for his dad, especially if they were going to settle down.

During the drive from Maryland to Ohio, Brock's dad told him what he knew about their new home. Brock wondered how he knew so much, but didn't ask.

Calhoun, Ohio, was built on a hillside overlooking a bend in the Muskingum River. The less desirable part of the town spilled across the river into what people called the Flatlands. The Flatlands were where—a hundred years ago—the town's factories had been built. Around the crumbling skeletons of those buildings, mashed together like garbage in a trash compactor, were the tiny homes used by factory workers of old. Today, those sagging neighborhoods housed the clerks from places like Walmart and Dollar General, the laborers in the newfound oil fields, and the folks who cleaned the office buildings for the lawyers, doctors, and engineers across the river.

"Where are *we* going to live?" Brock asked.

His father chuckled softly. "The wrong side of the river, I guess. I told you, money is going to be an issue with us. We'll start out in the Flatlands and see if we can't work our way up."

"I'm fine with that." Brock meant it too. He didn't care where he lived. Having his dad around and not running off in the middle of the night for days on end would be enough for him to be happy. He wondered if it could really be true, then pushed that from his mind the way he had the face of the evil Russian, Boudantsev.

Hours later, when they pulled into town, the rain came down so hard on the car's hood that it sounded like distant firecrackers. The stores on Main Street crouched under the dark sky. As they crossed over an old steel bridge, the muddy river below twisted and shivered under gusts of rain. While the charcoal-gray sky draped the surrounding hilltops with a frayed and dirty mist, the ruined factories crowded the riverbank like a row of giant rotten teeth. It was as ugly a place as Brock had ever seen.

"I bet it's a lot prettier in the sunlight," his father said, turning down a narrow street and passing a corner bar whose red neon light promised draft beer. They pulled into the tiny driveway of a narrow, pale-blue two-story house, jammed into a street packed with homes as close as candies in a box.

The sunny beach was a lifetime away. They unpacked the few things they'd acquired over the summer, climbing the unsteady steps of the front porch, then up the narrow stairs just inside the door. Brock had a tiny bedroom at the top of the stairs, his father the slightly bigger one in the back. They'd share the bathroom in between, with its old claw-foot tub and separate hot and cold faucets in the sink. The bathroom smelled like damp wood. Downstairs, a slumped and musty couch looked out the front window through a long diagonal crack. In the corner the bare cables for a TV lay like dead snakes. The kitchen was in the back, with a tipsy round table where they could eat. That was it. This was their house. It wasn't much bigger than a double-decker storage container, but it was home.

Brock was tired. Even though all he'd done was ride in the car all day, after he ate a sandwich with his dad, he crawled right into his new bed. The rusty springs beneath the old striped mattress creaked and groaned as he settled in. He tried to sleep, but couldn't, so he decided to read and turned on the light. The bed complained loudly as he tried to get comfortable with the pillow behind his back so he could sit up against the wall. He opened a paperback copy of *Big Red* but didn't get very far before the book slipped from his hand, jarring him awake enough to shut off the light. The rain drummed the roof and pattered against the windows.

As Brock drifted off to sleep, his only thought was that this didn't feel like home.

Brock woke early, threw on some sweatpants and a T-shirt, and wandered down the hall. His father lay with an arm over his eyes, feet sticking out from the covers, and mouth wide open, snoring softly. Brock used the bathroom and tiptoed down-stairs. There were two granola bars on the kitchen table along with three bottles of Gatorade from the drive. Brock ate a bar and sipped some orange Gatorade, then got up to explore their new home. There wasn't much to see. A rickety set of stairs around the corner by the back door led down into a smelly stone basement. A rusty water heater stood next to a greasy furnace. Old and dusty cobwebs bearded the underside of the floor above.

"Disgusting," Brock mumbled. He didn't want to poke around, even though the old shelves were filled with hardware and interesting knickknacks from another age. He climbed up the stairs, then let himself out the back, down a broken set of concrete steps. The small patch of damp crabgrass hemmed in by rusty fence held nothing for him, so he circled the house, turning sideways to squeeze past their car. He stopped when he reached the cracked sidewalk. A huge puddle stretched from the edge of the grass into the middle of the road. He looked up and down the street. Broken and severely wounded cars hugged the curb and filled the other narrow driveways. The sky was nearly white and the glow beyond the nearest factory wall promised sunshine.

It wasn't what he'd call pretty by any means, but it didn't look as bad as it had last night. The small crisp breeze rustled through a thick coat of leaves on the maple tree across the street. The rain seemed to have washed away the worst of the grime. Last night he'd thought he was moving into a war zone.

The clank of changing bike gears got his attention. He turned to see a big kid coming up the street on a small ten-speed bike. He wore a football uniform, head to toe, including cleats and a helmet. His gold padded pants were stained with dirt, and the bright-green helmet matched his jersey with big gold numbers that read "72." The bike wavered beneath the boy as if the equipment cost him his balance. Their eyes met as the kid steered past. The player looked back and the bike handle nicked the side mirror of an aging compact car. The handle spun, the bike tilted, and the hefty football player flew over the handlebars, crashing with a bang on the pavement below.

"Ouch!" The football player rolled onto his back and grabbed at his knee. "You dummy! What are you doing?"

Brock stepped out into the street, avoiding the puddle.

"Why am I the dummy? You weren't even watching where you were going. That's *my* fault?"

"You just jump out at me like that?" The hefty football player sat up, then rolled to the side, gathering himself before lunging to his feet.

"What are you talking about? I just stood here," Brock said.

"Oh man." The player growled and reached for his fallen bike. "Look at this. You bent the doggone rim!"

"I just stood here!"

"Staring."

"It's my street as much as yours." Brock stood his ground. He might not have as much bulk as this kid, but Brock was just as tall and more muscular if he had to bet.

The big kid waddled over to Brock, standing toe to toe and eye to eye.

"Yeah?" the kid said.

"Yeah." Brock nodded his head, and a fire burned in his gut. Even though he knew this was no way to get started in a brand-new neighborhood, he couldn't keep quiet. "What are you gonna do about it?"

The football player's scowl faded. He tilted his head. "Yeah, you're right. I'm just bummed. I *can't* be late for practice. I'm on the first team, but I won't be if I'm late. You know what a hard case Coach is."

"I have no idea what you're talking about."

"Coach Hewitt. The seventh-grade coach? Don't tell me you didn't play for him last year? With your size?"

"I'm not from around here. We came in last night."

"Hey, I'm new too. Not last night. We moved here last winter. Matthew Koletsky. Mom calls me Mattie. Friends call me Mak 'cause on the football field, I'm like a Mack Truck, only I spell it M-A-K. That's 'cause I'm Matthew Alexander Koletsky. Glad to meet you." Mak's smile lit his face and he seemed to have forgotten about his broken bike or being late. "I figured you were an eighth-grader at least. You're huge."

"Look at *you*."

"Yeah, I'm bulky huge." Mak patted his gut. "But you're like Hulk huge."

"Not quite."

"For seventh-grade you are. Did you repeat a grade?"

"No."

"Man, you gotta get to practice too. You could still be eligible for the first game. I mean, with your size, you could be first team too."

Brock rumpled his brow. "First team?"

Mak huffed. "A starter. It's a big thing around here to be first team. What's your name?"

Brock hesitated. "Brock. Brock Barrette."

"Is that your car?" Mak pointed with his thumb toward Brock's driveway.

"My dad's," Brock said.

"I know *that*. Is he going to work or anything? Maybe he could drive me to the field. I'd make it on time and you could meet Coach and get signed up. My dad works nights, so I gotta ride my bike. Does your dad work nights? No, well not last night because you didn't get in until last night. He didn't go right to work, did he?" The more Mak talked, the faster he talked, and Brock had to digest his words before he could answer.

"My dad might be able to give you a ride, but I'm not a football player," he said.

"Not . . ." Mak frowned. "You're huge. You gotta play football."

"I've thrown it around with my friends, but I never played in a league or anything. I played baseball. I'm a pitcher. A lefty."

"Not in the fall, you're not." Mak shook his head violently. "This is Calhoun. There's no baseball in the fall. I don't think it'd be legal. That's part of why we came here. It was here or Hensonville and my dad said, 'Kid as big as you, we gotta go to Calhoun for the football program alone.' Wish we lived on the right side of town, though."

"What's the right side?"

"Other side of the river." Mak angled his head toward where Brock knew the bridge and the river were. "This is the Flat-lands. Most of the guys on the first team tend to be from town. They start 'em young across the river. Age five, they're playing in this fancy flag league. Costs a lot to join. Your parents gotta have some bank to travel around and afford the equipment. Hey, can you get your dad to drive us now? You think he'd mind?"

"No, my dad won't mind." Brock had no idea if his dad would mind or not. Everywhere they'd been before, him just meeting some kid on the street was unthinkable. Before, he'd always been careful to take things slow with people, make few friends, and never talk about his family life. This was different, though. They were here to stay. He'd only be the new kid until some other new kid came along.

So, he went around in the back of the house because the front door was locked, then, from the bottom of the stairs, called up. "Dad? You up?"

"I am now." His father's voice was scratchy, but he didn't sound mad.

"Can we help my friend?"

40

"Friend? What are you talking about?"

Brock could tell by the thump from above that his father had gotten out of bed. "I just met him. He crashed his bike and he needs a ride or he'll get bounced off the football first team."

His father's head appeared at the top of the stairs, hair wild from sleep. "I don't know what you're talking about, but I'll be right down."

Brock went out the front door to wait. Mak had already dragged his ailing bike up into their driveway and leaned it against the side of the front porch. "Good?"

"He's coming," Brock said.

"Awesome. My goose was gonna be cooked."

"You want to take that helmet off?"

"Nah. I gotta get used to it, you know? I slept in it last night. That's commitment. That's what my dad says. Commitment is one of the most important virtues of sports. My dad says 'virtues' is a fancy word, but you don't have to be a fancy pants to talk fancy and—"

Thankfully, Brock's dad came out jingling his keys and Mak stopped talking. Brock's dad looked at the bike while Brock explained what happened and introduced him to Mak.

"Got a football game?" Brock's dad surveyed Mak's full equipment.

"Practice. Can't be late. Coach Hewitt—I was just saying— he's a hard case. Some people say a hard something else." Mak patted his backside. "But my dad doesn't go in for a garbage mouth."

41

Brock's dad gave Brock a look like he better be listening and Brock shrugged.

Mak kept talking. "That doesn't mean he judges other people who talk like that. My uncle Mike. Whew. You should hear him talk."

"We better go if you're not gonna be late," Brock's dad said as he got into the car.

"You guys made it just in time." Mak slid into the backseat. "Brock could get signed up today and play in the first game. He'd be able to get in enough practices. You gotta have ten. I got three already. Coach doesn't like you to miss any. But you just moved in. He's a hard case, but not unreasonable. My dad says that's part of being a good coach."

Brock's dad looked in the rearview mirror. "You talk kind of fast, don't you?"

"When I'm nervous."

"We'll get you there." Brock's dad backed out of the driveway.

Mak directed them over the bridge and through the center of town before taking a left and continuing through the treelined streets of fine homes until they reached a big brick school. They circled the school to the football fields out back. More than two dozen fully padded players already dotted the field in their gold pants and green helmets and jerseys.

Mak popped open the door. "Come on, Mr. Barrette. You got to meet Coach Hewitt and bring Brock. Coach will love him. Look how big he is."

Mak took a quick breath and talked even faster. "We could play on the line together. We could open up holes in the line so

42

big my grandmother could run through them. And my grandmother can barely walk. She hurt her hip. My uncle Mike
promised to get the ice off her steps. But he didn't. Well?"

Brock turned to his dad. "Can I?"

In Brock's mind were all the other times he'd asked to do something and the answer had always been no. He knew his father said things would be different now, but the pattern was stamped so hard into his brain that when his dad said, "Yes," he had to ask him to repeat himself. "What?"

"I said, sure. Why not?"

Brock took a deep breath and let it out slow, with a grin on his face.

"Nice," Mak said. "Come on, I'll introduce you to Coach. Being able to introduce someone new is an important skill. My dad says you gotta look everyone in the eye, though. Just introducing isn't enough. That's only half the battle. That's what he says, anyway. My dad."

They walked toward the goalpost, where Brock saw a man wearing green-and-gold Calhoun Fighting Crabs shorts and a

T-shirt get down into a three-point stance and fire out at a blocking dummy one of Mak's teammates tried to hold up. The coach pumped his short thick legs like dueling jackhammers. He drove the bag and the player holding it right through the back of the end zone, stopping only when the player tumbled to the grass with the big bag on top of him.

"Now that's the way you drive a dummy," the coach barked from one side of his mouth. He had a gray crew cut and a barrel chest, and stood no taller than Brock. The coach looked down on the fallen player with his hands on his hips. "Head up. Back flat. Legs never stop pumping."

Mak stepped forward. "Coach, I got a new kid from my neighborhood, wants to play football." Mak put a hand on Brock's shoulder. "My bike broke and they gave me a ride."

Coach turned. His blue eyes quickly absorbed Brock, then swept over to his dad before holding out a stubby-fingered hand that looked like a wedge of stone. Brock's dad shook the coach's hand and the veins in both men's arms jumped in their skin.

"Pete Barrette." Brock's dad's eyes met the coach's eyes with equal intensity. Brock's dad looked like a soldier poorly disguised in a regular person's clothes. He was like a concrete post, upright and formidable.

"Dale Hewitt." Coach broke off the handshake. "You got a big boy. Seventh-grader?"

"He is," Brock's dad said, nodding.

"Nice. You can never have too many linemen."

"You should take a look at him for quarterback," Brock's dad said. "He's got a heck of an arm."

Brock glowed at the sound of his father's praise.

Coach Hewitt snorted through his smile. "I can look, but I got a quarterback. Two, in fact."

Brock's dad shrugged. "Well, take a look and see what you think. What do I have to do to get him signed up?"

"Is he registered with the school? Physical, all that?"

"Did it all online last week," Brock's dad said. "His legal name is Robert, for the paperwork, but we call him Brock. It was Bob, but he didn't like that so we called him B. Then, he started getting big and strong and it was B the Rock, then someone started calling him B-Rock, then Brock, and it stuck."

Brock tried not to grin at his father's story and he wondered if it was made up on the spot, or something his dad had thought about.

Coach didn't seem to find it funny or interesting. He looked at Brock's feet. "You'll have to get him some cleats, but he can run through the noncontact stuff with us this morning in his sneakers and it'll count as a practice. He'll need three practices before I can give him pads."

"Mind if I watch?"

Coach shrugged and pointed at the bleachers. "It's a free country."

Brock's dad didn't blink. "Nice."

Coach pinched the whistle hanging from his neck between two sausage fingers, brought it to his mouth, and blew it loud. "Let's go! Line it up!"

Mak tapped Brock's arm. "Come on."

His dad said, "Good luck."

Brock muttered a thanks and hustled along behind Mak as the team fell into five lines across the goal line facing the field. Without fanfare, Coach Hewitt began tooting his whistle, and every time he did, another row of players would march off down the field, knees high reaching for the sky. Brock kept up and ignored the stares. He'd grown used to them. The new kid always got stared at. He let the looks pass through him like light through a window. From active stretching they went to agility stations. That's when Brock realized there were two more coaches, one even shorter than Coach Hewitt and who smiled even less.

"That's Coach Van Kuffler," Mak whispered.

Coach Van Kuffler wore the face of a mean chipmunk, something Brock didn't think possible.

"Get on the line," Coach Van Kuffler snarled, and it took Brock a second to realize the coach was talking to him.

He jumped like he'd stepped in hot lava. "Sorry."

"Flatty." Coach Van Kuffler's disgusted mutter hardly qualified as a word, but Brock was nearly certain he'd said "Flatty."

Brock ran through the row of bags, in and out, chopping his feet until he cleared the last one, grunting with effort and nearly tumbling when his sneaker slipped out from under him on the grass.

"What's that mean? Flatty?" Brock whispered to Mak at the back of the line.

"Don't call *me* Flatty." Mak glowered.

"I didn't. I just asked what it meant," Brock said.

Mak's face relaxed, then his lips puckered. "Flathead. A dummy. A boob. Someone from the Flats . . ."

"From . . . oh," Brock replied, realization creeping into his head.

"Don't take that junk from nobody." Mak lowered his voice to a growl. "You let people push you around 'cause you're new, and you're dead meat. Stick up for yourself. Smash them right in the mouth."

"Easy, Mak. It wasn't a kid." They were nearly back to the front of the line as the players ran back through the row of bags in the opposite direction. Brock shot a nervous glance at Coach Van Kuffler. "It was the coach."

Mak clenched his teeth. "He wouldn't say that junk around my dad, I'll tell you."

"It's so bad?" Brock asked.

"It's the worst."

"Get the lead out, Koletsky," Coach Van Kuffler snarled.

Mak turned and worked his way through the bags. Brock took his turn and did his best, but slipped three times.

"New kid looks like a clod." Coach Van Kuffler grinned at a couple of the players in front, showing off his long yellow front teeth. "You ever play football before, New Kid?"

Brock stayed silent, but shook his head.

"Ha. How'd I know?"

A couple of the kids in the front of the line snickered.

"It's just my shoes." The words slipped free from Brock's mouth before he could think.

"You back-talking *me*?" The coach's little face turned red. His front teeth pushed out from under his top lip like the sideways peak of a roof.

Brock shook his head.

"I say you were, New Kid. TAKE A LAP!" Coach Van

Kuffler's voice hit a hysterical high as he pointed toward the far goalpost.

Brock took off at a jog.

"FASTER!" the coach screamed at the top of his lungs.

Brock ran faster. On his way back, he glanced up and saw his father frowning from the bleachers. Brock shrugged at him and raised his hands, palms up.

"Don't talk back." His father's voice floated down on him like a chilly mist, stern, but too quiet for the others to hear. "This isn't baseball."

Brock clamped his teeth together and wondered if leaving this place after a few months might not be so bad after all.

The rest of the practice, Brock kept his mouth shut and tried his very best to do everything right. Still, whatever set Coach Van Kuffler off against him, no matter how small or silly, it seemed to be permanent. Even though Coach Hewitt was the head coach and ran the defense, he gave complete control of the offense to Coach Van Kuffler. So, when the team broke into skilled and strength positions on offense, Coach Van Kuffler laughed out loud when Brock tried to go with him and the quarterbacks, receivers, and running backs.

Coach Van Kuffler stuck a finger in his ear and worked it around before he pointed toward the other end of the field. "Go on, get down there with Coach Delaney and the line. You're a lineman. If you're anything at all."

Brock looked down toward the other end of the field. Mak and the rest of the big guys were gathered around who he guessed was Coach Delaney along with Coach Hewitt and some yellow blocking dummies.

"Can I just show you how I can throw, Coach?" Brock didn't consider a harmless question talking back at all, but Coach Van Kuffler's face twisted up and he leaned toward Brock.

"You got a problem with me?"

Behind the coach, the skill players stood in a small half circle. Brock knew that the one with the football in his hand was likely the quarterback, and he wore a smirk on his face that was less than nice. The boy was nearly as tall as Brock, but not as thick. Brock studied the quarterback's pale-green eyes for some indication if the coach was serious, or just kidding around. The quarterback didn't even blink.

Brock shifted his stare into Coach Van Kuffler's yellow-brown eyes. The left one had a ragged edge around the inside of his pupil and it gave the coach the look of a mad dog.

"I got a good arm, Coach." Brock dressed his words in a simpering tone of apology.

"There's an orangutan in the Columbus Zoo with a good arm," Coach Van Kuffler said through clenched teeth. "You think I'm gonna have an orangutan play quarterback for me?"

Brock could only shake his head and turn to go. Behind him, he heard Coach Van Kuffler barking orders to the remaining players, telling them the formation he wanted them to line up in. When he got to where the linemen were, Coach Hewitt, Coach Delaney, and the rest, even Mak, ignored him. They were too busy. Brock couldn't wait to get the pads on and be a part of it. At least he'd be able to take his frustration out on someone. He watched with envy as Mak lined up and smashed people around, knocking half the other linemen to their backs when he blocked them.

When the whistle blew, Mak would trudge back to the line, red-faced, glazed with sweat, and grinning like a fool. Once he winked at Brock, which made Brock feel at least a little better. There was someone who wanted him around, anyway.

At the end of practice, they ran sprints until a third of the players lay retching in the grass. Brock held up, but he wondered how he would fare once he had to do all the contact work before the sprints. Coach Hewitt blew his whistle and called them all together.

"We're not working hard enough." The coach glowered at his team. "Guys falling down? Puking themselves because we run twenty wind sprints? Is that what you're gonna do in the fourth quarter? We open in less than three weeks against Moravia and I promise you, they are outworking you guys."

Brock looked around. Everyone hung his head.

"All right. Don't forget, tonight is the Mom's Club meeting in the cafeteria for their bake sale. It's not just the seventh-grade team, it's for eighth, freshman, JV, and varsity, so make sure your moms are there and I don't get a call from Coach Spada asking what's wrong with the seventh-grade team. You all got that?"

Brock looked around. Everyone seemed good with this Mom's Club thing. He wanted desperately for someone to raise his hand and ask—like he wanted to—what they should do if they didn't *have* a mom. Brock couldn't believe he was the only one. He kept looking, but no one spoke. Brock's stomach knotted, and when everyone broke up, he walked toward Coach

Hewitt, but veered off when the head coach stopped to talk with Coach Van Kuffler.

Mak put a hand on his shoulder. "So, what'd you think? Hey, can I ride back with you guys?"

"Sure." Brock watched his dad walking down out of the bleachers to meet them.

"Yeah," Mak said, cheerfully. "I heard that stuff about quarterback. You better forget that, though, and just get ready to play the line with me."

"I got a really good arm. No one's even seen it."

"Yeah, but that don't matter." Mak chuckled in a friendly way. "You could have an arm like Ben Roethlisberger, but you won't play QB on this team."

Brock frowned and stopped Mak in his tracks. "But why not?"

Mak angled his head back toward the field. "Is anyone throwing pass patterns with a couple of the receivers back there?"

Brock looked around his new friend and saw a small handful of guys getting in some extra work after practice. "Yeah. A couple of them, and Coach Van Kuffler. I can stay after too. That's no big deal."

"Yeah," Mak said. "Coach Van Kuffler. You know who the first-team quarterback is?"

Brock shook his head. "No idea."

"Wally Van Kuffler. The coach's nephew." Mak took Brock by the arm and led him toward the bleachers. "It's not polite to stare."

Brock dug in his heels to look back. Mak kept leading him away.

"*That's* his nephew?" Brock stopped again to watch Wally throw a corner route to Xaviar Archangel, one of the wide receivers. His uncle stood beside Wally, two inches shorter, with his arms folded across his chest and his Calhoun Football cap pulled down tight on his head. Wally's pass wobbled and arced through the air. He missed the receiver by three yards. The ball hit and bounced, then rolled to a stop right at Brock's feet.

"Which is why you better set your sights on lining up at

guard, right next to me." Mak tugged at him again and talked with enthusiasm. "They'll call us the Big Bang Theory. We'll mangle people!"

Brock shook free and scooped up the ball. Coach Hewitt had been talking to another player and he was on his way toward the school, already ten yards beyond Coach Van Kuffler and his nephew.

"Coach Hewitt!" Brock hollered, and the head coach stopped and looked back.

Brock was fifty yards from the coach. He took a step and rifled the football. It arced up into the air, spinning in a tight and perfect spiral. Coach Hewitt's hands shot up in front of his face and he caught the ball. Brock smiled to himself, turned, and walked toward his father without saying anything else. Mak caught up to him.

"That was like, fifty yards! You're a lefty?"

"I told you," Brock said.

"You got some arm," Mak said.

"He does." Brock's dad patted him on the shoulder and the three of them headed for the car.

"How far can you throw it?" Mak asked. "That was like a perfect spiral."

Brock shrugged. "I have no idea. I never really tried. I've mostly just thrown a baseball except for fooling around a little with a football."

"Let them chew on that." Brock's dad unlocked the car and they all got in.

Mak chattered excitedly as they drove back through town.

"Hey, the library." Brock's dad slowed the car and turned

into the parking lot of a tall old brick building with a clock tower. Since the clock read 2:35 and it wasn't yet noon, Brock knew it was broken.

"I could use a couple books," Brock's dad said. "Brock?"

"Yes."

"You read, Mak?" Brock's dad looked up into the rearview mirror and locked eyes with Mak.

"Uh, sometimes. Kinda."

"Got a card?" Brock asked.

"Not yet," Mak said.

"You can get one with us," Brock said.

"I got all this smelly equipment," Mak said.

"Come on." Brock climbed out and opened the rear door. "They won't care. You might want to take your helmet off, though."

"Yeah, my dad says that too." Mak removed his helmet and laid it on the backseat. "He says I shouldn't wear it in public places. My dad says manners are very important."

Brock stared at the purple indentations on Mak's forehead.

"What are you looking at?" Mak raised an eyebrow.

"Doesn't that hurt?" Brock pointed.

"What, these?" Mak touched the marks. "Adaptable. That's me. You can get used to anything. That's what I'm doing. Making my equipment *part* of me. My dad says the human race only exists because we're adaptable. Pretty cool, huh?"

Brock couldn't even reply.

They all went inside and signed up for library cards, accepting temporary ones that would work until they got permanent ones in the mail. The librarian had a fiery head of curly red hair. She wore a purple dress with pink flowers that matched her lipstick, but Brock decided he liked her smile and the soft way she spoke. She did sniff suspiciously for a minute when she handed Mak his card, but then smiled, pretending he didn't smell like spoiled milk, even though he kind of did. Brock's dad thanked the librarian and disappeared in the grown-ups' section while Brock led Mak into the corner where the librarian said they kept the middle-grade books.

"Check this out." Brock pulled a book by Gordon Korman from the shelf and handed it to Mak.

"*Ungifted*?" Mak wrinkled his brow.

"It's hilarious." Brock took down two books he'd been meaning to read, *When You Reach Me* and—for a laugh—Jon Scieszka's *Knucklehead*.

"Hey." Mak pointed to *When You Reach Me*. "That looks like a girl book."

Brock twisted his lips. "There's no 'girl' books or 'boy' books. Come on, Mak. You sound like a caveman."

"Well, I don't know." Mak looked around the empty library. "People here are kind of . . . old-fashioned, in a way."

"Like calling people flatheads?" Brock asked.

"That's different." Mak's face grew dark and his hands clenched.

"What's that all about?"

Mak relaxed a bit and shrugged. "Just garbage. Some people think they're special 'cause they live this side of the river. It's not everyone, but a lot in football."

"Why football?" Brock sat at the reading table and Mak sat down across from him.

"This town lives for football. I told you, the kids start playing at five."

"Five years old?"

Mak nodded. "There's a bunch of travel teams from the time kids are five until middle school, when you can play on the seventh-grade team. They're expensive."

"Can't you sell magazine subscriptions or something, though?" In Oklahoma, Brock and some classmates sold magazine subscriptions to pay for a trip to the Grand Canyon, a trip he never got to go on because they moved.

"I guess, but they don't. The fathers who run it are crazy. They *try* to keep kids out, I swear. Kids from the Flats. They make you fly all over and if the parents can't go because of work or the money, well . . ."

"That's stupid."

"My dad says that's life." Mak nodded wisely.

"Anyway, we're in the school now," Brock said.

"It's still political. Wally Van Kuffler has been QB since the age of five."

"They can't have that much money. His uncle is a teacher."

"His dad's an accountant. They live right off Main Street, but more than that, everyone knows he's the nephew of one of the middle-school coaches. The fathers on the travel teams just roll over when they see one of the real coaches coming, or their kids or family."

"So, Wally Van Kuffler is gonna be the quarterback because of his uncle and where he lives?"

"In Calhoun he is."

Brock shook his head. "If this place is all about winning,

58

they're gonna play the best player. You're on the first team. You live where I do."

"Sure, but you gotta be *way* better if you're from the Flats. They don't expect you to be first team. They expect the kids who've been in the program all their lives. And if you are *that* good, they're not gonna make you quarterback. *Maybe* running back, but not QB. They save that for the rich kids."

Brock pointed at the book in Mak's hands. "You ever really read a book before? A whole book, first page to last? Be honest."

Mak's face reddened and he shrugged. "Not really."

"Well, you know what they say, right?"

"What?"

A grin crept across Brock's face. "There's a first time for everything."

Brock got up and Mak followed him to the checkout counter in the front of the library. The long wooden counter stood empty. A small fan whirred, pushing warm air across their faces before it rotated away. A notice about a summer book club fluttered on the wall, struggling to free itself from the pushpins holding it to the corkboard. Brock stretched his neck and looked around for a sign of the librarian. When no one appeared, Brock reached out and struck a chrome bell with the palm of his hand, and the ding cracked the silence.

From the doorway behind the counter, a girl emerged. Brock caught his breath. A pink headband pulled the long blond hair off her face and it fell behind her ears, straight to her shoulders, shiny as gold. Her big blue eyes sparkled in a friendly way and the whiteness of her smile was enough to make Brock's eyes blink while his heart raced. She might be his age, but she might be older. She stood tall and straight, like a track athlete, maybe a basketball player. She wore white shorts and a pink sleeveless shirt that matched her hair band.

"Hi." She looked at Brock with an intensity that made him blush as she scooped his temporary card and the books from the counter. She fired a laser beam at the card, then the books' inside covers, checking them out with a beep like a cash register.

Brock was suddenly very aware that Mak smelled like roadkill and he wasn't much better in his sweaty T-shirt and shorts. He looked over at Mak, who grinned wide from behind his face mask. "Laurel? What are you doing here?"

"Why wouldn't I be here, Mak?"

Mak shrugged and looked around. "I guess I figured you'd be riding horses or something."

Laughter rolled off her tongue like the gurgle of a fast stream. "Community service, Mak. It's for college."

"College? College is for football." Mak nodded his head to back up his words.

"Who's your friend?" Laurel looked at Brock, and he felt his throat tighten.

"He's new. Real name's Bob, but he's like a brick so they call him Brock." Mak grinned with pride at his faulty recollection of the story.

Brock wanted to melt.

Mak pointed at each of them, making eye contact, and giving a proper introduction, per his father's advice. "Brock Barrette, Laurel Lehman."

"Hi, Brock Barrette." Laurel raised an eyebrow and pushed

the books and card back across the counter. "A boy who not only reads, but drags Mak Koletsky into the library?"

She clucked her tongue and checked out Mak's book. "I thought I'd seen everything."

"We just came from football practice." Mak accepted the checked-out book along with his temporary card.

Laurel sniffed the air and looked down at Mak's wet and grubby pants. "Really? And I thought someone threw up in the book return again."

"You can watch for him and me on the line together." Mak puffed his chest. "First team."

"First team?" Laurel raised her eyebrows. "Nice."

"Quarterback." The word escaped Brock's lips from he didn't know where. The sound of it made him jump and clamp his lips tight.

Mak laughed and slapped him on the back. "He's funny."

"Everyone loves the quarterback. You're tall enough." Laurel kept her eyes on his and Brock could say no more. He thought of Bella, the first girl who ever made his brain tingle. This girl was nothing like Bella, who was more compact and tough, but she did the same thing to him and he marveled at it.

"You ought to come see practice sometime," Mak said. "School spirit. Colleges love that."

"Maybe we could get some ice cream sometime?" Brock said, startled by his own words. It was like an alien took over his body and he could see that not only Mak, but Laurel, too, was surprised.

Before anyone could say anything more, Brock's dad appeared with half a dozen books and they all went quiet.

Laurel checked out his books and kept her eyes on her business until she pushed Brock's dad's books back to him with a smile. "Have a good day."

"You too." Brock's dad turned and they followed him out.

At the door, Brock glanced back—still under alien control—and waved.

Laurel smiled, and waved right back.

As they crossed the river, Brock's dad asked, "What's with you and that girl?"

Brock's mouth hung open and he couldn't help staring in total disbelief at his dad. "Nothing."

Mak leaned forward and planted his face between the two front seats. "Don't worry, Mr. Barrette. That happens to everyone. When Laurel Lehman walks down the halls in school, guys wilt like flowers on a grave."

Brock's dad glanced back at Mak as they pulled into their driveway. "Flowers on a . . ."

"Grave. That's what Coach Hewitt says when someone gets crushed on the line." Mak scrunched up his face and made his voice gruff, talking out of one side of his mouth. "'He wilted like flowers on a grave.' That's how he talks."

"Yeah, I heard him." Brock's dad shut off the engine and they all got out.

"Don't mind Coach, Mr. Barrette," Mak said. "Everyone says his bark's worse than his bite. He teaches freshman English. You should hear him talk about *Romeo and Juliet*. I hear he gets tears in his eyes. Can you imagine? I mean, who'd poison themselves over a girl? My dad says to stay away from girls as long as you can. Nothin' but trouble. That's what my dad says."

"Mak, you're an interesting guy." Brock's dad shook Mak's hand. "Maybe you'll join us for dinner?"

"Sure I will. Maybe lunch too?" Mak looked around hopefully. "It's gotta be noon."

"Better get a shower first." Brock's dad waved his hand in front of his nose.

Mak's face brightened and he looked down at his grungy pants. "Yeah, after three days of dirt and sweat it's time to get a wash in."

"Yes, three days is." Brock's dad smiled. "But come by for dinner if you want."

Mak nodded, picked his bike up, and trudged up the street, guiding it along on its crooked wheel.

"Nice boy."

"Funny," Brock said. "Now what?"

Brock's dad slapped his hands together. "I'll make us sandwiches, then I gotta go find a job. I'll pick you up some cleats on my way home."

They went inside. Brock filled two paper cups with milk and sat at the table while his father laid out slices of ham onto white bread he'd slathered with mayo.

"What will you do?" Brock asked. "For a job, I mean."

His father came over to the table and laid down the sandwiches on two paper plates. "Probably construction if I can find it. Something that pays cash."

"Cash?"

His father bit into his sandwich and spoke through the food. "Just to be safe. I don't need any paperwork going to the government. If I get paid cash, there's no record of me."

"I thought we were going to live a 'normal' life." Brock couldn't help the edge in his voice.

"Relax. Plenty of people live on the fringe. Cash jobs. Cash payments. There are some things you can't do, but not much."

"Like what?" Brock asked.

His father shrugged. "You can't buy stuff online. No credit cards."

"What about our library cards?" Brock asked.

His father laughed and swallowed. "I like the way you're thinking, like an operative. No, library cards aren't linked into anything anyone can search on a national level."

"But you said our identities were, what'd you call them? Clean?"

"They are clean. Everything the government does is in computers. Some people—like me—know how to get inside those computers and make stuff up. I did all that when I was still working there, made up stuff for you, me, and your mom. Just in case. That's how I got a driver's license in Maryland and your birth certificate as Robert Barrette, which let me register you for school. What I don't want to do is get a job where my social security number gets entered into the IRS database. Your mom and I are the only ones who knew the names I made up, but I like to play things safe. It's a habit, and I don't like having any connection to government computers."

Brock absorbed that, again wondering if it really was possible for them to have a whole new way of life. To change the subject, he said, "That coach doesn't like people from the Flats."

"Who told you that?"

"Mak."

"Coaches yell, Brock. They're trying to motivate twelve- and thirteen-year-old boys. I'd yell."

"It's not that. It's the way . . . I don't know. I get a feeling."

"If I got upset every time someone gave me a feeling, I'd be in a rubber room." His father got up and put his plate in the trash. "It's football. Football is different than baseball. It's more . . ."

"Mean?" Brock suggested.

"Intense. Like the army. Taking orders." His father reached into the cupboard. "You want an Oreo?"

"Sure," Brock said. "Speaking of cookies, there's something called a Mom's Club meeting tonight at the high school cafeteria. I guess all the players' moms get together for some bake sale."

His father turned his way with the Oreo package in his hands and froze. He spoke soft and gentle. "Well, you don't have a mom. I'm sure not everyone does."

"Apparently they do. And Coach said everyone's mom had to be there. Everyone needs to help."

His father forced a laugh. "I'll go then."

"You?" Brock didn't know if he was serious.

"Sure." His father opened the package and jiggled three cookies onto Brock's plate before pouring more milk into his cup. "If your mom *was* here, I'd be doing the baking anyway. She could barely butter bread."

His father laughed, but this time it was cheerful, like he was remembering good times without the pain.

It made Brock sad, and he could only imagine the reaction from people when his father from the Flatlands showed up at the Mom's Club.

The next morning, Mak appeared at Brock's back door in his football gear, still grungy and stained, but heavy with the smell of laundry soap instead of the stink of old sweat. Brock let him in and Mak stood in their kitchen with his helmet on, watching Brock and his dad finish breakfast and looking around the kitchen while he waited for a ride.

"Still wearing the helmet?" Brock's dad asked after a glance at Mak. Mak had shown up to dinner last night before the Mom's Club meeting with the helmet on as well. After Brock's dad assured him their home wasn't a public place, Mak had only taken it off to eat.

"That was great fish last night." Mak sniffed the air as if he could still smell their dinner. "My mom never gets fish from Hooligans. Too expensive."

"Do you want me to fry you an egg?" Brock's dad shoveled

in the last bite of his breakfast.

"No," Mak said, still looking around with his nose tilted up. "We gotta get to practice, but thanks."

Suddenly, Mak froze like a beagle. "Hey, what are those?"

Brock's dad turned around and looked to where Mak pointed. Brock put his face in a hand.

"Gingersnaps." Brock's dad cleared his throat and stood up to throw away his cup and plate.

"Can I?" Mak started for the pile.

"Sorry, buddy." Brock's dad put a hand on his shoulder. "They're for the Mom's Club bake sale tomorrow."

"Oh, yeah. My mom said everyone was talking about how funny it was that you showed up at that meeting last night." Mak snapped his mouth shut and his face reddened. He looked at the floor.

Brock's dad laughed it off. "I was a fish out of water, but they'll like my cookies."

Brock wanted to crawl in a hole, but he acted normal. "We'd better go."

They got into the car and Brock's dad took them to the school. This time, instead of watching practice, he said he was headed out to find a job.

"You guys grab a sandwich at Subway in town after practice," Brock's father said, giving Brock a twenty-dollar bill as they got out of the car. "Then you can hang out in the park and I'll pick you up there around one."

They were only halfway across the hot dusty football field when Coach Hewitt blew the whistle and got things started. Brock was glad for his new cleats. He was able to move faster and better. No one said anything to Brock about the throw he'd made after practice the day before, even though he gave Coach Hewitt an eager look every chance he got. It must have worked though, because when warm-ups and agility drills were over and Brock started to go with Coach Hewitt, Coach Delaney, and the linemen, Coach Hewitt stopped him. "No, you go with the skill guys."

Coach Hewitt then shouted over Brock's shoulder at Coach Van Kuffler. "Coach, let's see how Barrette does at quarterback. When his pads go on we can always put him on the line, but with an arm like he's got, we should at least see how he takes to it. Good?"

"Sure, Coach." Coach Van Kuffler looked anything but happy. When Brock joined the group, Coach Van Kuffler wore the stitched-on smile of a scarecrow.

"Just try to follow along and watch today. I don't want you slowing things down," he growled.

Coach Van Kuffler looked at Brock the way a caged dog looks at a cat, then he blew his whistle and everyone fell into place. The backs and receivers made two long lines. The first- and second-team quarterbacks pretended to take snaps from a center, then threw various passes depending on the patterns Coach Van Kuffler called out. Brock stood and watched, aching to be able to throw some passes himself. He was pretty sure he could, and he knew he could do it better than Wally Van Kuffler and Kurt Wentzel, the second-team quarterback who was even worse than Wally.

Eager to show what he could do, Brock felt the pressure building up inside him. Every time Coach Van Kuffler came close to him, he imagined himself asking if he could throw some passes, but every time, the words froze in his throat. His hands began to sweat from nerves. Finally, when Wentzel put a pass right into the dirt and Coach Van Kuffler was barking at him to finish his throwing motion and keep his head up, Brock burst out.

"Coach, can I try?"

Coach Van Kuffler turned and glowered at him, obviously mad, but it seemed he was also mad at Wentzel. Coach Van Kuffler's lip quivered under his long front teeth; then he pointed at the spot where Wentzel stood. "Sure. Go. You can't be worse than Wentzel."

Wentzel hung his head and stepped aside.

"Let's go, receivers! Give me ten-yard out cuts!" Coach Van Kuffler bellowed.

Brock watched Wally's receiver run ten yards down the field, then break out toward the sideline. Wally threw it behind his receiver. Brock stepped up to Wentzel's old spot and pretended to take a snap of his own. He dropped back, crossing his feet and nearly falling down so that by the time he regained his balance the receiver was dangerously close to the sideline. Desperate, Brock reared back and fired the ball like a fast pitch.

The football whistled through the air and Brock knew it was a good throw. When it hit the receiver's hands, though, the receiver yelped and the ball kept going.

"Wentzel! Get back in there!" Coach Van Kuffler barked.

Brock's mouth listed open. "B-b-but I . . . I . . ."

Coach Van Kuffler glared at him. "What?"

"I thought it was a good pass, Coach. I know I threw it a little late, but . . ."

Coach Van Kuffler began to mangle his lower lip with his teeth. His eyes bulged even more than they already did. "Now you're gonna tell me how to coach?"

Brock stayed silent, but that only seemed to make Coach Van Kuffler more mad.

"You think I care if you got a strong arm?" Coach Van Kuffler stabbed a finger into the space between them. "You gotta *complete* the pass. You threw a bullet your receiver couldn't catch. The object is to make plays. It's a *team* game, not a track meet. Now, stand back and watch and see if you can figure that out."

It was Brock's turn to hang his head. He wanted to tell the coach he'd missed a step and needed to throw it extra fast before the receiver reached the sideline, but he remembered his father's words and knew he'd said too much already.

"You better pick your head up and pay attention," Coach Van Kuffler said. "I'm going over our base pass plays just for *you*. Everyone else knows them, but Coach Hewitt wants to see if you can even learn this stuff."

Brock did his best, but it was hard. Coach Van Kuffler talked in a language the other boys seemed to understand, but Brock had no idea.

"Z has to break that post at twelve!" Coach Van Kuffler shouted at a receiver after Wally threw another incomplete pass.

After a while, Brock sorted out that Z was the wide receiver on the right. X was the wide receiver on the left. When Brock got up the guts to ask Coach Van Kuffler if that was correct, the coach replied, "What's it look like?"

Brock had no idea what the difference between H and Y was because Brady Calenzo, their compact and fleet-footed running back, seemed to be H sometimes and Y other times, and Brock wondered how that could be. When they took a water break between periods, Brock found Mak and asked him for help.

Sweat poured down Mak's face. He was huffing to catch his breath and he shrugged. "I don't know that stuff. I just gotta know who to block. Ask Coach Hewitt for a playbook, though. We can go over it after practice and maybe I can help you figure it out."

"Great." Brock watched Mak slurp down some water from the hose. He hadn't done all that much, so he wasn't thirsty, but to be like the others he took a turn and gulped some down as well.

After Coach Hewitt blew the whistle again, he shouted, "Linemen with Coach Delaney! Skill players with me and Coach Van Kuffler, seven on seven!"

Brock followed the rest of the skill players—everyone who wasn't a lineman—and stood in the back while Wally took charge of the seven-man huddle, called a play, and went to the line against a defense that also had no linemen. Brock scowled in concentration, taking in every last detail he could, but he was still generally confused after the first ten plays.

Coach Hewitt seemed to be running the defensive side of things, coaching the linebackers and defensive backs on their coverage assignments and techniques, but after Kurt Wentzel ran five plays, the head coach shouted across the field, "Coach, let's see Brock!"

Coach Van Kuffler hesitated, then shouted back, "He's got no pads, Coach."

Coach Hewitt waved a hand impatiently. "We're not hitting. He can take a snap and throw a pass."

Coach Van Kuffler shrugged and grit his teeth, but quickly forced a smile. "You got it, Coach. Brock, take the huddle."

Brock hesitated, not knowing what it meant to "take" the huddle, but he assumed he should just do what the others had done.

"Okay," Coach Van Kuffler said. "Call an X Cross Z Post on two; you know this, right?"

"I . . . I think I do. Yes."

"Sure you do, it's the first play I taught you and you watched it about a dozen times during individual period." Coach Van Kuffler had raised his voice so that everyone could hear him clearly, including Coach Hewitt.

Then Coach Van Kuffler lowered his voice so the defensive players couldn't hear him and he stepped into the huddle. "Go ahead, Strong Left, X Cross Z Post. Let's hike it on one to make it easy for you. Just say what I said and break the huddle."

Brock felt like he was walking into a trap. He didn't know why, maybe it was the overly nice voice or just the look on Coach Van Kuffler's face, the kind of eager look a dog has when it hears the rattle of food in its bowl, but he called the play and walked toward the line, stopping in the shotgun position three yards behind the center.

"Why don't you try and hit the post, okay?" Coach Van Kuffler said, then changed his voice as if he were talking to a three-year-old. "That's the Z. He'll run up the field, twelve yards, then break for the post. That's that big yellow H in the end zone."

Some of the kids snickered.

Brock ignored them and nodded. He went to the line and began his count with a color and a number, using the same combination he'd just heard Wentzel use. "Blue 22, Blue 22 . . ."

Brock looked left where the X receiver was. He'd do a cross, up the field, then crossing from one sideline to the other. Then Brock looked right—where the Z receiver was. The Z would run a post straight up the field for a ways and then break at an angle toward the goalpost. Brock's heart fluttered in his chest. It was all incredibly exciting, like the first time you got up on a bike, balanced, free, and moving faster than ever before.

"Set! Hike!"

The center fired the ball between his legs. Brock caught it and looked at the Z receiver. The player ran up the field, but instead of breaking at an angle for the goalpost, he cut straight across the field. In that split second, Brock didn't know if he'd heard everything wrong, or if the receiver was just doing the wrong thing. He waited, hoping the receiver might break his route up toward the goalpost. Even late would be better than never, but the receiver kept going, straight across the field for the other sideline. Brock glanced at the X receiver, who, instead of crossing the field, had broken for the goalpost, the post pattern.

Brock hesitated again. He didn't know if he should throw the ball to the wrong receiver running the correct route, or the correct receiver running the wrong route. There was no right answer. A little bark of panic escaped his lips, and he just threw the ball up for the post. By then, he was so late that the covering defenders had figured out the play, and the uncertain pass—wobbling like one of Wally's—was snatched from the air by the free safety who zipped past Brock like a rocket, all the way to the end zone. The defensive players hooted and cheered and slapped high fives.

Coach Hewitt looked at the ground and shook his head.

Brock looked to Coach Van Kuffler and opened his mouth to explain.

All Coach Van Kuffler did was smile.

20

"What were you thinking?" Coach Hewitt's voice was calm, but demanding.

Brock blinked. "It was a Z Post."

"Yeah?" Coach Hewitt nodded.

"Z ran a cross. X ran the post, so I got confused and didn't know where to throw. By the time I did throw, it was too late."

"It was too late all right." Coach Van Kuffler stepped between Brock and the head coach and began gesturing with his chipmunk arms. "We just spent the last half hour going over Z and X."

Anger pushed Brock's senses aside. "Yeah. Z is on the right and X is on the left, you said."

Coach Van Kuffler smiled in a mean way. "I never said that, son. I would never say that. Z is strong side, X is weak side. So, if it's strong right, Z is right. If it's strong left, like that just was, Z is left. Now, you gonna tell me I said different than that?"

Brock's mind whirled. Coach Van Kuffler didn't say Z was right, Brock had said it and the coach didn't correct him. All the players stared at him, choking Brock into silence.

Coach Van Kuffler turned to Coach Hewitt. "Coach, I can't be wasting my time on some new kid who isn't going to even pay attention."

"I paid attention." Brock's voice was weak because he knew as the words came out that he was doing it again, talking back, making excuses. This was football, not baseball. Intense. Like the army.

Coach Van Kuffler tilted his head and flicked his arms in Brock's direction. "Well, if you paid attention and you still don't know it you must be pretty du—"

"Coach!" Coach Hewitt glared at Coach Van Kuffler and shook his head.

"Okay, Coach," Coach Van Kuffler said. "What's the acceptable term? Mentally challenged? Learning disabled? Slow? I know we can't say stupid, idiot, or moron. I'd never do that."

The two coaches locked eyes until Coach Hewitt cracked a smile, blew some air out of his tight lips, and walked away.

Brock's ears burned and the other two quarterbacks chuckled.

Coach Hewitt blew his whistle and the practice continued. Brock stayed in the back and figured his days as a quarterback had ended before they even began. After they'd run their sprints and Coach Hewitt had dismissed the team, he grabbed Brock's shoulder.

"Hey, Brock. I want to talk to you about this quarterback thing."

21

Coach Hewitt looked Brock in the eye.

"Let's not give up. If I hadn't seen you throw that pass, I'd say you're a lineman for sure." Coach Hewitt let go of his shoulder. "But you can really sling it. Let's see if you can't get at least some of this stuff down. I want you to stay and work with Coach Van Kuffler and the other quarterbacks after practice. That's part of playing that position anyway, you have to keep working when everyone else goes home. What do you think?"

"You wanna see me throw it again?" Brock smiled.

"I do." Coach Hewitt tossed the ball he had under his arm up into the air.

Brock caught it and pointed at the far goalpost. He took a step and zipped the ball. It flew up and away in a whizzing spiral and didn't come down for over fifty yards. Coach Hewitt chuckled. "I like it. Now let's see if you can get it going to the right guy in the right place at the right time, huh?"

"I can." Brock's confidence suddenly bloomed, just because of the way Coach Hewitt looked at him.

"Good." Coach Hewitt pointed to the other end zone where Coach Van Kuffler, Wally, and Wentzel were gathered with three of the wide receivers. "Go join the crowd. I got a meeting with the varsity staff to go over scouting assignments."

Coach Hewitt walked off and Mak, who had been standing by, came over.

"What's up?" Mak was sweaty and hunched over from heat and work.

"Coach wants me to work with the QBs a little."

"Nice." Mak patted him on the back. "I'll just hang in the shade by the press box and watch, then we can go get food. Good?"

"Sure." Brock slapped Mak a high five and turned toward the small group. But as he walked toward the team, the confidence pumped into him by Coach Hewitt deflated quickly, step by step, as he approached Coach Van Kuffler. When he reached the other players, Coach Van Kuffler stopped talking and stared at Brock for a beat before speaking.

"Yes?"

"Well, Coach Hewitt said I should work with you guys some."

"Really?" Coach Van Kuffler's eyebrows disappeared under the bill of his cap. "Well, you've got a lineman's mentality, don't you?"

"Sir?" Brock had no idea what he was talking about.

"Linemen." Coach Van Kuffler grinned around at the other

players. "They bang their heads together until they can't think straight, then they bang them some more. You already can't think straight, right?"

Everyone laughed.

"Huh?" It was the only thing Brock could say.

"Huh?" Coach Van Kuffler tilted his head and made his voice slow and stupid. "Huh?"

Everyone laughed some more.

"I'm only kidding." Coach Van Kuffler slapped Brock on the shoulder, sounding suddenly nice. "We'll get you into the mix here. You want to work like a QB, right?"

"I can," Brock said.

"Great." Coach Van Kuffler blew his whistle. "All right, guys, extra push-ups."

Everyone got down into push-up position.

"You want to be strong to throw the ball? Okay, down, one! Receivers, you want to bang on those defensive backs when they're pressing you at the line?" Coach Van Kuffler barked. "Down, two! We gotta get strong!"

Coach Van Kuffler counted out twenty push-ups for them before blowing his whistle. Everyone got to his knees and started to rise. "All right. On your feet, boys. Quarterbacks, on the line. Go right through the passing *tree*. Five throws for each pattern."

Coach Van Kuffler turned suddenly to Brock. "Whoa, Brock. Where you think you're going? No, no, no. You get down and keep going. You missed the first five days, you gotta get caught up. We can do that, though. Ready? Down, one! . . . Down, two! . . ."

While Wentzel and Wally threw passes, Coach Van Kuffler made Brock do five more sets of twenty push-ups. It took quite a while because after the first two sets, Brock had to rest between reps while Coach Van Kuffler screamed at him for being weak. When he finally finished, sweat bled into Brock's eyes and filled his mouth like salty tears. He staggered to his feet and Coach Van Kuffler tossed him a ball. The other players stopped to watch.

"I saw you showing off to Coach Hewitt." Coach Van Kuffler gave Brock a twisted grin. "Let's see how far you can throw it now. Go ahead. Show us that cannon."

Brock gripped the ball, still huffing with exhaustion. Furious, and determined to disappoint Coach Van Kuffler, he gripped the ball as hard as he could and launched it down the field. The ball wobbled and dropped short of thirty yards.

"That's not so impressive." Coach Van Kuffler bit the end of his thumb and spoke in a mystified voice, then he suddenly brightened. "But let's see how you do with some live targets. Come on, you want to be a quarterback? You gotta be a team leader. Imagine it's late in the fourth quarter. Everyone's tired, but you gotta make a play. Come on. Throw a post, that one you couldn't figure out earlier."

Brock nodded and stepped up to the line. One of the receivers got in his stance. Brock called out the cadence and pretended to get the snap. He waited for the receiver to get to twelve yards and break for the goalpost, then he let his pass fly. It wobbled and sailed behind him. The receiver spun to get it, but it was too far off. He barely nicked it with his fingertips before it fell to the turf.

"Not so good, but let's try again." Coach Van Kuffler spoke in a voice that was as false as it was kind. "See if you can get it."

Brock looked at him and sighed. The other quarterbacks stood and watched while Brock threw. He threw wide, high, and low, completing just two of about twenty passes. Still, they kept on. Brock had no idea why Coach Van Kuffler kept it up. He'd already humiliated Brock thoroughly.

Then, Brock saw Coach Hewitt come out of the building and march toward the field. When he got to the sideline, Coach Van Kuffler shouted over to him. "Take a look!"

Brock saw Coach Hewitt staring at him and he knew he had to perform. This was his chance.

Coach Van Kuffler turned to Brock. "Go ahead. Let me see a go route."

A go route sent the receiver up the sideline as fast as he could run. Brock barked the cadence and threw the pass. It wobbled and fell short. Brock couldn't even feel his arms. His stomach suddenly felt like he'd swallowed a box of ants.

"Okay, not bad." Coach Van Kuffler spoke in a friendly tone that belied everything he'd been doing to Brock. "Let's see a hitch."

A hitch was the easiest throw a quarterback could make. The receiver simply stood at the line and caught the ball before running, but it was like Brock's arms were filled with Jell-O and he threw a bad hitch pass. His stomach crawled. He sniffed back hot tears, determined not to break down, even though what Coach Van Kuffler was doing to him was so wrong.

The coach kept calling out different routes.

"A cross."

Brock missed on the cross.

"Post."

He missed it.

"Swing."

Brock missed again, and with that, Coach Hewitt shook his head and walked away.

At the end of practice, Brock dragged his feet off the field. Mak met him at the bottom of the bleachers.

"What happened?" Mak's eyebrows disappeared up into the football helmet he still wore.

"Did you see all those push-ups he made me do?" Brock tried to snarl so he wouldn't cry.

"Yeah, that was sick. Was your arm just jelly?"

"It still is." Brock raised his left arm and let it fall back down, limp.

"Yeah." Mak turned and the two of them started to walk toward the center of town. "The line isn't so bad. You'll be with me."

They left the school grounds and tramped down the sidewalk. They passed big homes with bright green lawns under the shade of tall trees. Birds twittered high above. The sun winked down at them through the leaves but heated the naked streets like the surface of a griddle. Boiling air waffled up and away, adding to the muggy warmth.

Up ahead, Brock could see the brick and stone buildings standing along Main Street. "I'm not playing on the line. I'm playing quarterback."

"What?"

"You heard me," Brock said.

"Yeah, but why so stubborn? You'll do good on the line."

"You've seen me throw the ball," Brock said.

"I saw you throw it just now. I could have done better, and I'm kind of a slob."

"That wasn't right and you know it." On a whim, Brock veered down a side street, heading for the library. Something in him wanted to see Laurel, just see her.

"Where you going? Aren't we going to Subway?" Mak stopped, but Brock kept on walking. "I'm starved."

"Library."

"Oh Romeo, oh Romeo, wherefore art thou, Romeo." Mak giggled and caught up. "You got guts, I tell you that. Quarterback and Laurel Lehman. You gonna run for class president, too, I bet."

Brock shook his head and smiled. He looked at Mak. "Do you ever feel silly walking around town with your full football uniform and that helmet on your head?"

"Don't get mad," Mak said. "I like your style. You remind me of me."

Brock glanced over at him and shook his head. He pulled open the door to the library and said, "After you."

"Why thank you . . . Romeo."

Brock slapped Mak's helmet. Mak took it off and the two of them giggled together as they tumbled into the musty library. When Brock looked up at the desk, he saw Laurel and froze. She wasn't alone. A boy leaned close to her with his arms braced against the top of the checkout counter. The boy was big, over six feet tall, and looked like an actor with his tan skin, blond hair, and blue eyes. Laurel pointed at Brock and said something he couldn't hear.

All Brock could think about was his blurted invitation to take her to ice cream. Obviously, this superhero at the counter was her boyfriend and Brock had made a run at his girl.

"Him?" The boy pointed at Brock.

Laurel nodded and Brock couldn't move—even though he was horrified—as the older boy marched toward him with a cold hard look on his face.

23

"You're Brock?" The boy stopped and folded his arms across his chest. His hands made the biceps bulge through the sleeves of his black T-shirt. Brock could tell he lifted a lot of weights. Brock wanted to deny that he was Brock but, just as he'd blurted out his invitation to take Laurel to ice cream, his head simply nodded on its own.

"Yeah." The other boy nodded back. "Laurel told me about you."

"I didn't mean anything by it." Brock's voice came out in a kind of squeak. He assumed that this kid viewed his invitation to Laurel for ice cream as asking his girlfriend out on a date.

"Pretty hard to say you didn't mean anything by it." The boy's stare was cold and hard. "You said what you said."

Brock looked over at Mak, who seemed to be enjoying the whole thing. Brock wanted to kick his new friend in the shin.

"Hey, Taylor." Mak raised and lowered his chin.

Brock glared at Mak. Couldn't he have told Brock about this guy? Instead, Mak quoted *Romeo and Juliet* at him, making the whole thing a joke. Mak should have warned him the minute he mentioned the library.

"Hey, Mak." Taylor looked at Mak before turning his attention back to Brock. "You guys gonna be any good?"

"We got a good line." Mak puffed up. "We'll see about the QB, though."

"How's the new kid look?" Taylor angled his head at Brock.

"Not too good today, but Coach Van Kuffler made him do about a million push-ups."

"That figures." Taylor frowned. "So, New Kid. Brock. Laurel says I got to help you."

"She said . . . help?" Now Brock was totally baffled. He thought Taylor was getting ready to knock him flat, now he was talking about help?

"You got any sisters?" Taylor asked.

Brock shook his head. "No."

"Yeah, well, you're lucky." Taylor looked over at Laurel and grinned.

"Hey!" She looked up from a stack of books she was working on. "Taylor Owen Lehman, I heard that."

"You're Laurel's brother?" Brock said.

"Taylor's the first-team varsity quarterback. Ohio State's looking at him." Mak beamed, proud of his information.

"The *varsity*?" Brock's mouth dropped.

"State champs last year." Mak said it like he was part of the winning squad and he pointed at a silver ring on Taylor's hand.

It had a green stone the size of a gumdrop. "That's where he got *that*."

Taylor blushed and cupped his hand so the ring didn't show. "You're gonna need some extra help if you're gonna try and break in around here, especially with Wally Van Kuffler in the same grade. You'll be swimming upstream like a fish with a hook in its gills."

"Help?" Brock didn't even want to think about the image of a hook in his gills.

"With the plays. Lots to learn," Taylor said.

"You could teach me?" Brock glanced over at Laurel, who was lit up like a merry-go-round at a carnival.

"We all run the exact same offense," Taylor said. "I've been doing it since I was five. I gotta go to practice now, but come over tonight. We can go through some footwork in the yard too."

"Why?" Brock couldn't keep the question from rolling off his lips.

"I don't know. Ask her." Taylor laughed and nodded toward the desk as he made his way out of the library.

Mak grabbed Brock's arm and tugged him into a quick hug. "Dude, do you know how cool that is?"

"Yeah." Brock had his eyes on Laurel. She was opening new books, pasting stickers on the inside cover and running the scanner over them with a beep. She acted like she hadn't even been paying attention, but her cheeks were flushed, and she was focused a little too hard on the books. Brock walked over to the desk. She didn't look up until he cleared his throat.

"Oh, hi," she said.

"That was really nice. Thanks."

"What do you mean?" she said, but the smile crept onto her lips. "No, I'm kidding. I like underdogs, that's all."

"Underdog?" For some reason, that made Brock mad. "Like community service? Helping out a poor Flatty? Must be nice to be so important. Princess and the pauper, right?"

"No!" She scowled. "I'd never say that. You're new, that's all."

Laurel got up and held out the book in her hands, open, as if presenting it to him. "And you're rude too."

She slapped the book shut, set it on the stack, and marched off into the back.

Mak tilted his head. "Dude, you just blew the whole thing. What is wrong with you?"

"What *is* wrong with me?" Brock asked the question out loud as he quickly exited the library. Mak paused on the steps to put his helmet on. Brock put his head in his hands. He couldn't just tell Mak he was a social misfit after years of living a life on the run with his father, fending off friends with a stiff-arm of secrecy and silence.

"Go in there and tell her." Mak shoved Brock back toward the library doors.

"Tell her what?" Brock let Mak push him along.

"Anything. That you got hit in the head. That you're suffering from heat stroke. Anything. Just say you're sorry, Brock. This could be your ticket, if you really want to play QB. *I* want you to play because I saw that arm and I want to grow up and win a high school state championship and go to Notre Dame and then the pros. Say 'sorry.' It'll work. You should see the stupid stuff my dad does, then bang. He says 'sorry' to my mom and it works like a charm. 'Sorry' is like magic with women."

Brock swatted Mak's hands away and stopped short of the door. "Do you realize how silly you look in that helmet?"

"Don't change the subject. Just do it. I'm telling you. And I'm not letting you leave here unless you do. I play defensive tackle too, you know. I can sack you right here and now, a quarterback sack on the library front steps. Sounds like a movie, and I'll do it." Mak crouched down and flexed his fingers like he was getting ready to make a tackle.

Brock looked at the sidewalk, wondering if he could make it. If he could, he'd outrun Mak and be clear of this mess, but then what? This was his home, now. He touched the skinny new nose on his face. They weren't running anymore.

He turned and went through the doors, but stopped at the sight of the gaping hallway that led to the library offices in back. "Who knows if she's even still in there?"

"Go." Mak pointed a thick finger and crouched down in his tackling position again.

Brock sighed and circled the counter. He stepped slowly into the offices. Fear buzzed in his ears—fear of being in a place he didn't belong, and fear of seeing her face. The librarian appeared suddenly from a doorway on the right down the wide hall. She didn't look happy.

"Were you mean to Laurel?" The softness was gone from the librarian's voice and the color of her cheeks matched her fiery hair. "She's here to help people, you know. No one's paying her."

"I'm . . . I wanted to say sorry."

"Well, that's a good idea." She said it like an order and pointed her finger toward the door she'd just come out of.

Brock marched down the hall. He passed an open office where a large man in a dress shirt sat with his back to Brock, typing at a computer. When Brock got to the door, the librarian opened it and marshaled him in.

"Laurel, this young man has something to say."

The room was a lounge of sorts with dusty old chairs, a couch, reading lamps, and a noisy refrigerator in the corner. Laurel stood at a sink built into the counter beside the fridge. She pulled coffee mugs out of the sudsy water and rinsed them in the steady stream of the spout. When she raised her chin, he thought she looked more angry than sad.

"Oh, man," Brock said. "I'm really sorry. Please. I swear the sun got to my brain. I'm just a mess of scrambled eggs between the ears, moving here and trying to play football and looking like a dork wherever I go. Why I'd take it out on you when you're being nice to me is . . . well, it's . . ."

She glared. "Inexcusable?"

"Exactly. It is."

She sighed and her face softened. "It's not easy to apologize."

"It's easier when someone as big as Mak is gonna smear your guts all over the library floor if you don't."

She laughed. "He's nice. A little crazy, but nice."

"You mean your brother doesn't wear his football helmet to bed?" Relief gushed through Brock's veins, cooling and calming him. She smiled at him and he knew at that moment that if she asked him to jump off a bridge, he'd do it.

"My brother can help you, you know."

"I do know. What I don't know is why you'd do all this for me."

"My mom tells us all the time to do random nice things for people."

Brock's face fell. "Oh."

"But it's more than that." She spoke quickly. "You just . . . seem nice. I like that you read and . . . *When You Reach Me* is one of my favorite books, but you're this big football player. Or, you want to be."

"Want to."

"Anyone tough enough to get Mak Koletsky into the library, then brave enough to check out a book that has a girl for the main character can be a football player," she said. "My dad used to play for the Bengals, so I should know."

"That's awesome," Brock said. "What was it like?"

She shrugged. "I don't really remember. He retired when I was only two."

"Mak says your brother might go to Ohio State," Brock said.

"Maybe. He's tough like that too. He doesn't care what he looks like or what people might say. He took a dance class once."

"Dance?"

"Jazz." Laurel nodded.

"Jeez." Brock didn't even know what jazz dancing was, but he had an image of the big blond Taylor twirling on a hardwood stage under some spotlights.

"No, jazz." She frowned.

"Yeah. I mean, that's cool."

"Well." Laurel wiped her hands on a towel. She moved toward the door, stopped and touched his arm. "I better get back to work."

Brock followed her out of the lounge and down the hall. Only a huff and a head wag from Mak could break her magnetic pull; otherwise, Brock thought he would have stayed behind the counter for the rest of the afternoon, just looking at her. Laurel jotted something down on a scrap of paper and handed it to him. "My address. Come over after dinner. Seven thirty? Taylor will work with you."

"I . . . what about a football? We don't use the same size ball as the varsity," Brock said.

Laurel rolled her eyes. "My brother could fill a barn with his old footballs. He'll have something. See you later."

She went back to her stack of books, but again, as Brock walked out through the main entrance he looked back and caught her smiling at him. Brock barely felt the flagstone steps beneath his feet.

"See?" Mak thumped him on the back. "Magic with women. Flowers is another trick my dad uses. Don't have to be roses, either. You can pick stuff from the side of the road, daisies, buttercups. . . ."

"Buttercups?" Brock couldn't contain a laugh as they turned onto Main Street heading for the Subway. "Listen to you . . . buttercups."

"Hey, I'm not the one with a girlfriend." Mak poked his arm.

Brock's heart buzzed like a bee, but he waved a hand. "She's just being nice."

"Yeah. Well. I'm not as dumb as I look."

"If you were, you'd have a hard time crossing the street. Seriously, you gotta lose the helmet, Mak. People are staring."

"Let 'em stare." Mak looked around and caught a little girl on the other side of the street holding her older sister's hand and pointing at him. Mak raised an arm and hooked his hand so his finger pointed down at the top of his helmet. "Take a look! Calhoun Middle Fighting Crabs. First team, girls!"

"Come on." Brock shoved his friend inside the sandwich shop and treated him to a chicken bacon ranch sub. They sat facing each other in a booth. Mak removed his helmet to eat. He set it down on the seat beside him, and they dug in.

"Stuff is awesome!" A slug of chewed sub plopped out of Mak's mouth as he spoke. The blob of food banked off his chest, bounced off the helmet, and hit the floor. Mak glanced around, bent over, scooped it up, and held it high between his fingers, examining it in the light as if it were a jewel.

Brock choked down a mouthful of milk. "Mak, you're not going to . . ."

Mak popped the blob into his mouth and chewed, rolling his eyes with delight as he gulped it down.

Brock leaned over and looked at the dirty floor, losing his appetite.

Mak raised his eyebrows. "What?"

"Dude. Disgusting." Brock set his sandwich down.

Mak took another huge bite and talked through the food. "My dad says everyone eats a pound of dirt over their lifetime. That barely hit the ground."

Mak took a swig of milk to wash down his food.

Brock wrinkled his nose. "That was gross. Even if it hit a clean plate, it looked like something that came out of the other end."

Mak burst with laughter, choked, and milk sprayed from his nose all over the table. Everyone looked. Mak howled even louder as he mopped up the mess with a handful of napkins. Finally, he caught his breath.

"The other end!" Mak grinned around at everyone else, delighted with the humor and expecting them to be too. People rolled their eyes and looked away in disgust.

Brock examined the rest of his sub, saw that it hadn't been sprayed, and folded it carefully in the wrapper to save for later.

"Where you going?" Mak blinked up at him.

"Not hungry anymore."

Mak shrugged, stuffed the rest of his own sub into his mouth, and jammed the football helmet back on his head before he rose to follow Brock with his milk in one hand and his garbage in the other. Brock waited for Mak to throw away his mess. When he turned around, he stood face-to-face with Wentzel, the backup quarterback, and two goons who looked like linemen.

"Hey, it's the son of the cookie man." Wentzel smiled like a boy who enjoyed pulling the legs off spiders. "Heard your dad likes to get in the kitchen and bake."

All three of them laughed.

Brock's stomach knotted up and he clenched his teeth.

"What's a matter?" Wentzel kept grinning. "You don't like it here? Maybe you should head on over to your side of the river? It's a little *flatter* over there, like your head."

Brock's hands coiled into fists. He stepped forward so that his chest almost touched Wentzel's.

Mak burst in between Brock and Wentzel with both hands. "Hey, guys. Come on, now. We're all on the same team. You know what Coach says. You fight, you're cut. Now, come on."

Mak dragged Brock away. They walked out into the sunshine and headed for the park.

"Don't fall for that." Mak shook his head.

"What?"

"You get into a fight with Wentzel, who wins?"

"Wentzel would get cut too if that's the rules," Brock said.

"Yeah. So, who wins?" Mak asked.

Brock thought about it and realized Wally would be the real winner. "Seriously? Wentzel would risk getting suspended for Wally Van Kuffler?"

"I'm not saying he wouldn't. Maybe it was one of those other guys who were gonna step in. Quinn can't play his way out of a paper bag and the other kid isn't even on the football team. They'd do it just to get attention, so keep away from that kind of junk."

"We moved around a lot," Brock said. "I got used to fighting, especially in the first week or two. Then people usually leave you alone."

"Well, don't fight here." Mak led the way to a bench under a big shade tree in the park next to a statue of a Union soldier on horseback. "Who cares what they say? Let them say what they want. Cookies? Who cares? That's so stupid it hurts."

Mak picked up a stick, sat down, and began to break it into pieces.

Brock sat next to him. In the silence, Brock noticed a big dark-gray car parked along the road. Four silver rings on the grill told him it was an Audi. The windows were tinted so that he couldn't see inside, but Brock had the sudden feeling that someone was watching them. He stared at the car and the lights went on as it revved to life.

"Is that someone you know?" Brock kept his eyes on the car so Mak would know where to look.

"Nice wheels," Mak said. "Not *me*. Why?"

Brock was overtaken by a feeling so strong it made him sweat.

He stood to go. "Come on."

Mak sighed. "Let me rest. Your dad said to wait for him in the park."

Brock kept walking. The car began to roll slowly forward, mirroring Brock's movement.

"Hey." Mak caught up.

Brock's mind did cartwheels. He didn't know if he should keep walking to pretend he wasn't aware of the car, or take off and run. Suddenly, he felt like his old life was back upon him—running, hiding, panic.

Brock broke to his left and bolted across the park, away from the car. He heard the yip of tires as the Audi took off behind him.

"Brock!" Mak hustled to keep up.

Brock looked back and saw the Audi turn the corner so that it could circle the park and cut him off. He broke back again the other way.

"What are we doing?" Mak had confusion in his voice and a touch of fear.

Brock didn't know what he was doing. That was the problem.

He reached the street and shot down a brick alley.

It was a dead end.

"Brock." Mak threw his hands up in the air, puffing. "You're crazy."

Brock was crazy, and when he turned and looked back up the mouth of the alley and saw the headlights swing into the narrow space, heading his way, he was so crazy he couldn't even breathe.

27

The car stopped.

It wasn't the Audi. It was another car, his father's. The horn beeped and the window rolled down. "Cut the nonsense and get in, will you?"

There was no urgency to his father's voice, no panic.

Brock swallowed and gulped for air.

"Dude, you're cracked." Mak huffed, and he whispered, "You scared me."

They piled into his dad's car.

"What was that about? Hide-and-seek?" His father switched on the radio.

"Just kidding." It was all Brock could think of to say. He felt so foolish. His father said they were going to have a normal life. Why couldn't he just believe it and let go?

"Yeah, well do me a favor, will you? Save the kidding for

Mak." His father glanced at him as he backed the car out of the alleyway. "I've got things to do at the house."

"Did you get a job?" Brock asked.

"In fact, I did." His father nodded and bit his lip. "Sanitary engineer."

"Man," Mak said, "sounds important. My dad's just a factory worker."

"A job's a job," Brock's dad said, turning back into the street.

Brock could tell by his dad's face that he should stop asking about the job. They were off the subject of hide-and-seek though, so he clamped his mouth shut.

"We'll get you a bike later on so you can start riding to practice with Mak," his dad said. "I'll be working all day."

"My dad's picking me up a new wheel today," Mak said brightly. "So I'm good to go too."

"How was lunch?" Brock's dad steered them across the bridge.

"Better than practice," Brock said.

"Why's that?"

"That Coach Van Kuffler doesn't like me, Dad." He had no plans on getting into the details because he figured his dad would only remind him that it wasn't baseball.

"Oh?" His dad rubbed his beard.

Mak leaned forward so that his helmet poked out between the seats. "But we got a plan, right, Brock?"

"A plan?" Brock's dad passed the broken-down factory and turned down their street.

Brock told his dad about Taylor Owen Lehman, the varsity quarterback, offering to help, and then he held out the scrap of paper.

Brock's dad glanced at it. "Very nice."

"Yeah," Mak said, "and his sister—"

Brock gave Mak a deadly look.

". . . is real nice too," Mak continued. "That's how we met Taylor. He was visiting her in the library and we just stopped in to . . ."

"Ahhh." Brock's dad smirked and looked over at him. "I see."

Brock sighed and shook his head, slapping Mak's helmet. "Now I know why you wear that thing."

"Why?"

"So when people want to smack you in the head—which is probably about every two minutes—they don't scramble your brains."

"When you're the first-team QB," Mak said, "you'll be glad your left tackle is comfortable in his helmet so he can concentrate on protecting your blind side."

"You're forgetting something," Brock said.

"What?" Mak asked.

"I'm a lefty, so my blind side is on the right."

"Oh." Mak chewed on the mouthpiece hanging from his face mask. "Then I guess you better watch your back."

"Is that what your dad would say?" Brock asked as they pulled into their narrow driveway.

"Oh, for sure. My dad says that all the time."

Brock nodded, because he had a feeling it was advice he'd need to follow quite a bit here in Calhoun, both on and off the field.

That evening, Brock and his dad headed over the bridge and through town on their way to Laurel's house. Highway 37 went north out of town along the river before veering toward a round-top mountain covered with trees. Thick woods bordered the road on both sides for half a mile before they came to the spot where Brock's dad's GPS said they had arrived at their destination. On their left, two fifteen-foot stone towers stood watch on either side of a gravel driveway. Big fancy coach lights capped the towers, their bulbs already burning bright in the shadows of late day. Brock's dad turned in, and just beyond the towers they saw a matching stone cottage with a slate roof. It looked like a gingerbread house.

"Wow. Nice." Brock leaned forward in his seat, looking for signs of life through the diamond-shaped windowpanes.

An older man in a tweed cap came out of the front door

carrying a walking stick. He seemed surprised to see them, but stepped right up to the car. Brock's dad opened his window.

The man leaned down. He had a thick graying mustache. "This is a private drive; you'll have to turn back."

"My son is supposed to throw the football around with Taylor. Are you Mr. Lehman?"

The man looked startled. "Oh, no, I'm Humphries. Master Taylor is at the main house."

The man pointed up the gravel road. Brock's dad thanked him and they drove on.

"Main house?" Brock hadn't seen many homes nicer than the stone gingerbread house Humphries lived in.

"I guess," his dad said. They rounded a bend and the trees opened up into a sprawling lawn where an enormous stone mansion fronted by a half circle of columns rested on a small rise overlooking the river. Off to the right, beyond a pasture spotted with dark-colored horses eating grass, was a crisp white horse barn trimmed with dark-brown beams and a slate roof of its own.

"Wow," Brock said.

"Wow is right." His dad swung the car into the large gravel circle and stopped.

One side of the wide front doors swung open. Laurel burst out and down the half-round stone steps. "Hi! Taylor's out back. Come on."

Brock got out and introduced his dad.

"Nice to meet you." Laurel held out a hand to shake, gave Brock a smile, and set off down a slate path that circled the big house, bringing them to the grassy lawn between the house and the river, which was cloaked in the shadows of the trees from the far shore. Beyond the river, the sky glowed orange as the sun set in the distant hills.

Taylor had a pile of footballs spilled out in the grass, and he was throwing each one into a net some thirty yards away. The net was strung with various red plastic circles for targets. He took a pretend snap, dropped three steps, and rifled a ball, striking one of the red disks with a pop. He gave his work a tight nod before turning to them.

"Hey, Brock." Taylor shook Brock's hand before addressing Brock's dad. "Sir."

Someone coughed behind them and Brock turned. Walking down the wide rounded staircase from a terrace above was one of the most beautiful women Brock had ever seen. Tall with silky blond hair that glowed in the late-day light, Laurel's mom moved like a deer, stepping smoothly and effortlessly as she came toward them with an outstretched hand.

"Well, hello." Her smile came easy and stayed. "I'm Laurel and Taylor's mom. You must be Brock. Laurel's told me about you, the football player who reads."

"Hey," Taylor said, "I read."

"Yeah, the sports page," Laurel muttered in a playful way.

Brock shook the mother's hand. It was long and smooth, but strong. Thin bracelets of gold jangled together on her wrist like tiny wind chimes. He was suddenly aware of the rip in the knee of his jeans and the color of his father's sneakers—once white but now a shabby gray. Still, his father stood tall and proud, like a stone monument that belonged right there in the middle of this fancy lawn.

"And, this is your father?" She extended her hand to Brock's dad.

"Pete Barrette. It's very nice of your kids to help Brock," his dad said. "We just moved into town."

"I'm Kim Dahlman. It was nice of you to bake cookies for our sale." Her smile quivered, and it mocked him.

The image of Wentzel's insults about his dad flooded Brock's mind. He realized how bad they must look, Flatties with no mom, a cookie-baking dad, here in this place with this rich and beautiful family. Brock also knew that as short and hot as his own temper was, his dad's was shorter and hotter. Right now, his father's face was blank.

Brock took a breath, and waited for the fireworks to begin.

Suddenly, Laurel's mom's smile bloomed into a toothy grin and she snorted at her own joke, making a noise that didn't fit anything Brock had seen so far. Then Brock saw his dad do something rare: he looked at his feet, blushed, and broke out into a silly grin of his own.

"I mean it." Laurel's mom touched his father's arm. "That was borderline heroic. Most men would have taken a big pass on that circus of hens."

Brock's dad shrugged. "You have to do your part, whether you want to or not. Especially when not."

Laurel's mom swept her hand toward the terrace. "Please, why don't we sit. We can watch the kids, and I can offer you coffee or something?"

"Coffee?" Brock's dad said.

"I have a fresh pot."

Brock's dad gave him a wink and a smile and followed the beautiful woman up to the terrace.

"Here." Taylor tossed a smaller football to Brock and he caught it. "Let me see how you hold it."

Brock spun the ball in his hands so that his fingertips touched the laces.

"Lefty, huh? Good." Taylor moved Brock's left hand back on the ball, just a bit. "Some people put their finger right on the tip, but you don't have to. Whatever feels right. Now, when you throw, you always want to follow through so that your thumb ends up pointing down."

"Um. I can *throw* it pretty good. I just don't know the plays." Brock didn't want to sound ungrateful, but he hoped Taylor would simply watch him throw and they could get down to business.

"Oh?" Taylor gave Laurel a look. "Well. Okay. Let's see. Throw it into the net."

"Which disk?" Brock asked.

"Disk? Well, if you think you can hit one, go for the one in the center."

Brock stood sideways to the target, drew back and fired the ball.

THUNK.

Taylor smiled and tossed him another ball. "Do that again."

Brock did.

Taylor grinned at Laurel and scratched his head. "Okay. Well, that was quick. What about the footwork on your drops?"

"Three step and five step?" Brock only knew from watching practice that a quarterback's footwork was important.

"Do you know that too?"

"No," Brock said. "I've seen it and tried a couple three steps, but I could use some help."

"Good. We'll work on that, then we'll go inside and work the whiteboard. I can show you how this offense works."

"Can you explain that Z and X and H and Y thing?" Brock asked.

Taylor waved a hand in the air. "That's easy. You'll see."

Brock threw well, not perfect, but strong for someone with so little experience. Taylor said so, and the beaming look on Laurel's face confirmed it. Brock glanced up at his dad every so often, but more times than not he was watching Mrs. Dahlman instead of them. After a time, Brock rubbed his shoulder.

"Sore?" Taylor asked.

"A little."

Taylor nodded. "Time to stop. When your shoulder gets sore, that's your body telling you you've had enough, and you have to listen. You're just not used to throwing. You'll be able to zing a hundred passes by the end of the season."

Brock opened his mouth to speak, then clamped it shut.

"What were you going to say?" Laurel asked.

"I was just thinking about Van Kuffler having me do all those push-ups," Brock said.

Taylor frowned and shook his head. "He's a rotten egg, that Coach Van Kuffler. Maybe I can help with that. We'll see. Let me think about it some more. Hey, let's go get on that whiteboard."

Brock helped Taylor—along with Laurel—retrieve the footballs that were spread across the lawn and stuff them into a big mesh bag.

"How do you know all this stuff?" Brock asked. "I mean footwork, and arm motion and all that? You're like a coach."

Taylor shrugged. "My dad was a quarterback."

"I told him he played for the Bengals." Laurel nodded with pride.

"Is he here?" Brock felt a small charge of excitement.

Taylor glanced at Laurel. She didn't say anything, so he spoke. "He's in Dallas. We don't really see him since they got divorced."

"Oh." Taylor's tone made Brock wish he hadn't asked.

None of them spoke after that. Taylor led them inside, through a double set of glass doors in the lower level of the huge house. He put the footballs away in a closet beside the entryway. They passed down a short hallway, then went right down another hall before taking another right and entering a huge room filled with Xboxes, flat-screen TVs, and thickly padded couches and chairs. On a wall by the window looking out at the river, a whiteboard hung in front of a small circle of desk chairs.

"Sometimes the offense comes over and we watch videos and go over plays." Taylor pointed to the chairs and Brock could imagine the high school running backs and receivers sitting around with serious faces.

Brock slipped into a seat, trying not to grin when Laurel sat right next to him. He watched and listened intently.

It was easy, the way Taylor explained it anyway. Before nine o'clock, Brock understood a dozen basic plays of the offense. It was a simple language based on letters and numbers so that the name of each play told the quarterback exactly what to do.

"This isn't so hard," Brock said. He'd just correctly diagramed a Spread Right Alaska 99 on the whiteboard.

"Well, you're pretty smart. Some people don't get it that quick," Taylor said.

Laurel's expression made Brock blush and he thought of his dad, up on the terrace with their mom. It was getting dark outside. Brock yawned.

"Yeah, I could do this all night. You'd better get some rest." Taylor set the marker down on the narrow tray beneath the board. "You're gonna be crazy sore tomorrow from the push-ups alone. Forget about our throwing."

"Maybe he should take it easy?" Laurel gave Taylor an eager look.

Taylor shook his head. "He should, but that's the trap. That's why Van Kuffler did what he did. He knew you'd be useless tomorrow, and if you bail out, he'll say you're not tough."

"They're getting ready to put me on the line anyway," Brock said. "Because of my size."

"That's not fair." Laurel scowled at her big brother. "He's got an arm. As good as *you* when you were his age."

Taylor shrugged. "You know what Dad always said. Life's not fair, and football's less fair than life."

"You can help him." Laurel sounded almost angry. "They

listen to you, Taylor. You know they do. Don't let Coach Van Kuffler end Brock's career before it even starts. You know he's good."

Taylor studied Brock and chewed on his lower lip. "He *can* be good."

"Then do something." Laurel slapped the desktop attached to her chair.

Taylor looked out the window. The light was nearly gone and the day had faded to charcoal gray.

"Maybe," Taylor said. "Let me see what I can do."

31

"Nice people," Brock's dad said. They were driving across the bridge, its steel ribs jutting up into the night, lit by random blue-white lights whose reflections glinted off the tar-black river below like huge stars. "I mean, they have everything, but you'd never know it. Very down to earth."

Brock had his window down, and he pretended not to hear. His mind had wandered into a world where *he* had a family who everyone respected, so that people like Coach Van Kuffler wouldn't dare to mistreat him. A nudge in his ribs startled Brock into the present. His father removed his finger from Brock's chest and returned his hand to the wheel. "I asked you a question, Brock."

"Uh, sorry. What?"

"I was saying how nice the Lehmans are. The whole family, and I asked you what you thought."

"They are." Brock glowed like the ring on a hot plate. He recalled the image of his dad and Laurel's mom on the terrace. After the whiteboard session, he and Taylor and Laurel had gone upstairs through a towering wood-paneled room with a marble fireplace you could stand up in, and out onto the terrace. In the faint light of the stars and a sliver of moon only inches remained between the thick wicker arms of his father's and Laurel's mother's chairs. They tilted toward each other, both looking out at the river, talking in low voices, coffee gone cold in cups resting on the small cocktail table before them.

He remembered his father's words about dating and how it would have to be a pretty special woman, but wasn't that exactly what Laurel's mom was?

It would be perfect. What could be better for gaining acceptance in such a small and hostile town than the richest, prettiest woman around falling in love with his father, and taking them both under her protective wing? Still, Brock knew better than to talk about such things, especially with his father.

"Taylor said he might be able to help me with Coach Van Kuffler." Brock nodded and they turned down their street.

"Really?" Brock's dad raised an eyebrow. "Well, it's just another example of how nice they are. Kim invited us to dinner on Friday. I'd say we're pretty lucky. First place we decide to stay and we meet people like them."

"Mak too," Brock said as they pulled into the driveway.

His father grinned. "And Mak."

Brock's new friend sat on their tiny front stoop in the dark, dressed in his football gear, head to toe. He stood when he saw them and stumbled toward the car. Brock's dad shut off the engine and they got out. Mak was blubbering like a wounded whale.

"Mak? What happened?" Brock's dad put a hand on Mak's shoulder pad.

Brock saw something gooey all over his friend, something glimmering in the light from the streetlamp.

"They . . . they made me . . . I didn't want to, but I had to." Mak gasped between words and he shook with distress and rage.

"Easy, Mak," Brock's dad said. "Just tell me what happened."

"I came over to see how everything went at Laurel's." Mak stifled his sobs. "They were egging your house."

"Who?" Brock's dad's voice went cold.

"It was Wentzel and his goons."

Brock now saw that the shiny goo on Mak was from broken eggs. Little shards of shell clung to his jersey and helmet. He saw too that the front of their house had been pelted with a dozen or so eggs, yellow yoke and clear dribbling goo scattered with shell fragments smearing the front door, siding, and windows.

"Wentzel did this?" Brock could barely believe it. "What about the whole teammate thing? Won't he get kicked off?"

Mak burst out with a fresh gut-wrenching sob. "*He* won't. *I* will."

"You?" Brock's father scowled.

"Wentzel didn't throw the eggs. That slick snake. He was just with them and he was laughing and when I yelled at them to stop, they threw them at me and ran, but that jerk Wentzel stood there pointing and laughing and . . . Oh!" Mak sobbed again and smacked a fist into his other hand. "I couldn't help it. I just *smashed* him, punched him right in the face. Now . . ."

Mak gasped again and shook his head violently. "I'm not gonna be on the first team. I'm not gonna be on *any* team."

The very next day before practice even started, Coach blew his whistle and called them all in. Brock stood with the rest of the team, listening to Coach Hewitt rant. Flecks of spit burst from his mouth like fireworks. His cheeks burned red and his hands flew through the air. Mak was demoted, off the first team and suspended for the first game.

The only good news was that he hadn't been thrown off the team entirely. That had been Mak's biggest fear.

The only rebuke Wentzel got was a general bit of life advice from Coach Hewitt to be careful the company you keep. Wentzel smiled smugly. Brock wanted to scream. No mention was made of the boys who egged his house. Brock's father had insisted that the best course was to not make a big deal out of it.

"Kids throw eggs," his father had said. "Let it go, Brock. If you don't, you'll look like a baby. Trust me."

Practice began with a sour intensity. Sharp whistles. Angry shouts. Players dug teeth into their rubber mouthpieces and moved and sweat and added some extra hustle to their steps. By the time warm-ups and agility drills were over, jerseys were dark with sweat and droplets of perspiration drizzled down cheeks like raindrops.

Quarterbacks peeled off from the rest of the team for individual drills where they began to warm up their arms and run through footwork drills for both run and pass plays. Brock's arm ached. He searched the bleachers and sidelines between breaths, stomach tight at the thought of Taylor Owen Lehman showing up with a varsity coach to champion his cause.

No one ever came.

Weighed down by confusion and a vague sense of betrayal, Brock did his best to throw, but his arm was weak from push-ups the day before and his extra throwing, so his timing was off. He did very little to win over Coach Hewitt, let alone Coach Van Kuffler, who couldn't contain his glee at Brock's miserable performance. Coach Van Kuffler didn't have to do anything to make Brock look bad, the damage was already done. It was as though the previous night never happened, and, as practice slogged along in the midday heat, Brock's entire fantasy seemed to melt like a Popsicle on pavement.

The repetitions he got diminished as the practice wore on. During team scrimmage, he seemed a forgotten man. Brock's spirits sank. He didn't think it could get any worse.

Then it did.

Coach Hewitt blew his whistle, calling his team into a tight cluster at the fifty-yard line, and went into a fresh rant. "That was *pitiful*. You want to come out here like a bunch of old ladies with walkers? Wilt like flowers on a *grave*? I tell you something. You waste my time like this and you will *run*. You will run like you never thought you could run. Line it up!"

Coach Hewitt's whistle set the tone. Loud and harsh and unrelenting.

They ran. And ran and ran until kids began to drop.

First the linemen went down, collapsing into heaps of trembling Jell-O.

When Mak went down, Coach Hewitt lorded over him, bellowing. "You quit! You're not a *team* player. You fight your own *teammate*? Now, you *quit*!"

The coach stepped over him like a pile of garbage and kept running them.

The third-string players went down next, then the big guys, except for Brock. Kids all around him snarled their resentment. *He*—without his full equipment—had barely practiced and *he* was making others look bad by running tall and proud.

It didn't feel right, but Brock faked exhaustion.

He slowed and huffed and doubled over and groaned. Something inside rattled its cage—it told him not to quit, not to slow down—but Brock couldn't stand the hateful mutterings. So, he took a dive, collapsing on the grass right next to Mak, who'd gone down a dozen sprints ago and lay gasping still, like the rest of them.

Finally, Coach Hewitt hollered at them to get some rest and some water because by God they'd better be back and ready to go a half hour early tomorrow. Then, he and the rest of the coaches stormed off. At the goal line, the coach spun on his heels and cupped his mouth with both hands to shout.

"Brock! Get up and get your butt into my office!"

Mak curled up to his knees, gasping for air until he could cast a questioning look over at Brock. "What'd you do?"

Brock got to his feet, turned over his empty hands, and shook his head. He hoped to God it had something to do with Taylor Owen Lehman arguing on his behalf. After what he'd done today, he'd need all the help he could get for Coach Hewitt to keep him at quarterback.

"Well, good luck." Mak patted Brock on the shoulder, but made no move to go with him.

35

Brock walked into the office. Coach Hewitt sat hunched over some papers with a pen, scribbling notes. He looked up at Brock as if he'd already forgotten why he asked him to come. Coach Hewitt made an impatient gesture toward the coach's locker room. "Coach Van Kuffler will get you your equipment. Tomorrow you can go full contact, so we'll get to see if you're really a football player or not."

Brock stood unable to speak.

"Well?"

Brock's mouth lagged open. "Umm."

Coach exhaled through his nose.

"Can I still try quarterback?" Brock asked.

Coach Hewitt rolled his eyes. "Come on, Brock. Really? Do I have to go through it for you? You had your chance."

He stared at Brock and Brock struggled for the strength to

explain everything Coach Van Kuffler had done against him, and then how he'd really learned the plays from Taylor Owen Lehman and how the varsity quarterback just might take him under his wing and help turn him into a superstar. His mind whirred and tripped over itself.

He *had* to say something.

"Taylor . . . Taylor Owen Lehman. He thinks I can be good . . . at quarterback."

Coach Hewitt raised his eyebrows. "Taylor? Taylor Owen Lehman?"

Hope sprang to life in Brock's heart. He nodded violently. "He showed me some plays last night and we threw at his house."

Coach Hewitt removed the whistle from around his neck and let it dangle in between them. "And . . . what's this?"

"Coach?"

"What's *this*? Is this Taylor Owen Lehman's whistle?" Coach angled his head down at the desk. "Is that Taylor Owen Lehman's desk? Are these his game-plan notes for opening day against Groton?" Coach Hewitt's mouth curled into a snarl.

"I don't know what you mean, Coach?"

"Just answer me."

"No."

"No. This is not his whistle, desk, or game plan. Do you know why?" Coach Hewitt leaned toward him so he could whisper. "Because he's not the coach. I am. Got it?"

"Yes."

"Yes, *Coach*." Coach Hewitt kept his voice soft, which was scarier than when he yelled. "Now go get your equipment and

130

I'll see you at practice tomorrow."

"Yes, Coach." Brock hung his head and started to let himself out of the office.

"Hey, Brock?" Coach Hewitt's voice was still soft, but something about it had changed.

"Yes, Coach?" The coach's face had turned soft like his voice and Brock let some air out of his lungs.

Coach Hewitt put a hand on Brock's shoulder. "I'm not mad at you. I'm a coach, that's all, and when people mess things up, I gotta be grumpy about it. I forgot for a second that you're the new kid and you don't know that my bark isn't the same as my bite. You'll be fine. Don't worry about the quarterback thing, okay? Let's get you going with some pads and see how you do. You're a big kid and with Mak out for game one, we could use some depth on the line. Maybe we can work on the quarterback thing in the off-season, when there's more time."

Brock nodded and smiled. "Okay, Coach." It felt like a ray of sunshine on a cold dark day, but he still wanted to play quarterback.

"But don't you tell the other guys I'm soft. Got it?"

"Got it, Coach." Brock turned again.

"And Brock?"

"Yes?"

"I am *not* happy with Wentzel." Coach Hewitt wore a snarl on his face. "Some things I can't say in front of the whole team, but I can say in private, and trust me . . . I'm no dummy. I know what he did and it makes me sick, and my bet is that he's not going to be bothering you anymore when I get through with him."

"Thanks, Coach."

"Okay, go get your pads."

Brock opened his mouth to talk. A flood of words was ready to burst, but he thought better of it. It sounded like Wentzel wasn't going to be a problem going forward. He'd quit while he was ahead and not get into the whole mess with Coach Van Kuffler. He'd let them put him on the line, but he wasn't giving up on quarterback. He'd learn it anyway and work with Taylor. Something might happen and, if it didn't, there was next year. Things were different now. He and his dad wouldn't be pulling up stakes in a few months. They were here to stay, and Brock knew he had the talent to play quarterback.

Taylor Owen Lehman told him so, and, maybe more important, so did Taylor's sister.

Brock got his equipment from a grouchy Coach Van Kuffler. He took the stack and jammed it all into his corner locker. Except for groans and heavy breathing and the slamming of lockers, things were pretty quiet. When the door banged open and Coach Hewitt's voice filled the locker room everyone jumped.

"Wentzel! My office!"

Brock couldn't help a secret smile as Wentzel skulked out, but he didn't stick around. Mak was waiting for him outside the locker room, sitting on a bench along the wall with his head tilted back against the collar of his shoulder pads. Mak was still puffing. Sweat drenched him like a garden hose and it still beaded on his cheeks, forehead, and nose.

"I'm dyin'," Mak groaned.

Brock rolled his eyes. "Can we just go?"

Mak looked at him like he was crazy, then slapped his hands down on the bench and rose. "I don't want to sound critical of my new best friend, but *you* didn't have to drive the sled today like me."

Brock removed his bike from the rack and started pedaling, but waited until Mak caught up before he spoke. "I will tomorrow."

"The quarterback thing is over, huh? Sorry, buddy. Hey, can you slow up a little?"

"Sure." Brock slowed down. "I just want to get into the shade is all."

"And I want to drink a million gallons of Gatorade is all," Mak said.

"In the shade." Brock reached the canopy of trees on the street across from the football field and looked back. Mak pumped his legs and rocked his body forward and backward, looking supremely silly riding a bike with all his gear on.

Mak coasted up onto the shady sidewalk. "Made it. Let's go to Quik-Mart. Gatorade. Must have."

They started down the sidewalk toward the center of town.

"Surprised you don't want to go get some more books, Romeo," Mak said as they passed the street for the library.

"Nah. I'm good." Brock didn't want to say that the real reason he didn't want to see Laurel was that he felt let down by Taylor.

"Good. You don't need to be distracted," Mak said.

"What do you mean?" They pulled into the Quik-Mart parking lot and got off their bikes.

"Well, tomorrow you start going full contact," Mak said.

"You're gonna be on the line. You know what that means."

Brock followed him into the store and picked a red Gatorade from the cooler. "Mak, what are you talking about?"

They paid for their drinks and Mak grinned through his face mask as he swung the door open and they plunged back into the heat of the day. "You know. Down and dirty. You're on the line, now. A grunt. A hog. You gotta eat your own snot and drink your own blood. You're half man, half animal. That's the life of a lineman."

Brock cracked open the Gatorade but held it only halfway to his lips, without drinking.

Mak slapped him on the back. "Welcome to football in the trenches, buddy."

Brock stayed up all night thinking about Mak's words.

The ache from his first three days of all the running and the push-ups didn't help either.

He thought about who he was and wondered if it was worth it at all, this football thing. He wasn't half man, half animal. He didn't like snot or blood. He liked Laurel's back lawn and the whiteboard. He liked throwing, using the arm he had—a gift, Coach Hudgens, his old baseball coach had called it. He remembered Coach Hudgens, the way he believed in Brock and his abilities. Coach Hudgens did everything he could to *help* Brock. And now—it was just so different. After a time, exhaustion dragged him down, and Brock fell into an uneasy sleep.

The next day was Friday. On Saturday, Brock and his dad would be going to Laurel's house for dinner, so Brock tried to think about that to keep him going while he practiced with the linemen. He was strong enough that he didn't get slammed to the dirt or knocked on his back, which was something. There were plenty of kids who seemed like little more than blocking dummies for the first-team guys. On the other hand, as he crouched and smashed and tried to drive his feet like pistons, the way Coach Hewitt showed them, he couldn't help glancing over at the quarterbacks, where he knew he should be.

Brock did okay, but he wasn't built for it. He knew that by the way Mak worked. Mak loved it. He snorted and smashed people and chuckled to himself when someone went down under his bulldozer treads. Brock heard two other players, Declan Carey and Bill Shafer, talking about Mak in the back of the line.

"He's out of his mind," Bill said.

Declan nodded. "Don't get matched up with him. Let the new kid do it. Mak likes him."

They were taking turns in a pit drill, a one-on-one blocking contest where two linemen faced off and basically tried to mash each other into the dirt. It was true, Mak did like Brock, so he let the other two kids budge the line in front of him so he had to face Mak in the pit instead of one of them. Coach Delaney blew the whistle, stopping the two linemen before him in the pit and calling for the next two.

Brock went out and got uncomfortably into his stance. Mak hunkered right down like a pig in mud, snorting and *growling*. Brock looked up at his friend through their metal masks.

"Easy, buddy," Brock said. "It's me."

Mak's eyes widened and he snorted two jets of snot from

his nose onto the mask. His lips tightened and an angry fire burned on his face.

"Set! Go!" Coach Delaney hollered.

Mak exploded into Brock. Brock did his best to get his hands into Mak's pads, but their helmets crashed. Brock saw stars and before he knew it, his feet left the ground. Mak lifted him up and slammed him down. Brock's breath left him, but Mak wasn't finished. Mak kept his face mask and hands pressed into Brock's body and his legs pumped furiously, and he rooted Brock along in the dirt like a wild hog digging up mushrooms.

Finally, Coach Delaney blew his whistle.

Mak popped up and helped Brock to his feet. "Sorry, buddy. That was great!"

Brock swatted some of the dirt off his pants. "Not for me."

"Yeah, you gotta be a little more edgy." Mak slapped his shoulder pads. "These are the trenches, buddy."

With that, Mak walked ten feet away from the drill and puked in the grass.

38

"I don't think I can do this, Dad." Brock let the fork clatter against his plate.

"Don't eat what you don't want," his dad said. He peered across the table at the steak he'd grilled in their tiny yard out back. "When you work out in the heat, it can take away your appetite. Did I cook it too long?"

"Not the steak, Dad. Football."

"Oh." His father cut a piece of meat and popped it into his mouth. He studied Brock while he chewed.

"That's it? 'Oh'?" Brock swigged down some milk. "Did you not hear the story I told you about Mak puking?"

"I like Mak." His father spoke as he chewed.

"I like Mak too, but I'm not Mak, right?"

His father swallowed and took a drink of iced tea. "Safe to say there's only one."

"I'm not a *lineman*."

"I wasn't either." His father took another bite of steak.

Brock looked up. "You played football? I thought you were a baseball player." It still amazed Brock how little he knew about his own father, and he wondered if his father was naturally close-lipped, or if he'd been that way because of years of training for his job.

"In college I played baseball. But I played the big three in high school. Lettered in all of them, football, basketball, and baseball."

"What position?"

"Point guard." His dad fought back a grin.

"In football."

"Oh, in football." His father played dumb, joking around. That too was something Brock wasn't used to. "Wide receiver."

"Really? I could throw to you if . . ." Brock's excitement suddenly melted away and he shook his head. "I'm not going to be a lineman."

"You'll quit?"

"I don't know. But why should I play for a team when the coach hates me?"

"Coach Hewitt sounds like a good guy. A little rough, but nice. Fair."

"He is. I'm talking about Coach Van Kuffler. Stop messing with me, will you?"

"I'm serious," his dad said. "Van Kuffler has nothing to do with you on the line."

Brock rolled his eyes. "I'm not a lineman. That's what I'm saying. These guys are nuts. They spend all practice smashing each other's heads in. I got an arm, Dad. I can *throw*. And I can learn the plays as well as anyone if they'd just teach me."

His dad put his fork down and leaned back. The kitchen was so small the back of his chair bumped into the countertop next to the sink. Without getting up, his father reached into the fridge and got a fresh can of iced tea. "Well, we did show up five days late, and it sounds like these kids have been working in the system since they could walk. You can't expect everyone to stop everything for the new kid."

"You're siding with *them*?"

"No, just trying to help you understand." His father's face turned serious. "If you slog it out on the line this year, you'll be a part of the team. In the off-season, you can work on your throwing and you'll learn a lot about the offense just being there, watching and listening. You'd be surprised how much we can learn by watching."

"From the trenches. You want me to watch from the trenches, where guys vomit during drills."

"It's not like he got any on you, right?" Brock's dad stared at him with a serious expression until they both burst out laughing.

"Oh my God. You should have seen it, Dad." Brock clutched his stomach. "Two other guys puked right after that just from the smell."

"Glad I didn't. Come on. Help me clean up." His father got up and Brock helped the way he'd done as long as he could remember.

"What's it like not to do the dishes?" Brock dried a plate and set it down in the cupboard.

"I have no idea." His father rinsed his hands and shook them off in the sink.

"Didn't Mom do the dishes?"

"I know I baked the cookies, but she actually did do the dishes. Yes." Brock's dad straightened up and stared at his reflection in the window over the sink.

Brock dried another dish. "You think you'll ever have someone do that again?"

His dad seemed lost in the reflection.

"Dad?"

"Huh? Oh, I have no idea." His father put his dish towel under the sink and walked into the next room where he turned on the TV and sat down on the couch.

Brock listened to the newscaster talking about a plunge in the stock market. He peeked around the corner and studied his dad's face in the flashing glow of the TV. His father looked old suddenly. The wrinkles stood out at the corners of his eyes and mouth, dragging his face toward the floor. Brock fidgeted with his own dish towel as he stepped into the room.

"Are you gonna wear nice clothes tomorrow night?" Brock asked.

His father looked up at him and blinked. "What?"

"Tomorrow, when we go to dinner at Laurel's. Should we dress up, do you think? I mean, like a tie or anything?"

His father barked out a laugh. "No. We're fine."

"They're kind of fancy," Brock said.

"But down to earth. Kim texted me today and said something about going out on the river after dinner, so I gotta believe jeans will be fine. Is that what you're worried about? You like that girl, don't you?"

"She's nice," Brock admitted. "Pretty."

His dad nodded. "So is her mom."

Brock's dad turned his attention back to the TV set. Brock had a plan. He had no idea in the world whether it would work, or blow up in his face.

The next day at practice was hotter than the day before. Brock and Mak rode their bikes together and got there early, already sweating. Brock wanted plenty of time to get changed in the locker room. Mak didn't need to change, but he promised to work with Brock on his blocking technique before things got going. Brock didn't want to play on the line, but while he was there, he figured he better keep from getting killed.

"You gotta explode up into him." Mak's eyes sparkled. "You gotta get your hands on his chest plate. Like this."

Mak blasted his hands into Brock's chest, his fingers biting into the edge of the protective plate just inside of each armpit. Brock gasped for air, but nodded that he understood.

"But your feet never stop moving. It all happens at the same time, see?" Mak chopped his feet and began to wheel Brock backward on the grass. "And, if you stay low and move your feet, you can drive anyone off the ball. Low man wins."

Mak stopped driving and let go.

"That's what Coach Hewitt says." Brock nodded, almost understanding now.

"Cuz you can't just quit." Mak took hold of Brock's shoulder pad and gave it a little shake. "Quitting's for losers."

"Losing's for quitters." Brock wanted to show he was on the same wavelength.

"Okay, so you try." Mak crouched and tapped the breastplate of his shoulder pads. "Fire out. Hands inside. Drive the feet."

Brock got down into his stance.

"Your feet are too wide."

Brock narrowed the space between his feet.

"Better. Ready? Go!"

Brock fired out, struck Mak's chest with both hands, which then slipped off, and he crashed his helmet up under Mak's chin, saw stars, reeled sideways, tripped, and fell.

Brock blinked up at Mak. Sunshine peeked around the cusp of his helmet, blinding Brock so he couldn't read Mak's expression. Mak sighed and extended a hand to help him up. "Okay, let's try it again."

Brock struggled to his feet, filled with shame and frustration. From the corner of his eye he saw a couple of other early arrivals pointing at him. Wisps of laughter floated across the empty field. Brock ignored them and kept working, struggling until most of the team was out on the grass.

"Well," Mak said, patting his back, "you're a little better, anyway."

Brock could only shake his head.

Coach Hewitt blew the whistle and got things going. Brock ran and bear-crawled and hit the sled with the other linemen. He fired out through a metal cage that banged his head the first several times until he kept his helmet low enough. He tackled a dummy, then drive-blocked another dummy, then shuffled in and out between more dummies. He felt like a dummy.

They lined up for an inside run drill. Since Mak had been demoted, Brock was next to him, and that was a good thing. Mak told Brock who to block, so, even though he did a poor job of it, at least he was hitting the right person. When someone substituted in for Mak, Brock tried to explain through his mouthpiece on the way to the line that he needed to be told who to block, but the other boy just gave him a confused look. The ball was snapped. Brock fired out straight, guessing.

Someone hit him from the blind side, knocking him over. Brock fell to the grass right in front of the running back, who tripped and tumbled to the ground. The running back got up and threw the ball at the ground.

"I had a touchdown if this clown isn't falling into the hole!"

The ball sailed up and then down, bouncing off Brock's helmet with a *thunk* that left everyone laughing except the coaches.

Coach Hewitt hollered at Coach Delaney. "Kevin! Get him out of there."

That made everyone laugh even more.

Then a whistle blew, short, sharp, and hard.

Everyone stopped.

Everyone looked past Coach Hewitt, who wore a mask of rage and confusion.

Brock looked too, and couldn't believe who stood behind their coach.

Coach Hewitt's snarl melted into a simpering smile. "Coach Spada!"

"Who's that?" Brock asked.

"That's Coach Bobby Spada," Mak said. "He's a giant in Calhoun. He coached for fourteen years and led the Fighting Crabs to six state championships."

Beside Coach Spada stood Taylor Owen Lehman, tall and proud. Fat state championship rings sparkled on both their right hands. No one could know what Coach Spada was thinking because his eyes were hidden by the big mirrors in his aviator sunglasses. His mouth gave away nothing either, but judging by the tone of Coach Hewitt's voice, Brock suspected that Coach Spada wasn't happy.

"Only thing fun about football is winning, Coach." Spada directed his words at Coach Hewitt who nodded vigorously.

"We hear that, Coach Spada. We all hear that, right, men?"

There was a smattering of agreement that caused Coach Spada to frown. "That doesn't look like winning to me. Who's the slip-and-fall guy?"

Coach Hewitt cleared his throat. "New kid, Coach. Just joined up, but he's got some size."

Coach Spada stared. A slight breeze ruffled the collar of his bright-green shirt and the wisps of graying hair bursting from the band of his hat. No one but Taylor Owen Lehman seemed comfortable. Everyone waited for the head varsity coach to speak.

Finally, he did. "TL says you got a quarterback I need to see."

Brock was confused, but only for a second before he figured TL was Taylor Owen Lehman.

Coach Hewitt chuckled in a puzzled way. "Wally Van Kuffler?"

"I think," Coach Spada nodded at Brock, "the new kid. The one you got tripping over the line. I hear he can throw."

Taylor nodded in case anyone was looking. Brock didn't feel as swell as he'd imagined. He wanted Taylor to rescue him from the line, but not quite like this. This was a public display of discomfort.

"He's got a strong arm, Coach." Coach Hewitt bobbed his head. "Needs a lot of work, though. Not enough time to get him going at this stage of the game."

Coach Spada tilted his head. "What stage?"

"Eight days before our opener, Coach."

Coach Spada bit into the right corner of his lower lip.

"How many days until playoffs?"

"Coach?"

Coach Spada repeated himself more slowly. "How many days until seventh-grade playoffs?"

Coach Hewitt wrinkled up his face. "Eight weeks, times seven . . . about fifty-six days."

"That's enough time," Coach Spada said. "*If* he can throw. That's what I'm here to see about."

"If he can throw?" Coach Hewitt gave Coach Van Kuffler an anxious glance.

"If he can throw." Coach Spada's head wavered a bit. His hands snapped up and clapped. A dead fly fell to the grass, causing the varsity coach to smile. "Got him. So, let's see it. You keep on with your inside run, Coach. Just give me the new kid."

Coach Hewitt pointed at Brock and then waved his finger over toward Coach Spada, then blew his whistle. "Go ahead, Brock. All right, the rest of you! Team period. Give me the first-team offense!"

Taylor smiled as Brock followed him and Coach Spada to the empty grass on the other end of the field. Coach Spada scooped up a seventh-grade ball from the ground and tossed it underhand to Brock as they walked. "Where you from, Brock?"

"All over, Coach. Maryland most recently."

"I don't love Maryland football. Lacrosse country isn't it?" Spada kept his eyes ahead.

Brock shrugged. "I play baseball in the spring, Coach."

Spada smiled. "Who's the best player ever?"

Brock swallowed. He wanted to say Albert Pujols, but he felt Coach Spada was more old-school, really old-school. "Babe Ruth."

"Correct." Coach Spada stopped. "Okay. Let's see you throw."

Brock warmed up, throwing the ball back and forth to Taylor. Taylor snuck a smile at him and a wink. Brock kept his face serious. His whole body was sore from hitting and playing on the line, and his shoulder was still aching from the treatment Coach Van Kuffler had given him, but the more he threw, the better he felt, and soon they were thirty yards apart and Brock was zipping it.

"Taylor, you run some patterns." Coach Spada stood with his arms folded across his chest. "Do a couple hitches, then a post, then three or four outs."

Taylor nodded and lined up on the thirty-yard line. Brock stood at the thirty-five, going into the end zone.

"Go ahead," Coach Spada said. "Call a cadence and run it."

Brock held out his hands as if he were receiving a shotgun snap. "Blue eighteen, blue eighteen, set . . . Hut!"

Taylor took a jab step and hopped back behind the line. Brock delivered a bullet. Taylor snatched it and pretended to run a couple of steps upfield before tossing it back. He ran two more hitch patterns, then a post pattern. Twenty yards downfield, Brock zipped it right into Taylor's hands. He never broke stride and took it into the end zone.

Coach Spada cleared his throat. "Nice."

Brock beamed.

"Now," Coach Spada said, "let's see you throw a ten-yard out. If you can't throw the out, you can't play quarterback at Calhoun. When we get it going, the defense just can't stop the out."

Brock tried to breathe deep while he waited for Taylor to jog back to the line. He had a feeling that these next three passes would determine whether or not he'd continue playing football.

Taylor lined up and nodded at him. Brock called out the cadence. Taylor took off. Brock stepped into it and let the ball fly, another bullet, right into Taylor's hands.

Brock couldn't help looking back over his shoulder. Coach Van Kuffler was watching and scowling. Brock tried not to grin, but didn't mind that much when he failed.

"I'm a little disappointed," Coach Spada said.

Brock attempted to hide his confusion. He wished he could see the man's eyes.

"Me too," Taylor said.

Brock's eyes went back and forth between the two of them, waiting to hear what he'd done wrong.

"How can you have an arm like this and put the kid on the

line?" Coach Spada glanced over at the seventh-grade team and snarled.

"I told you, Coach," Taylor said. "And I'll work with him too."

"You're not the only one who's gonna work with him. Come on." Coach Spada tugged his hat down tight and marched toward the other end of practice.

Coach Hewitt saw them coming and he blew his whistle and stopped everything and waited for Coach Spada to speak. Coach Spada stood like a statue.

Brock wondered if he was maybe changing his mind? Whatever he was doing, no one was comfortable, coaches and players alike, except for Taylor, who simply waited, smiling, and kicking at something in the grass with the toe of his cleat.

"Who's your backup quarterback, Coach?" Spada directed his glasses at Coach Hewitt.

"Kurt Wentzel," Coach Hewitt said, glancing around until his eyes found Wentzel.

Spada looked Wentzel over. "Not very thick, is he?"

Coach Van Kuffler stepped forward, surprising everyone. "He's got a good head on his shoulders, Coach. Makes great decisions."

Coach Spada tilted his head at Coach Van Kuffler. "Decisions?"

"Yes," Van Kuffler said.

Coach Spada looked at Wentzel. "Which one's correct, Wentzel? Three and two *are* six, or three and two *is* six?"

Coach Spada started snapping his fingers at Wentzel. "Come on, son. Quick. Decisions. Decide. Which is it?"

Wentzel wore a panic-stricken face. "Three and two *are* six, Coach."

Coach Spada turned to Coach Van Kuffler. "Kind of panics under pressure, Coach."

Coach Van Kuffler stood his ground. "Coach, all due respect, grammar's got nothing to do with football. *I* didn't even know it was three and two *is* six."

The corner of Coach Spada's mouth quivered, suggesting a smile that never came. "Three and two are five."

Coach Spada turned to Coach Hewitt. "You got yourself a new backup quarterback, Coach. I want him ready for the playoffs in case your starter goes down. Or . . . maybe he beats out your starter? Kid's got a cannon for an arm."

Coach Spada walked away with Taylor beside him.

Just before he stepped off the field, Coach Spada turned and pointed at Coach Van Kuffler. "Don't disappoint me, Coach."

They marched off.

Coach Hewitt stared at Brock.

Brock's hands and eyebrows went up like they were attached to puppet strings.

"All right!" Coach Hewitt seemed determined to regain command of the field by being loud. "Brock, you're a QB now. Wentzel you're—"

Coach Van Kuffler stepped forward with his hands in the air. "Coach, I can use three . . . in case Brock's not ready and something happens with Wally. What if Wally gets hurt today? Wentzel knows the offense."

Brock raised his hand. "I can—"

Coach Van Kuffler charged Brock like a mad bull and

pulled up right in front of him with his boiling face just the other side of Brock's mask. "You shut your pie-hole! You think because you kiss some butts and get the varsity coach down here to watch your circus act that you're something *special*? You're a *player*, and you keep your mouth *shut! RUN A LAP! NOW!*"

Brock glanced at Coach Hewitt, but by the look on his face it was clear he wasn't going to help, so Brock took off to the distant shouts of Coach Van Kuffler for him to run faster. When he got back, the team was already back in the full swing of practice and Brock stood in the back, as close as he dared to Coach Van Kuffler, trying to listen and learn.

When Coach Van Kuffler saw him, he gave Brock a look so nasty that Brock knew if looks could kill, he'd already be dead.

Brock only got three reps in practice at quarterback. He ran with the second team, as Coach Spada had insisted, but a grinning Coach Van Kuffler only put the second team in for one play at a time before he replaced them with the third team, then back to the first team for the bulk of the reps. So, Brock was back at quarterback, and on the second team, but anyone could see that with Van Kuffler running the offense, it wasn't going to do him much good. Brock kept trying to catch Coach Hewitt's eye, but he was busy with the defense and when he wasn't focused on them, when it came to the offense, he seemed to only pay attention to the line.

Coach Hewitt carried on like Coach Spada had never appeared. They ran hard at the end of practice, but only two kids lost their breakfast. When the quarterbacks and a few receivers stuck around for some extra work with Coach Van

Kuffler, Brock stayed too. He figured if ever there was a time for him to get some instruction, this would be it. Instead, Coach Van Kuffler acted like Brock wasn't even there.

Brock just stood there, feeling furious and sickened at the same time. Finally, Coach Van Kuffler gave a toot on his whistle and told the players he'd see them tomorrow. Brock walked away too.

That's when Van Kuffler called his name.

Brock turned and shuffled back, standing face-to-face with Van Kuffler.

"That was a good trick," the coach said, "getting Taylor Owen Lehman to drag Coach Spada down to our practice, throwing the ball around like that."

"What?" Brock didn't know what to say. He could feel the rage oozing from Coach Van Kuffler. Brock stepped back and shifted uneasily.

"Only problem with that is . . . Lehman and Coach Spada aren't going to be here day in and day out." Van Kuffler gritted his teeth. "I am."

"Coach, I just want to—"

Van Kuffler silenced him with an upraised hand. "No. I know what you want. You want what everyone wants. First team."

Coach Van Kuffler looked around to make sure they were alone. The field was empty.

"This is a small town, Barrette. It takes years to belong here, generations really. You don't just move into the Flatlands and think you're God's gift because you can sling the ball. That's not how it works. You're from the wrong side of town. No one's gonna stick their neck out for you. Maybe you got Taylor Owen Lehman to make a little noise with Coach Spada, but that dog won't hunt day in and day out. Day in and day out, you're with me, and you know what I think of you? I think you're a pain in the neck Flatty who doesn't know his place.

"So, until your daddy lives in a mansion on the hill, you just settle into your place on the bench."

Brock blinked and Van Kuffler suddenly broke into a wicked smile.

"That's all, boy. That's all."

Brock slogged into the locker room. Most of the players were gone already, and it stunk from so many boys and so many sweat-soaked pads that simmered day and night in the stuffy room. Brock shed his pads and crammed them into the locker. He changed into regular clothes, stuffed his dirty jersey and pants into a duffel bag he slung over his shoulder, and got out of there as fast as he could. Mak sat waiting on a bench in the shade near the bike rack.

"Hey." Mak stood up slowly. "Get some good extra work in?"

"Even less than I got in team period." Brock removed his bike from the rack.

"Man, that Van Kuffler better watch it. Everyone heard what Coach Spada said. You gonna tell him?"

"What? Me? Go tell Coach Spada?" Brock shook his head. "I can't see that."

"Well, you can tell Taylor." Mak got his bike too.

"I don't know," Brock said. "I'd have to be going to them every ten minutes with Van Kuffler."

The two of them started to slowly pedal toward town.

"Too bad this isn't the Old West," Mak said.

"Old West?"

"Yeah. I could see your dad slapping Van Kuffler across the face and having a duel or a bar fight or something. Your dad'd wallop him."

"How do you know that about my dad?"

"In case you haven't noticed, the guy looks at me and I'm scared. Everyone else too, I bet. He's nice, don't get me wrong, but there's something dangerous about your dad," Mak said. "Maybe you don't see it, because he's your dad."

"No. I see it. But we're not in the Old West, are we?" Brock said.

"Well, there's gotta be something you can do," Mak said.

"Maybe," Brock said, and left it at that.

Brock stopped by the library with Mak. Laurel was in the back and couldn't come out. This made Brock nervous, but when he texted her to ask if they were still on for tonight, she replied that she couldn't wait, and that they had a surprise. When Brock expressed his excitement as they rode toward home, Mak rolled his eyes.

"Girls," Mak said. "You gotta be kidding me. My dad says girls are a slippery slope."

Brock turned his bike onto the bridge. Tar bled from seams in the road. Their tires made a sticky sound as they went.

"Laurel's different," Brock said.

"That's what they all say," Mak said. "That's what my dad says."

"I gotta meet your dad, Mak. He says a lotta things."

"You will."

"Just not tonight," Brock said.

"Yeah, tonight is all mushy mushy." Mak laughed and made kissing noises.

"Whatever," Brock said.

"I guess, at least it got you out of being a lineman," Mak said. "No matter how much of a jerk Van Kuffler is to you, you're still a quarterback."

Brock bit his lip and nodded without smiling.

They hung out that afternoon until Brock's dad got home.

"You gotta take a shower, Dad." Brock sniffed the air.

"I will. What are you worried about?" Brock's dad took off his shirt. His skin was tan from their time at the beach and stretched so tight over his muscles they might have been stone.

"And we gotta dress nice." Brock slipped in front of the mirror and patted his hair.

"Kim said jeans were fine," his father hollered from his bedroom.

"But nice shirts and *new* jeans. Come on, Dad." Brock stared into the mirror until his father agreed and bumped him out of the bathroom so he could shower.

When they arrived at Laurel's house they drove right past the caretaker's house. When they reached the opening, the place looked just as big as it had before, maybe bigger. There was a black Volvo SUV in the circle and Brock worried a bit if there'd be other guests. Their tires crunched the gravel as they pulled to a stop in front of the big stone steps. This time, they walked right up. Laurel swung the door open and yelled back into the house.

"They're here!" She grinned at Brock's dad and took Brock by the hand. "Wait till you see the surprise."

"It's one of my favorite things," Laurel said. "Oh, I better not say that. It's not Splash Mountain at Disney World or anything, but it's just fun. First dinner though, anyway."

Laurel led them through the house and out the back. A table draped with a white cloth had been set out on the terrace under a billowing white tent. Candles burned in the middle of flowery centerpieces.

Brock nudged his father. "Your collar."

"Right." His father felt for the collar of the polo shirt Brock made him wear and he straightened it.

In a small circle of padded wicker chairs Laurel's mom stood up, along with Taylor and a very pretty girl with long dark hair. Laurel's mom took his father's hand and kissed his cheek. "Well, hello. Don't you look sharp? This is Taylor's girl-friend, Gracie."

"Hi." Gracie extended her hand. "I'm Gracie White. Nice to meet you."

"Nice to meet you too," Brock's dad said, before shaking Taylor's hand as well.

Laurel's mom sat back down in a love seat and patted the cushion next to her. "Sit, please."

They all sat down like three couples.

"You're blushing." Laurel poked his arm.

"No, I'm not," Brock protested.

A young man dressed as a waiter brought around trays of appetizers while another took drink orders from everyone. Brock followed Taylor's lead and asked for a grape soda, then leaned back into the thick cushion of his chair, took a deep breath, and let it out. The evening was cloudy but with enough breaks in the sky for the sun to cast an occasional beam on the nearby woods, hills, and river, lighting up patches of green like discarded emeralds.

At first, they talked about all the colleges recruiting Taylor—including Ohio State—and the outlook for the Calhoun varsity team, then the three couples broke off into conversations of their own.

Laurel beamed at Brock and leaned close to whisper. "So, my brother got that first-team thing back on track today?"

Brock hesitated, but quickly recovered. "He did. Yes."

Brock turned to Taylor. "Thank you for today."

Taylor smiled and hugged his girlfriend closer. "Hey, my pleasure. You made me look good. That'll straighten that Van Kuffler out good, huh?"

"For sure." Brock turned to Laurel. "I'm second-team QB. I

wanted to tell you in person."

"Sorry about the library today. We got a shipment of books in and Mrs. Hubble won't stop in the middle when she's unpacking a new shipment."

"That's okay."

Laurel looked around at her brother and then her mom and his dad. "So, this is kind of perfect, isn't it?"

"It's great. You must love living on the river."

She looked out at it, wide and green, and as she did, a beam of sunlight made the surface dance with a golden light. "It's always different. I like it even in the winter when it's dark like licorice and the trees are frosted with snow. Sometimes it smokes like it's burning underneath. Sometimes it's so still I swear you could walk on it."

"You're lucky," he said.

"I am." She turned her blue eyes on him and everything inside him shifted. It made his throat tight and he coughed and looked around for one of the waiter guys and held up his empty glass with a questioning look that sent the waiter on his way for a fresh one.

"I feel kind of bad," Brock mumbled, and looked at her apologetically. "I can get my own drinks, right?"

Her laugh was soft as the breeze. "It's okay. Everyone likes to work for my mom. She feels bad too, so she overpays by a lot, and she treats everyone like an old friend."

"She's really nice." Brock looked over. Her and his father sat leg to leg, and she had a hand on his near shoulder.

"She likes your dad," Laurel said.

Brock tried to keep cool. "My dad's tough to get to know."

Laurel stared at their parents, who didn't even notice. "My mom's tough *not* to know."

"Opposites attract, right?" Brock said.

"You think we're opposites?" Laurel raised an eyebrow. "I thought you and me were kind of the same. We both like sports and books, right?"

"You're rich and I'm not," Brock said.

"We're both nice."

"Everyone knows you, and I got one friend who's a crazy man," he said.

"Neither of us has both parents. That's a big one."

"You look at the bright side, and I'm always worried," he said.

She pinched his arm. "You're right. We are opposites."

"Is everyone ready for dinner?" Laurel's mom stood and motioned then toward the billowing tent. "Shall we?"

They got up and started to move toward the table, and Laurel whispered to him. "I guess that's why I like you."

Brock looked around. No one else could have heard Laurel, but his face felt like it was on fire. He couldn't look at her, and when she sat next to him and poked his leg under the table, he could only stare down at the shiny plate and bite the inside of his mouth.

"Yup." She giggled. "Opposites."

Dinner was served by two older waiters, dressed in black jackets and ties. They served each of the four courses from fancy silver trays. Everyone, even Brock's dad, acted like that's how they ate every day, using the big silver serving utensils to fill their plates while the waiters . . . well, waited with gloved hands firmly supporting the massive trays. The food also made Brock nervous, until he tasted it. There was a squash soup that tasted of cinnamon, soft-shell crabs over a bed of lettuce, small handmade raviolis in a cream sauce with mushrooms, and thick slabs of poached salmon dressed in colorful sautéed vegetables.

For dessert, one of the waiters brought out a soufflé crested with blue flames. It tasted like vanilla from heaven.

Brock felt like a king.

The grown-ups had coffee and then Laurel's mom tapped her water glass with a spoon and cleared her throat. "So, one of the great summer traditions in Calhoun is Three B's. Laurel's been counting on the fact that you *haven't* heard of it. Have you?"

Brock and his dad looked at each other and shrugged.

"Wonderful. Laurel?"

Laurel put her napkin down on her plate. "Three B's are the Brass Bank Band, and we go by boat! So for us, it could be the Four B's, or five I guess: Brass Bank Band by boat."

Laurel stood up at her place and looked around. "The Bank is the park in town that's right on the river. Have you seen it?"

"I think so," Brock said.

"With the gazebo?" she asked.

"Sure." Brock had a vague image.

"So, every Friday in the summer, the Brass Bank Band plays in the gazebo. It's like a big party. Everyone goes! It's so fun. Come on." She started away from the table and down the steps that led to the lawn.

Everyone followed her to the stone boathouse, a smaller version of the main house. They went down the stone steps and into the boathouse where a rich wooden boat rumbled and filled the air with blue smoke. A man in a white captain's hat stood at the wheel in the open cockpit. He helped them down into the boat where two long leather-cushioned seats faced each other inside a cabin with an open roof. As they backed out onto the river, Brock could see the stars. In the very back of the boat was a seat facing front. Laurel's mom motioned to Brock's dad and that's where they sat.

"I'd like to drive this thing, but Vincent won't let anyone touch his baby." Taylor sat down heavily on the seat across from

Brock and nodded toward their captain.

"It's so much fun just to ride," Laurel said. "I love to see the town from the river, especially at night. It's all little lights, like the stars. Don't you love it, Gracie?"

"I do," Gracie said.

"You see?" Taylor leaned over, put a hand under Gracie's chin, and gave her a kiss. "The perfect girl."

Laurel nudged Brock. She winked at him and rolled her eyes. He ran his fingers along the smooth wood. The engine droned like a monster bee. They surged through the water and Brock saw that there were other big homes on the water, but only on Laurel's side of the river.

"Why isn't anything on this side but trees?" he asked.

"When it floods, that's where the water goes," she said. "It's mostly woods and farm fields."

"The Flatlands," Brock said.

"Well, when you get closer to town, there's the bank where the old factories were built and beyond them, yes, that's the Flatlands. It used to flood pretty regularly, but they built a levy in the thirties."

"No more floods?"

She gave him a confused look. "I don't think so. Look, there's the Kents' place. Their great-great-grandfather and mine started the timber company together."

Brock studied the mansion that was built in a much different style than Laurel's place. The Kents' place looked like a southern plantation with a big brick body, towering white columns, and a wide flat roof.

"Wow. Nice." Brock didn't know what else to say.

They rode for a couple of minutes, chugging along, the drone of the motor drowning out the other conversations.

"Hey." Laurel nudged him again. "I'm sorry. I don't care about all that stuff."

"What stuff?" Brock thought he knew.

"The Kents. The lumber company. Big homes. It's fun, but it's not what's important. People are important. Like you." She tapped his knee.

"Why do you say that? About me?"

Laurel shrugged. "My mom always said I was a good judge of people. I can see right into them."

"Oh yeah? What do you see?" He looked into her blue eyes.

Her face got serious and she spoke that way too. "I see quiet. Secretive . . . I'm not the first girl you ever liked, but I scare you. You love your dad and you respect him a lot. I think you're playing football to fit in, but you're excited because you also know that you could be really good."

Brock's mouth lagged open. "Wow."

"You asked."

"What's there for me to say? I can't tell you anything about yourself except you're nice and you're the prettiest girl I think I've ever seen."

It was her turn to blush.

"Hey. What'd you say to her Brock?" Taylor laughed and

spoke over the motor. "Laurel doesn't blush for anyone. Now you? Looks like they got sunburned, don't they, Gracie?"

"Stop. Leave them alone." Gracie laughed and tugged on Taylor's arm.

"Look." Laurel pointed as they passed under the bridge. "Town."

Yellow lights sparkled through the trees. The hum of music from the band floated on the breeze. Brock smelled cotton candy and popcorn. People milled about on the grass, many of them spread out on blankets. Colored balloons bobbed on strings tied to children's wrists. It was a giant party. The long L of a concrete pier jutted out into the river. They weren't the first boat to arrive, but there wasn't another one quite as nice as their shiny wooden craft.

The captain pulled up alongside the pier, tossed some bumpers over the side and with expert precision nudged the edge. He hopped out, lashed the boat, then helped them off. Brock's dad offered his arm to Laurel's mom. When Taylor did the same to Gracie, Brock felt his face burning, but offered up his arm to Laurel. She grinned and took it with a squeeze. Brock straightened his back and was very aware of the looks people gave the six of them as they walked off the pier and into the park, moving among the people and making their way toward the concession stand to buy ice cream cones.

"You want a balloon?" Brock licked his cone and pointed to a man dressed in red and white stripes with a tank of helium and a bundle of colorful balloons who bobbed his head to the tune of the brass band.

Laurel laughed. "My dad used to buy me balloons and I'd

set them free on the river on the way home. He said the angels would watch me especially hard when I sent them balloons. He said angels love balloons."

Brock dug into his pocket and came up with some rumpled bills from the allowance his dad always gave him. He bought two balloons, a red and a blue, and tied them to Laurel's wrist. Laurel's mom had a blanket under her arm and they found a place on the grass where she spread it out with one hand, balancing her ice cream cone in the other.

As they sat down, Laurel turned to Brock. "You want to walk around a little?"

"Sure." He offered his arm again.

"Don't be gone all night." Laurel's mom turned her cone around and around.

"We'll come back," Laurel said. "Promise."

Brock had Laurel's arm, but it was she who led him toward the shops on Main Street. Most of the people were in the park, so only a handful of other people also wandered the street, looking into the shop windows. They reached the end of the shops where the sidewalk turned from brick to concrete and people's homes began, then crossed the street and started back down the other side. Brock scanned the faces of the people they saw, just wishing for Wentzel or Wally Van Kuffler, or even Coach Van Kuffler himself, to see him walking arm in arm with Laurel Lehman. That would give them something to think about. They were halfway down the street when the wooden door to a place called Young's Irish Pub flew open and two men spilled out onto the sidewalk.

They nearly tripped over Brock and Laurel, excusing

themselves as they walked on past. Brock took only two more steps before he stopped and looked back. They talked funny, and something about one of the men reminded him of someone. He couldn't place who or where, but when he turned around, the man was staring coldly at Brock and it hit him.

Brock turned away, and tightened his grip on Laurel's arm.

"Come on." His voice was low and urgent. "Let's get out of here."

"What's wrong?" She stumbled in her effort to keep up.

"Maybe nothing," he said. "Maybe everything."

47

Run for your life. Brock's father's words echoed in his mind.

Brock tried not to run. He didn't want to excite any attention, but he had to get back to his father, fast. Stray balloons escaped skyward. Couples held hands, some swinging children between them. Brock dodged and darted and Laurel kept up with a look of worry tugging down the corners of her mouth.

When they reached the blanket, Laurel's mom finished telling a story that made the rest of them laugh. The band stopped playing at the same time and they all clapped politely along with everyone else.

"Dad." Brock had to catch his breath.

His father looked up. His face went from a lazy smile to serious state of alert in an instant. "What happened?"

"Can I, um . . . talk to you?" Brock motioned with his head.

His father got up. "Just a second. I'm sorry."

Laurel's mom laughed. "That's fine. You men."

Brock's dad put an arm around him and they walked out of earshot.

"I saw him. I think I did," Brock whispered, and tried to convey his anxiety through the look he gave his dad.

"Who?"

"Remember in the newspaper? After you did whatever it was you did?"

"The *Washington Post*?"

"Yes. Boo-dant-suv, the Russian."

"Boo-don-seeve, what about him? You *saw* him?" His father scanned the crowd around them.

"I think I did. I'm not sure. He . . . he looked at me."

"Brock, are you *sure* he looked at you? No one knows what you look like now, right?"

"I'm not sure. I'm pretty sure it was him and I'm pretty sure he looked at me, but we bumped right into him, so maybe that was why. I stopped and looked back, though, and he was still looking, Dad. And there was that Audi too."

"Audi?" His father crumpled up his face.

"Remember that day when you got your job? You said you'd pick us up in the park and we ran into that alley?"

"I do, but what's that got to do with it." His father waved a hand impatiently. "Get to the point."

"I saw an Audi with blacked-out windows watching us. That's why I was running, not from you. You just saw us running and followed. Maybe it was him in that Audi? I don't know. Dad?"

His father's face had gone blank. It was a look Brock hadn't seen in some time.

"Okay. You're sick. Got that? Migraine headache. Go with it." His father steered him back toward the rest of their group, stopping at the edge of the blanket. "I'm sorry, but we have to go. No, don't get up. Don't let us ruin your night. Brock is embarrassed about it, but he gets migraines. He has medicine he's supposed to carry with him, but you know kids. We need to get him home. Maybe the boat could take us to the house and then come back for you all."

"No, that's silly. We're fine." Laurel's mom got up and brushed the grass off her dress. "We see Three B's all the time, and this was nice. It's more something to see than anything and now you've seen it."

Brock's dad helped fold the blanket, but his eyes darted around so quick they seemed to almost vibrate. As they walked through the crowd toward the pier, his father snuck glances back over his shoulder.

"Is everything else okay?" Laurel's mom sounded concerned.

"Yeah, fine." His dad spoke in a tone that didn't invite a second question.

They got into the boat and pushed away. Brock put his head in his hand and faked a headache. It wasn't hard. His head was spinning with all the possibilities. Were they in danger? Were they leaving? Could they ever be safe?

Laurel lightly rubbed his back and clucked her tongue.

Laurel's mom said something to the boat captain and he took off at a clip, the bow rising up over the dark water and a wake of white foam cascading from the stern. Brock stole a look at his dad, who now sat with his arms on his knees, staring at the darkness on the river's shore, thinking . . . planning.

They pulled into the boathouse, got off, and started up the lawn at a quick pace.

"You're sure there's nothing we can do?" Laurel's mom asked.

"Kim, thank you so much for everything. This was a wonderful night, dinner, the boat, the band. Brock'll be fine. I just need to get him back to lie down and to take his medicine."

"You'll call me?" she asked.

Brock's dad paused.

"To tell me how Brock is?" she said.

"Of course." His dad swung the car door open and Brock got in.

As his dad rounded the car, Laurel leaned into the open door and gave Brock a kiss on the cheek, then whispered to him. "I know it's not a headache. Call me when you can and tell me. I want to help, Brock. I'm scared."

Brock's dad got in and started the car. Brock looked up at Laurel, unable to speak. She closed the door and his father pulled away, leaving Laurel and her family in a small spray of gravel and dust.

Brock wondered if he'd ever see her again.

Brock's dad pulled the car over on the street two blocks away from their house.

"Wait here." His father started to get out.

"I can't come?"

His father gave him a look, then closed the door. Brock sat, waiting and wondering, hoping that his mind had simply played a trick on him. Maybe the whole thing was just a crazy coincidence. He'd heard somewhere that everyone had a double, a random person out there in the world who looked exactly like you.

"Why did he look at me like that, though?" Brock asked himself aloud. "And he talked funny."

A car drove slowly by. Brock slid down into the seat, watching it across their own car's dashboard as it pulled around the corner in the direction of Brock's house. He worried about his father, but told himself that his father above anyone knew how to take care of himself. Brock remembered the airplane, the crash, and the hospital. His father's abilities seemed to have no limit.

From nowhere, his father appeared and flung open the door. He threw a duffel bag over the seat into the back, climbed in, and took off.

"I got you some things."

"Did you get what you needed?" Brock asked him, leaning into the turn as his father swerved out onto the main boulevard, heading south, away from the bridge and town.

His father shook his head and slapped the wheel. "I can't believe this. I just can't."

"Maybe I'm wrong."

His father glanced over. "I'm glad you're cautious."

"I thought we didn't have to be."

His father just kept shaking his head and he gave his tongue one big cluck.

"I thought we could stay." Brock tried to sound hard to keep from whining.

"Let's not get ahead of ourselves. I just need to get you clear of town *in case*."

"For how long?"

"Two, three days." His father shrugged.

"What about football? We've got practice tomorrow. If we come back, they'll kill me for missing."

"You got a migraine, remember? I'll call the coach and give them a doctor's note."

They drove for over an hour in the dark, and his father

occasionally consulted a paper road map until they pulled off the highway and rode up a rough dirt road into some woods. A handful of small log cabins lined the path. His father told him to wait and went inside the main cabin, which had a light on the outside big enough that Brock could read the license plates on the cars in the parking lot—Ohio, but also Tennessee, Pennsylvania, and West Virginia. His father came out several minutes later and drove them up the dirt road to the cabin at the end.

"This is it." His father got out and unloaded the bag. "You'll be safe here."

It was pitch-black. Brock heard his dad fumble with the keys and get the door open before a light went on inside. Brock went in and sat down on a musty couch. He wanted to put his head in his hands and cry, but he knew better. From the bag, his dad removed some fresh clothes and his book. Brock cracked it open and began to read.

"I'll be back by morning and I'll bring some food." His father turned to go. "Lock the door. You can read a little, but get some sleep."

"What? Dad? You're leaving me here?"

His father stopped. "I know it's not ideal, but hang in there, buddy."

"I want to go back." Even the thought of Coach Van Kuffler couldn't drown out the image of Laurel and Mak. "I mean, to stay."

"I know. Me too," his father said. "Let me scout things out and make sure it's safe."

He stared at his father. Brock was used to being left alone.

He'd been left alone his whole life. What he never knew until a few months ago was that there were people trying to kill his father. Brock had seen them, one up close. He remembered the dark shape of the man outside their previous home who had tapped on the car window with his gun, with Brock alone in the dark, waiting. He remembered his father thumping the man on the back of the head and them racing away.

He remembered the airplane and the sparkles of light that were gunfire. "What if you don't come back?"

His father took a deep breath and let it out in a long thin stream. "I always come back. Don't even think about it."

His father left. Brock closed his book and set it down.

Because whether his father would come back or not was all he *could* think about.

49

Brock wandered into the bedroom and looked at the quilted bedspread. He opened a window. The scent of pine rushed in to wrestle with the musty smell of bedclothes and furniture that hadn't seen the sun in years. He lay down on the bed to read, but a million pine needles whispered to him in the night breeze outside the open window, and he grew so tired that he slept.

When he woke, the sun was already high enough to filter down through the trees and dapple the mossy rocks and pine boughs with golden light. Brock threw the covers aside and realized by the coffee smell that his father had returned. He got up and opened the bedroom door to find his father sitting in the kitchen at his computer.

"Sleep good?" his dad asked in a cheery tone which encouraged Brock to relax a bit. "I got some cereal for you, milk's in the fridge."

"You didn't find anything?" Brock asked.

"That doesn't mean too much, yet." His father sipped coffee from a thick white mug.

"How do you even start looking for someone?"

His father set his mug down. "Well, Boudantsev is a wanted man. He isn't going to stay in one place for very long. If he knows we're here, it's because he somehow got a line on us. I can't imagine how, but things happen, and if he had a line on us, he'll find out where we live quick and make a move. I put cameras on the house to watch."

His father's words made Brock shiver. He knew "make a move" wasn't like a board game. It meant someone was going to try and kill them.

"Couldn't he just go away and come back?" Brock asked.

His dad shook his head. "It'll never happen. Don't forget, he has no idea we're here to stay. If he knows where we are, he'll do something about it now. He'd stay someplace close. Try to get in and out, so I spent the other half of the night checking out every hotel and motel in the area. No sign of him."

"How do you check out hotels? You can't just ask for him, can you?" Brock found a bowl and a spoon. He shook out some Raisin Bran and doused it with milk before sitting down.

"Not by name, but Boudantsev isn't a guy to go unnoticed. He's got a unique look."

"A scary look." Brock slurped his cereal.

His dad nodded. "And he doesn't speak English all that well."

"So, if he's not staying anywhere, maybe he was just passing through. Maybe it wasn't him at all, that's what I keep thinking." Brock couldn't help being hopeful, despite what he knew he saw.

His father rubbed his beard. "I doubt he was passing through Calhoun, Ohio. That's too much of a coincidence. I'd normally say we're all clear, but you said he was with another person."

Brock winced. His father had asked him several times to try and remember something distinguishing about the other man, but he simply couldn't. He didn't know if the man was tall or short, heavy or thin, red-haired or black-haired. The image of Boudantsev's glare burned so deep into his brain that everything else was faded.

"I'm pretty sure he was," Brock said.

"So, it's possible that person is the front, doing all the talking, getting a room, and Boudantsev just sneaks in and out unnoticed by almost everyone."

"I could be wrong about the whole thing, though." Brock poked his cereal, thinking of Laurel, and still hoping.

His father bit his lip and studied Brock. He spoke soft. "You've been through a lot, so . . . yes, I'd say it's possible someone just looked a lot like the man you saw in the newspaper. He looked back at you because you bumped into him. That's entirely possible, Brock. But, I've stayed alive and kept you safe for the past ten years by being careful. Give me a couple days. If nothing turns up, then we'll be fine."

Brock took another spoonful of cereal, then spoke through his food. "Mak. I should tell him."

"Let me," his dad said. "Give me his number. I'll call your coach too when I get out on the road."

"But we're not even home. What if he stops by?"

"I'll tell him you're in bed. Shut down, and can't see anyone. That's how migraines are anyway. I'll make the calls when I get out on the road. First, I'm going to close my eyes for a few minutes."

Brock finished his breakfast while his dad lay down in the other bedroom. Brock cleaned up and sat on the couch to read his book. He couldn't help laughing out loud as he read Jon Scieszka describe himself and his brother as kids peeing on the space heater to put it out like a campfire. He looked at the author's crazy picture on the back of the book and heard a shuffling in the next room.

"What's so funny?" His father was bleary eyed and scratching his beard.

"Sorry. Jon Scieszka, the author. Didn't meant to wake you up."

"I gotta go anyway."

"Do you have to call in sick to your job?" Brock asked.

"I did."

"I'm going to finish this today." Brock held up his book. "Can I download something? Do you have your iPad?"

"I thought you only liked 'real' books." His father reached into the duffel bag and handed Brock the iPad before changing into a new shirt.

"I do, but . . . it's better than nothing. I'm guessing you don't want me to leave the cabin."

"Correct. Tell you what. I'll take it down to the highway and stop at a gas station and download it there."

"Why?"

"I don't trust these things. They're just as dangerous as using your phone with a location service on. When you enable a wireless connection to download something people know where you are."

"What people?" Brock asked.

"The government for sure," his dad said. "And if the government knows, anyone can know. I'm just playing it safe, that's all. Even if Boudantsev does have a line on us, I doubt he's in that deep, but you never know. Once you uplink an iPad, you're location is marked. You can't undo it. What do you want me to download?"

"*The Lightning Thief.* Get the next couple in that series too."

His father finished changing, then left with the iPad before returning twenty minutes later and handing it to him. "Enjoy. I got a package of bologna and some bread. It's nothing great, but it'll hold you over. Don't worry if I don't come back tonight. It might be tomorrow."

"Don't you need to sleep?" Brock asked.

His father's mouth was a flat line. "Not when I'm working."

"Working." The word had an entirely different sound from when his father was talking about his new job as a sanitary engineer. He'd thought that variety of the word had been put away forever. "Good luck."

His father winked. "See you soon."

Brock was thankful for the ebooks. They were good ones, and kept him occupied for the next day and a half. It was Sunday night and Brock had already put himself to bed when he heard a car roll slowly up outside the cabin. His blood froze and he clenched his hands. Something told him to run.

He remained frozen, like a deer in headlights.

He heard the cabin door swing open.

"Brock?" his father's voice floated in from the main room.

Brock exhaled. "In here."

His father walked into the bedroom and flipped on the light. Brock's dad's eyes were red and watery, but he kept his chin high and his back straight. Concrete. "How'd you like to go home?"

Brock threw off the covers. "Really? It's okay?"

"I wouldn't say it if it weren't."

"I know. Yes. Let's go. I can go to practice tomorrow."

His father chuckled. "For a guy who hates his coach as much as you, I'm surprised you didn't want another day off."

"If I'm here, I got to play." Brock went into the bedroom and started stuffing his things into the duffel bag, raising his voice so his dad could hear him. "It's what everyone does, and I've only got one season with Van Kuffler. After that, I'll be moving up. I've been thinking about it while you were gone. I mean, what if Percy Jackson just gave up when things were hard?"

"Who?" his dad asked.

"Percy Jackson," Brock said. "He's the main character in those books I'm reading. Wild stuff."

"Well, good." His dad followed him and stood in the door-way. "I can't stand the idea of quitting just because of someone like Van Kuffler. There are Van Kufflers everywhere. It's like stepping in dog poop. It happens to everyone and you just have to keep walking. Eventually, it wears off and the smell goes with it."

"I like that." Brock grinned. "Mak's gonna laugh when he hears you called Van Kuffler dog poop."

"Technically, I didn't. That would be disrespectful."

"Come on, Dad."

"Hey, that's your interpretation." His father's smile was weary, but filled with relief and joy. "I can't help that. Come on."

"Can I turn my phone back on?"

"Why don't you wait until we get home. This was a good

place. Not that we'll need it again, but it's good to know it's here."

"Sure," Brock said.

They left in the dark and didn't get back to their tiny house until after midnight. Brock turned on his phone and saw seventeen texts from Laurel along with three voice messages. He read and listened to them and responded with one simple text.

Sorry. I ws totally out of it

better now ☺ c u tmrrow

Brock smiled to himself, yawned, and got to bed, happy for the creak of the springs and even the smell of the place. Almost losing it made it now seem that much more like home.

When Brock woke the next day he saw a text from Laurel saying how glad she was that he felt better and asking that he stop by the library after practice. Mak was already downstairs with his father, fully dressed in his football gear and eating a piece of toast with cream cheese on it through his face mask.

"Hey!" Mak's face brightened when he saw Brock. "You're okay?"

"Now I am."

"Wow, my dad says those migraines are the worst." Mak fished the toast through his mask and took another bite, talking through his food. "His cousin used to get them so bad they had to put him in a *rubber room*. Man, I was worried when your dad said you couldn't even come to the door. Did you see me waving from the street?"

Brock looked at his dad.

"He was really out of it," Brock's dad said. "We had him in total lockdown."

"What was that, blankets over your bedroom window?" Mak crunched down his last bit of toast and wiggled his fingers into his mask to lick them clean.

"Light is like a hammer with a migraine," Brock's dad said.

"And he's all right to practice today?" Mak asked, looking at Brock's dad.

"Once it's over, it's over." Brock's dad shrugged and opened his newspaper.

Brock got some cereal and ate it quickly while Mak talked about how the kid who replaced him on the line wasn't worth his weight in pee. "Be the last time *he* ever sees first team. My dad says my temper is part of what makes me a good lineman, but I'm not going to let anyone—not that clown Wentzel or anyone else—draw me out into a fight or anything that gets me suspended. That's over, and my dad says it's a good lesson to learn now instead of when I'm on varsity."

"Your dad's right." Brock's dad sipped his coffee. "Again."

Mak beamed.

Brock put his things in the sink and they took off on their bikes, heading for the school. Brock changed into his practice gear, which, although smelly, had the chance to really dry out over the weekend. A couple of his teammates asked how he was doing, but for the most part, people went about their business and got themselves into the right frame of mind for another tough football practice in the heat.

As he trudged out to the field, Brock felt a hand on his shoulder pad.

192

"How you doing?" Coach Hewitt actually smiled at him.

"Good, Coach. Better." Brock tried not to sound guilty about the lie.

"Those things are nothing to mess around with," Coach Hewitt said. "Don't push yourself too hard in this heat, and I don't want you running after practice. You're not going to have enough practices to be eligible to play in the opener anyway, so let's ease you back into things."

"Okay, Coach." Brock's chest filled with gratitude, and it was the first time he really felt like he was a true part of the team.

"Good." Coach slapped his shoulder pad and pointed toward the end zone. "Go get warmed up with the other quarterbacks. Coach Van Kuffler's waiting for you."

Coach Van Kuffler glanced across the field at where Coach Hewitt was going over his practice plan with Coach Delaney. "Well, well . . . is our little headache better?"

Brock bit into his mouthpiece. "I'm fine."

"Of course you're fine." Coach Van Kuffler spat his words out, before mumbling, "Pathetic."

Brock stood there, waiting for instructions. None came. Coach Van Kuffler worked with his nephew and Wentzel, coaching them to turn their thumb down more or step into their throw, but all the while pretending like Brock wasn't even there. So, Brock just stood and watched and fumed and planned his revenge.

He remembered the looks on people's faces when he and his father had walked off the pier with Laurel and her family, the respect in their eyes. Van Kuffler hadn't been there to see, but if Brock had his way, they'd be spending a lot more time around town with Laurel and her family. Maybe his father and her mom would become an item, get married?

The thought of being part of Laurel's family made his heart gallop. Van Kuffler *would* see, then. Everyone would see. And if that ever happened, Van Kuffler would have to choke on it and know that whatever plans he had for his nephew, Wally, would be ruined by Brock.

After nearly an hour of standing and thinking about how Coach Spada would chew Van Kuffler's leg off if he only knew how badly his instructions were being disregarded, Brock became emboldened. He had nothing to lose. Van Kuffler couldn't treat him much worse. So, when Coach Van Kuffler started the seven-on-seven session where the offense worked on its pass plays, and after Wally had run the first ten plays with only moderate success, Brock took a breath and walked right up to Coach Van Kuffler.

"Coach," he said, "I think you should give me some reps."

Coach Van Kuffler turned and stared a Brock. When the disbelief cleared from the coach's face, it curled and twisted into a nasty grin. "Oh, you think you should get some reps, do you?"

Van Kuffler's hatred felt like the heat of the sun and Brock actually stepped back from it. He couldn't speak, but he nodded and croaked.

Van Kuffler leaned so close Brock could smell the stale coffee on his breath and something spoiled that stunk so bad it made Brock blink.

Van Kuffler spoke in a whisper. "Now you're gonna start

telling me what you think? *That's* your next move?"

Brock didn't know what to say. He wished he could undo the last minute of his life and he wondered what in the world could have prompted him to say anything in the first place.

Then, behind Coach Van Kuffler, he saw the cavalry riding in to save the day.

52

Coach Spada marched straight out into the middle of the field. Taylor Owen Lehman wasn't with him, but that didn't matter. The way he made a beeline for Brock let everyone on the field know why he was there. Brock tried not to grin at Coach Van Kuffler, but couldn't help it.

"Van Kuffler!" Coach Spada shouted and slapped Brock's coach on the back. "How's the arm looking?"

A giddy sound of delight burst from Brock's throat and he eagerly glanced around to see if Mak was catching the show. Mak was in a pit drill, so he wouldn't see, too bad, but Brock took a deep breath and widened his eyes. He didn't want to miss a thing.

Van Kuffler straightened like a wooden soldier. "Coach? How are you, Coach? Glad you came to watch a bit."

"I said I would." Coach Spada laughed. "How's the Arm?"

"The arm?" Van Kuffler wrinkled his brow.

"Not 'the arm,' THE ARM. This kid." Coach Spada beamed. "Never seen anything quite like it on a twelve-year-old, have you? No."

"Well . . ." Coach Van Kuffler hesitated. "He's doing pretty well."

"I don't want you undermining me, Frank." Coach Spada scowled at Coach Van Kuffler as he used his first name. "You know I can't stand being bucked. It won't do."

"You know I wouldn't buck you, Coach." Van Kuffler licked his lips and his eyes darted nervously at Brock. "The Arm is about to take his reps, so you should just see for yourself, right?"

Coach Spada folded his arms across his chest. "Nice."

Brock's spirits soared. He stepped into the huddle and Coach Van Kuffler read the play off his sheet.

"Heavy Right 367 Bama."

"Bama?" Brock's gut clenched.

Brock should have known Van Kuffler wasn't going down so easily. His mind spun. He knew he'd heard about Bama, but no one had shown it to him, not even Taylor.

"Uhh."

"What's the problem?" Coach Spada demanded.

Van Kuffler repeated the play.

"Uhh, Bama?" Brock gave Coach Spada a hopeless look.

Coach Spada turned his glare from Brock to Coach Van Kuffler. "Don't think I'm blaming the Arm, here. *You're* the coach, Frank. You're responsible for your doggone backup quarterback to know the plays . . . you've got a game in four days, Frank."

Coach Van Kuffler nodded innocently and turned his hands, palms up, begging forgiveness. Brock was still delighted, but he was more wary now. He trusted Coach Van

Kuffler only to be devious and mean.

"Well, I did teach Bama, and he's *not* my backup quarterback, Coach."

Coach Spada's face turned red and he leaned toward Coach Van Kuffler, speaking in a snarl. "I *said* I wanted him on second team."

Coach Van Kuffler wagged his head up and down violently. "I know, Coach, but he can't *play* in the opener."

"What do you mean? Coach Hewitt told me he'd have ten practices." Coach Spada smacked a fist into his open hand. "He's fine to play."

Coach Van Kuffler snuck a mean smile at Brock and shook his head slowly. "No, Coach. He was *supposed* to have ten practices, but he missed Saturday—that's also when I put Bama in. He can't play in the opener, so I thought—exactly what you said—I need to get my backup quarterback plenty of reps. Brock's been practicing, but I thought—in the interest of the team—that I should get Wentzel ready to go if Wally goes down. Moravia is one of our tougher opponents."

"Wait." Coach Spada held up a hand. "You didn't tell me *why*. He *missed* a *practice*?"

Coach Spada turned toward Brock now, his face still distorted and brilliant in color.

Brock opened his mouth. His dreams coming to a rapid end, jumping the tracks for nightmare city.

It was Coach Van Kuffler who answered the question.

"Well, Coach . . . he had a headache."

54

Brock couldn't speak.

He wanted to explain that it was a migraine, but even that, he knew, was a lie. Coach Spada's look of disappointment and—was it disgust? Probably, yes—forbade Brock from saying anything anyway.

Coach Spada twisted up his mouth and shook his head. "I don't care what position you play," he said to Brock. "Football player's gotta be tough. That's before anything."

Coach Spada walked away.

Before the varsity head coach even reached the sideline, Coach Van Kuffler called out, "Can I get a quarterback who knows what Bama is?"

Wentzel barged into the huddle, practically shoving Brock aside. Practice continued. Brock stood, shoulders slung low, watching. As he fumed over the injustice of it all, Brock threw all his hope into his master plan. Coach Spada still knew Brock had a good arm—he called him THE ARM! And a missed practice was something that everyone had at one time or another. All Brock needed was an advocate, someone who wasn't just a part of the community, but a *pillar*. A pillar of any community was a person so important that whatever they said or did affected the entire town. And Brock knew Laurel's mom was a pillar.

The whistle ending practice finally blew. Coach Hewitt called the players together.

"School starts Wednesday, guys. So today and tomorrow are our last summer practices. After this, we've got a lot less time to work, so let's get a lot done tomorrow. We've got Moravia on Saturday at their place and we need to set the tone. Outside of Groton, they may be our toughest opponent all year. Bring it in, guys. Nothing is fun about football but winning, so give me three 'wins.'"

They all held their hands up and chanted with their coach. "WIN! WIN! WIN!"

Brock jammed his gear into the corner locker and stormed out. Mak was waiting on a bench by the bike rack, also scowling. They mounted up and rode their bikes in silence to the library. Mak, Brock presumed, caught up in the funk of his suspension, and Brock eager to find comfort after a disastrous practice. He felt fairly certain Laurel would be glad to see him, and that would help.

The librarian was at the desk right behind Laurel, so Laurel didn't yell out or anything. Her mouth stayed tight, but her eyes rang out with joy.

"Hi, Brock. Hi, Mak."

"Hey, Laurel."

"I'm really glad you're feeling better." She stopped scanning books and spoke quietly. "I know your dad said it was a migraine, but I saw the way that man we bumped into looked at you, Brock. Is everything okay?"

"It's fine." Brock forced a laugh and angled his head toward Mak's look of curiosity and confusion. "Don't worry. Just a coincidence."

Laurel studied him for a moment and seemed to finally get that Mak knew nothing about the man. "Well, I didn't say anything, Brock. You can trust me. Anyway, my mom was going to call your dad to see if you guys wanted to have dinner tonight. It's the second-to-last night of summer vacation."

"Summer vacation ended for us when football practice started." Mak pounded his chest plate with a fist, rattling his pads.

Brock ignored his buddy. "I can't see him saying no."

"Nothing fancy this time. Just a cookout."

"We love cookouts."

"Hey . . . me too?" Mak waved his hand.

"Sure, Mak. We'd love to have you." Laurel sounded like she meant it.

Brock cringed, hoping she wasn't going to invite Mak's dad too. Brock wanted to meet Mak's dad, but not tonight, when it would ruin the chance for his dad and Laurel's mom to be together.

"I'll ask." Mak's smile shone through his face mask. "Can I

ride with you guys, Brock?"

"Of course."

"What you reading?" Laurel asked Brock.

"I finished the two I got here and downloaded a couple of Rick Riordan's. I forgot to bring the ones I finished with me to return, or I'd get something else."

"You can get one." Laurel glanced over at the librarian and spoke quietly.

"Two book limit," Brock said.

She winked. "I got you covered. Here, take this."

Brock took the book from her hands. "*The Fault in Our Stars*?"

"Gracie, my brother's girlfriend, was reading it. It's very romantic," she said. "But I want you to read it."

She scanned it with a beep, somehow checking it out for him despite the limit. Brock looked at the cover.

Laurel's eyes sparkled. "It'll make you happy to be alive. It'll make you cry too."

"Oooh-kay." Brock dragged the word out slowly.

Laurel turned to Mak. "How about you, Mak? How's *Ungifted*?"

"Funny, but I'm not done."

"It's good you're working on it," she said. "Well, I better get back to it. See you tonight, hopefully. Both of you, and I'm glad you're better."

Before they reached the bike stand, Mak grabbed the book from Brock's hands. "Let me see that."

Mak cracked it open and moved his lips as he read. Then, he looked up to make sure he had Brock's attention. "See? This is what I was afraid of. *I fell in love the way you fall asleep: slowly, then all at once.'* Dude, you cannot read this kind of stuff. It'll poison your mind. She's a *girl*. You're a *football player*."

"I thought football players liked girls." Brock snatched the book back.

"In the off-season, they do. You gotta focus. I thought you wanted to be first team. With me."

"You're second team, remember?"

"For the moment. They're gonna wish they had me when they get to Moravia. Same with you. Wally will get whacked around and something will hurt him." Mak climbed on his bike and started pedaling. "You'll get your shot."

"Are you at the same practices I'm at?" Brock removed his bike from the rack, kicked the stand, and caught up. "I'm second team, but Wentzel gets more reps at third team."

"Trust me." Mak thumped his chest with a fist as they rode. "I know how this goes. The tide is turning for you. You got Coach Spada on your side."

"Did you not hear what happened during seven on seven?" Brock asked.

Mak wrinkled his brow and shook his head. "What?"

Brock told him how everything went.

"Well," Mak said, "he called you 'the Arm.'"

"I know. That's good, right?"

"No, that's great," Mak said. "And, you got Taylor Owen Lehman behind you. What I really wish is if Laurel's mom got onto the Brock Barrette bandwagon."

"Laurel's mom?" Brock wondered if Mak suspected what he was planning.

Mak shrugged. "Well, she's the president of the Mom's Club. You think, 'oh, big deal' but it is a big deal in Calhoun. The Dahlmans have practically owned this town since it began. Then she marries an NFL player? Talk about the perfect storm. I know it's crazy, but if things keep going good with Laurel, maybe you could ask her mom to . . . you know, put in a good word, let Van Kuffler find out she's got her eye on you. That'd put the whole Van Kuffler clan into line."

Mak stopped his bike at the light in the center of town and looked over at Brock. "But *don't* start that kissy face stuff. That is *not* the way to help the situation. Just be her friend. Get the mom to love you. You're in a great spot, my friend. You've got a path to the top unlike any new kid I've ever seen, especially from the Flatlands."

The light changed and they crossed Main Street on their way to the bridge.

Brock grumbled under his breath. "Kissy face."

Mak glanced over and must have heard him. "Don't think you can fool me. I see the way you look at her and I see the way she looks at you."

Brock pretended disgust, but inside, his heart seemed to spin.

Dinner at Laurel's was a huge success.

Mak couldn't make it because he had to watch his little sister.

Brock secretly watched his father and Laurel's mother. They sat close to each other at dinner, on the terrace, and then they took a boat ride alone up the river with the captain silently piloting from the front. Brock and Laurel watched the boat pull away and disappear into the night and Brock thought he just might have seen his father lean toward her mother in the backseat to kiss, although he couldn't be sure.

Brock and Laurel stood on the grass, cool now in the dark. The moon was settling into the treetops and had decorated the water with bright flickering ghosts.

"It's so . . . beautiful, right?" Laurel took his hand.

Brock stiffened, thinking of Mak's words.

Laurel led him to a pair of low chairs on a tuft that jutted out over the riverbank and kept his hand as they sat to watch the light show.

Brock cleared his throat. "Mak says you gotta focus on football if you want to be first team."

Laurel's laughter danced out across the water, mixing with the moonlight. "Have you not noticed that Mak doesn't take his football equipment off?"

"He ate a piece of toast through his face mask this morning." Brock tried to hold back his laughter, but it squeaked loose and they giggled together.

"I love Mak, though." Brock sniffed.

They sat quiet for a long time and Brock realized he could no longer hear the chug of the boat motor. "How far can you go up the river?"

"There are locks all the way up to Coshocton. That's where the river starts." She laughed. "They could be gone all night."

"They won't be gone all night." Brock didn't know why he said that.

"I know. I'm just saying, the Muskingum River used to be a major waterway and they kept the locks operational ever since."

They sat quiet again.

"I think they like each other." The words jumped from Brock's mouth without a thought.

"I haven't seen my mom like this before. Ever. Not even with my dad."

"They don't even know each other that well." Brock wanted his heart to settle.

"I think people like you and people like us . . . they just sense something about one another." She took a breath. "Good people. That's all. People who care. People who are kind."

"Thank you."

"Thank *you*. You're the ones who appeared out of nowhere."

Brock thought about that and he wondered if they ever could become part of another family, let alone part of a community, because . . . if that happened, didn't you have to tell people about your past? Could you ever really be close with someone and not tell them who you really were, where you're really from? But then, Laurel hadn't questioned him anymore about being spooked on the street by the man who looked like Boudantsev.

Maybe people *could* just cut off their past life and start new.

"So," she said, "did you start *The Fault in Our Stars?*"

"I'm almost done with *The Titan's Curse.*"

"But you'll start it before you finish the series, right?"

"I will," he said, still thinking of Mak's warnings. "Tonight."

"Good. Are you worried about school?" she asked. "Everything is so new, I mean."

"No." Brock couldn't help a small laugh. He ached to tell her how many times he'd started at a new school, sometimes twice in one year, and once, three times.

"Yeah," she said, "you know all the football players already."

"Not so much." Brock didn't want to get into how isolated he felt, but he didn't want to exaggerate his acceptance into the team either. "Not everyone's like you."

"How are they not like me?" She lowered her voice to a raspy whisper and her eyes glimmered at him, stealing his breath.

"You're just . . . ," he said in a hushed voice. "So nice."

That's when she leaned over and kissed him.

57

The next morning Brock's eyes shot open, the way they always did on the first day of school. When Mak rode up to Brock's house so they could bike to school together, Brock didn't recognize him. Mak's blond hair was combed over, greased down with some kind of gel, and split by a part so perfect it looked like a crease in his skull. He also wore a stiffly starched white dress shirt with a red bowtie.

"Holy moly." Brock could only stare at the tie.

"Yeah." Mak tugged at his shirt collar. "My mom did this. See, my dad says you always let a woman dress you, unless you got style yourself, and my dad says if you don't know the answer to whether or not you got style, then you already got your answer."

Mak looked down. He couldn't see the tie beneath his chin, but he made an effort to straighten it anyway.

"And your hair." Brock smoothed his own hair down, feeling a bit sloppy.

Mak looked up at the hair he couldn't see. "I know, but my dad says the first impression is the one that lasts forever."

Brock thought about Mak riding down his street a few weeks ago, weighted down by his football gear, and crashing his bike. "Your dad's right. Come on. Let's get going, or we'll be late."

Brock kept his eyes roving wherever he went. He remembered the last new school he went to and a wild kid named Nagel who picked a fight with him on the first day. Even though they'd eventually become friends, Brock didn't forget the lesson of being ready for anything.

It was odd to see teammates whose faces he'd grown familiar with. They all looked different without their helmets or their hair matted down from sweat. Many acted different too. Declan Carey, a big offensive lineman who snarled and snorted on the field, was soft-spoken and polite. Brady Calenzo, the team's running back who laughed like a madman and chattered throughout practice, insulting anyone who tried to tackle him, kept his nose in a book and was so shy that he didn't seem to talk to anyone.

Brock had science class with Laurel, but that was it, and he saw her very little in school. Thankfully, Mak was in his lunch as well as gym, English, and math classes. It was weird for Brock all day, seeing Mak in regular clothes with no helmet on his head. He got used to it by the end of the day, though, and he got along with the other students better than he normally did the first day at a new school.

After science class, he didn't see Laurel again until after football practice, in the evening. They all had dinner together before the parents took another boat ride. When they were alone, Laurel wasted no time at all asking him how he liked *The Fault in Our Stars*.

"I like it okay." Brock tried hard to sound enthusiastic.

"What's wrong? You don't like it?"

The two of them were down at the boathouse, dangling their feet off the end of the dock.

"I feel like it's gonna be sad." He looked off at the trees over the water.

"Well." She paused for a minute. "Life is sad when it ends, and it always ends."

"There's no sports in it," Brock said. "I like sports."

"He used to be a basketball player." She sounded hopeful.

"Sports *action*."

"Oh."

Brock looked over. He knew he'd disappointed her, but he thought it was important to be honest. He held out a fist. "Opposites?"

She smiled, then looked at him and he felt the pull of those pretty blue eyes, and bumped his fist. "Attract."

"Because my dad always says if you don't love a book, you shouldn't force yourself to read it."

"That sounds okay to me. Maybe one day." She sounded disappointed, but soft-punched his shoulder anyway.

What he didn't tell her was that when the girl in the book started to like the guy, the whole thing just freaked him out. Exactly why, he didn't know. Maybe it was because of the way he felt about her, and that she'd kissed him. He felt like reading the book she'd given him would just take him that much farther into the uncharted territory he was afraid of. Also, he'd rather read about spies, pitchers, or alien worlds, places he'd want to be if he could. His own life felt difficult enough without diving into the world of a book that had even more problems.

58

There weren't too many nights when they didn't have dinner at the mansion on the river, and it was pleasant for Brock—who still suffered under Coach Van Kuffler's mistreatment—to plan his football breakthrough once his dad and Laurel's mom solidified their relationship.

Brock wasn't quite certain what that meant, or exactly how it would happen, but he felt he'd know when it did. He'd heard of people getting married just months—or even weeks—after they first met, but he didn't need all that. A simple commitment between them—announcing that they were a couple—was all Brock was waiting for. When that happened, he was going to go right to Laurel's mom with his problem. It made him giddy to think of her watching his practices day after day from the bleachers and the blowout she'd have with Coach Van Kuffler who would retreat from her vigilance and her wrath like a wounded rat . . . maybe a chipmunk.

Brock wanted to be a football player. Mak was right. He wanted to fit in at Calhoun. He also wanted to win the affections of Laurel, and for that matter everyone around him. Still, he only wanted football the way you might want to win a really good door prize, something like a signed Peyton Manning jersey or an Xbox. When he and his dad went with Laurel and her mom to watch Taylor's game on Friday night at the Calhoun High School stadium, though, that all changed.

Traffic was thick through town, but when they got to the high school, Laurel's mom showed a special pass and the policeman let them go straight while all the other traffic had to take a right into the fields of parked cars. Brock didn't know if it was because she was the president of the Mom's Club, or that her son was the starting QB, or just because she was so rich, but whatever the reason, they parked right up next to the stadium in an empty spot. Brock's dad raised an eyebrow at Brock, but said nothing. Parked cars stretched as far as Brock could see, most of them bursting with families decked out in green and gold, many flying Crab Nation flags from folding chairs, and cooking burgers or dogs on mini grills. They too wore green and gold. Laurel and her mom had number seven jerseys—replicas of Taylor's, and Brock and his dad had Calhoun Fighting Crabs T-shirts. It was a carnival.

Inside the stadium, only half the seats were full, but people started streaming in for real as the Calhoun Fighting Crabs took the field for warm-ups. The crowd cheered at the very sight of them. When Moravia's varsity came out wearing visitors' white jerseys with touches of dark blue and gold, the crowd booed like they were villains. Only a small slice of blue and gold in the visitors' end zone tried to overcome the boos with cheers.

"How many people does this place hold?" Brock's dad asked Laurel's mom.

She waved a hand through the air in an offhanded way. "I think twelve thousand. Isn't it twelve, Laurel?"

"I think so, Mom." Laurel took Brock's arm as they weaved their way through the throng, up the middle of the bleachers to their seats on the fifty-yard line.

All around, Brock could feel people's eyes on them. He didn't know if it was just because of Laurel's mom and who she was, or if it was Laurel's mom and who *they* were, the new kid and his dad from the Flatlands. Whatever the reason, Brock had to bite the inside of his cheek not to grin when he saw the stupid look on Kurt Wentzel's face, sitting with what looked like his parents, all dressed up in green polo shirts with fancy gold sweaters tied around their necks like it was a country club party rather than a football game.

From the moment they sat, Laurel's mom fixed her eyes on Taylor. Even when she spoke or stood to cheer, or order a drink from the popcorn and soda vendor, she looked only at her son. A lot of people looked at her son.

Taylor was all business and obviously in charge of things. He looked back and forth from the sideline to his own play-ers in the huddle and commanded the field like a general. He marched his troops up and down the field, and while Moravia was able to score some points of their own, it wasn't enough to keep Taylor Owen Lehman from another all-state performance and a big win in the Calhoun opener.

Brock loved baseball, the crack of a bat, the polite applause from a nice crowd on a sunny day, but this was something entirely different. Sometimes during the game, the crowd got so loud that Brock couldn't hear Laurel even when her lips tickled his ear and she shouted at the top of her lungs. When it all ended, the home crowd began singing a song Brock didn't recognize. Laurel told him it was the alma mater and that most of the people in the town had gone to Calhoun themselves.

"People from out of town usually learn it too." She offered him an apologetic smile, like she didn't care whether he learned it or not.

What struck Brock was the scale of it all. It wasn't just the colors or the sounds of cheering or when people stamped their feet so hard he could feel the bleachers vibrating beneath his feet. It was the passion people had, the light in their eyes when they talked to one another about *their* team or *their* quarterback. As a high school senior, Taylor Owen Lehman was as big a star in Calhoun as Tom Brady was in Boston.

As they walked out of the stadium, people shouting congratulations to Laurel and her mom for Taylor's performance and the big win, Brock set his jaw and decided that he too was going to be Calhoun's star. It would take some time, true. He'd need to get over some obstacles—that was always the case in sports. But one day Brock Barrette would be a name the people of Calhoun would come to know and admire. That was his dream. That was his wish.

It wasn't just a door prize anymore, it was an obsession.

On the bus to the season opener at Moravia Middle School the next day, Brock sat next to Mak, who wore his school clothes rather than a uniform because of his suspension. Mak glowered the whole time, but Brock was still thankful for his company and his coaching on what to do. Brock had never played on a school football team before, and the silent grim faces of everyone around him were nothing like the bus rides he'd been on with his travel baseball team last spring. Those rides were festive, with plenty of chatter and a good dose of laughter sprinkled in.

As they pulled into the parking lot next to Moravia's football field, Brock could hear the grind of gears and the hiss of the bus brakes. Mak nudged him and they stood, following the others off the bus in total silence. The team assembled in two lines, then marched out onto the field and through the goalposts before they split off into eight fresh columns on the thirty-yard line, facing the four team captains on the forty. Wally Van Kuffler was one of those captains.

The entire team barked out numbers, counting out jumping jacks, then an assortment of stretches before running through agilities and some actual plays. Finally, they poured over onto their sideline where an undercurrent of nervousness and excitement filled the air. Coach Hewitt called them all together in a tight group. His trembling face went red. "This is a violent game, boys. I want you to go out there and *smash* them. You got that?"

Coach Hewitt glared around at them with crazy eyes.

Brock remembered his last coach, Coach Hudgens, who was nothing like this. Of course, that was baseball, this was football.

"Now you go out on that field and play your *guts* out. You got that?"

The team murmured that they did get it.

"*What?* I can't hear that!" Coach Hewitt screamed. "Say it like you mean it! Are you ready to play your guts out!"

"YES, COACH!" the team shouted right back, Brock included, and he felt the thrill of it.

"Bring it in." Coach Hewitt held a fist out for everyone to touch. "Three wins. Ready? One, two, three . . ."

"WIN! WIN! WIN!"

Brock yelled with everyone else, then found Mak and joined him on the bench. The two of them stared across the field at the Moravia team, dressed in dark blue and gold and looking much bigger than Calhoun.

Mak leaned close and spoke low. "I hate to say this, because it's our own team, but I got a bad feeling about this."

Calhoun won the coin toss and elected to receive the kickoff.

The stands weren't packed for a seventh-grade game, but there were enough fans from both sides to make some noise, and with cheers and jeers that made it hard to hear, the Moravia kicker sent the ball up and end over end, through the air. Brady Calenzo, the Calhoun running back, got under the kick, caught it, and took it right up the middle of the field. He hadn't gone ten yards before a Moravia defender crashed into Brady like a runaway train.

Pads popped and crunched. The crowd gasped and the ball squirted out of Brady's hands like a watermelon seed. Players from both sides piled on to where Brock last caught sight of the ball. The refs sorted it out and the one in the white hat flashed his arm in the direction of Calhoun's end zone, giving Moravia the ball.

Players and coaches all around Brock moaned. Mak gave Brock a knowing look and took a swig from the cup of Gatorade he'd served himself from the drink table. Moravia scored four plays later.

Coach Hewitt went ballistic. He stomped up and down the Calhoun sideline, popping his players' helmets with an open hand, warning them to wake up. Moravia kicked off again. Brady muffed it, but dove on the ball himself this time. At least Calhoun had possession.

Mak shook his head, then spoke in a low tone to Brock. "Hate to say it, but they deserve this . . . suspending *me*? I would have been blocking the guy who made Brady fumble on that first turnover. They should have suspended Wentzel, not me."

"Well, maybe they'll get it together." Brock tried to sound optimistic, but secretly, he didn't want things to go well without him or Mak in there.

Wally Van Kuffler took the snap and dropped back. The guy replacing Mak whiffed on his block and Wally got smashed to the turf. The Moravia crowd went wild, sounding air horns and rattling coffee cans full of coins amid the howling. Brock tried hard not to enjoy Wally's pain. Wally got up slow and returned to the huddle where his head jerked back and forth, obviously chewing out Mak's replacement.

"Ugly." Mak cracked his knuckles and fought back a smile.

The next play was a pass as well. Moravia blitzed. Mak's replacement failed again, and Wally just threw the ball over his receiver's head and out of bounds before getting blasted. Mak choked off a laugh and pretended to cough. No one could hear anyway. The home crowd unleashed a storm of bloodthirsty cheers.

On third down, with seventeen yards to go, everyone knew it had to be another pass. Brock gripped the edge of the bench, uncertain how he felt.

Wally Van Kuffler took the snap, dropped back, and heaved the ball up into the air.

Three people jumped for it; two were Moravia defenders.

As Wally Van Kuffler's pass wobbled down from the sky like a busted flying saucer, the two Moravia defenders smashed into each other and dropped to the turf. The ball bounced off one of their helmets, up into the air and into the arms of Brady Calenzo, the Calhoun running back. Surprised by the ball, Calenzo turned and ran for his life. Because the rest of the defense had stopped to watch, no one could catch Calenzo and he scored. The Moravia crowd got quiet, but the visitors' stands took their turn making noise and everyone on the Calhoun sideline jumped in the air. Everyone but Mak and Brock, who blinked at each other in disbelief before belting out some half-hearted cheers.

"Can you believe the luck?" Mak spoke softly between twisted lips.

Brock shook his head. "No way."

It was almost scary. After that, everything that could go wrong for Moravia, did. When they scored, a holding penalty brought it back and the next play they fumbled. Driving for another touchdown just before halftime, their runner failed to get out of bounds on the two-yard line and the clock ran out.

On the other hand, everything that could possibly go right for Calhoun did. If a Calhoun player fumbled the ball, it would end up in another Calhoun player's hands. When Wally threw an errant pass into the arms of a Moravia defender, it would bounce off his pads. When Wally threw an interception, the defender ran it back, heading in for a score. Then, on the two-yard line, Mak's backup stumbled, fell, and knocked into the defender so that he fumbled the ball. It bounced across the goal line and out of bounds, giving the ball back to Calhoun. A short screen pass by Wally resulted in a touchdown on the very next play.

"I'd rather be lucky than good, that's what my dad says." Mak rubbed a hand over his face and slung an arm around Brock's shoulders as the final whistle sounded and Calhoun players lifted Wally Van Kuffler into the air to celebrate their 34–21 victory.

On the bus ride home, Brock spoke in a low tone to Mak. "Why did everyone pick him up? He played like junk."

Mak shrugged. "You and I know he played like junk, but anyone who looks at the numbers will peg him for an all-state quarterback on the rise."

"Moravia must have dropped three *easy* interceptions." Brock's voice hissed with passion. "The three touchdowns he threw were garbage. One should have been picked off. The other two were screen passes where Calenzo ran for about fifty yards."

"I was sitting right next to you, remember?" Mak said. "The bad thing is that Coach Spada's gonna see those numbers and think Wally Van Kuffler is a great quarterback. Did you see Coach Van Kuffler's face? He looks like he won the lottery and got elected president of the United States in the same day."

"Won't Coach Spada know? Won't he watch the video?" Brock asked.

Mak snorted. "He's not gonna watch any seventh-grade video. He's getting ready for the varsity games. He'll get the box score, that's for sure. Van Kuffler probably already texted it to him."

The next week in practice, Coach Van Kuffler started switching third-team players to second team and the normal second-team guys to the third team. That way, Brock had to play quarterback with the worst players. Brock was second team in name only. The linemen, receivers, and running backs he practiced with were the bottom of the barrel, third-team scrubs. That meant that most of the time Brock's receivers ran the wrong routes. When they did do the right thing, they typically dropped the pass anyway.

When the second-team offense practiced as a whole unit, it went against the first-team defense. Surrounded by the worst players, Brock and his group got slaughtered by the first team. Defensive linemen swarmed Brock like bees and, more times than not, his offense went backward.

Meanwhile third-team offense practiced against the

third-team defense. So Wentzel basically quarterbacked the second-team offense against the scrubs. There wasn't much Brock could do about it. He was the second-team quarterback and the explanation sounded lame, especially for a kid who had missed the opening game eligibility for a headache.

Meanwhile, it took Mak just one practice—where he sent five teammates to the trainer's office with fresh injuries—before Coach Hewitt moved him back up to first team. Mak beamed at Brock when it happened, and Brock couldn't help feeling happy, even though he knew it meant he was alone, again.

That Saturday in their home opener against Liberty Middle—Calhoun's weakest opponent of the year—the first team got pulled off the field in the fourth quarter with a 54–6 lead. When Coach Hewitt sent the second team in, Brock's fingers trembled. As he jogged out onto the field, he looked up into the stands. His father sat with Laurel and her mom. Taylor was at a varsity weight-lifting session, after having pounded on Liberty's varsity the evening before.

They all waved to him. His arm felt numb as he flung a hand up in their direction.

Coach Van Kuffler stood with his arms crossed on the sideline. Brock looked at him, waiting for the signal. The ref blew the whistle that began the play clock. Coach Van Kuffler stood, staring at Brock, a smile slowly curling the corners of his mouth. Precious seconds ticked by.

On the sideline, Coach Hewitt finally yelled at his offensive coach. "Coach! Let's go! Signal a play!"

Van Kuffler's arms flashed a quick signal. Brock wasn't sure if it was a Light Right 651 Play Pass or a Light Right 651 Trap.

He gritted his teeth and decided to call the pass. Brock knelt in the huddle and barked out the play to his wide-eyed teammates, normally third-stringers who didn't see live action in a game. They broke the huddle and moved like a ragtag army to the line of scrimmage.

The ref raised his arm and began to signal the last ten seconds before Brock would get a delay of game penalty. Brock hurried to the line.

His left guard turned around and gaped at Brock in confusion. "What's the protection?"

Brock could only shake his head in disbelief. "I have no idea. *You're* the lineman, not me."

The seconds ticked away in Brock's head. He noticed now the Liberty defenders who'd been pounded on all game long were licking their chops at the sight of the Calhoun backups. The nose tackle—an enormous kid built like a bear—growled and snorted and his coiled legs trembled like springs.

Brock waved his guard into a stance and got under center. He barked the cadence, knowing he had no choice if he was going to avoid a penalty. He took the snap and pivoted. The running back was supposed to fake taking the handoff. Brock held it out momentarily before pulling it back in, but the runner panicked, grabbed at the ball, and Brock fumbled.

He scooped it up quickly and saw the giant nose tackle break free through the line. Brock dashed back and turned, looking downfield. His primary receiver ran a five route, breaking to the inside instead of a six route, which broke outside. The mistake drew the safety directly into his other receiver's seven route. Brock knew the one route, a hitch to the outside, was his only hope. As the nose tackle slammed into him, he rifled the ball to the outside receiver. As Brock fell, he saw the ball bounce off the receiver's hands into the air.

Brock smashed into the ground with the enormous kid on top of him and saw a world of stars. He heard the visitors' stands erupt into cheers and as he struggled to his feet, he got to see the Liberty cornerback who'd intercepted the pass waltz into the end zone, backward.

Brock jogged off and Van Kuffler met him at the white line. "You can't throw the one when the cornerback's pressed up like that! You gotta know better than that! That's basic!"

Spittle flew from Van Kuffler's mouth like little missiles. Brock blinked and looked past the red-faced coach into the stands. His father, Laurel, and her mom all frowned sympathetically. Brock felt a hand on his shoulder and turned.

"Easy, Coach. He's just not ready," Coach Hewitt said.

"Coach, I . . ." Brock couldn't finish his sentence.

"I *told* you, Buzz," Coach Van Kuffler snarled at Coach Hewitt.

Coach Hewitt snarled right back. "Coach Spada wanted him second team. That's that."

"Well, let me put our third string in, then." Van Kuffler leered at Brock.

"Go ahead," Coach Hewitt said, turning and walking away. "Do that."

Brock hung his head and slumped down on the bench.

For the next offensive series, Wentzel went in with the "third-string offense," who drove down the field, mostly running the ball since Wentzel only completed one of five passes, and scored a touchdown to make it 63–12.

Brock sat, sickened by it all, and burning with rage at the injustice.

Up in the stands he saw the only ray of hope he had.

Laurel's mom put her arm around his dad and rested her head on his shoulder.

63

It was Thursday evening when Brock's dad and Laurel's mom left the dinner table on the terrace and walked together toward the barn. Brock never knew his dad could ride a horse. But he'd never known his dad could fly a plane, either, yet he had done just that to help them escape the men who'd hunted him. Brock stared out at the river and ran a finger along his nose and the side of his face. That plane ride seemed like a lifetime ago.

"Ready to throw a little?" Taylor got up from the table and set his linen napkin down next to the fancy silver goblet that had held his ice cream.

"Sure." Brock looked at Laurel and got up when she did. They followed Taylor down the steps and fired a couple dozen balls at the targets on his net. Afterward, they went inside and worked on the whiteboard for a half hour until some of Taylor's teammates showed up to go over some plays and watch one last bit of video of their upcoming opponent, Bradley West.

"You guys can stay." Taylor gave Laurel a one-armed hug.

"That's okay." Laurel squeezed him back. "I want Brock to meet Sea Saw."

"Oooo." Taylor raised his eyebrows. "She's taking you to meet Sea Saw. This is serious. Next thing you know, she's gonna kiss him."

Brock's face burned at the thought of Taylor finding out that Laurel had *already* kissed him. He knew Sea Saw was Laurel's horse. He'd never seen the animal, but thought nothing of not being introduced.

"Leave me alone." Laurel shrugged her brother off and took Brock by the hand to lead him out back. "I can introduce Brock to Sea Saw. I was a little girl when I said that stuff."

Taylor laughed and explained to his teammates who were lounged in their desk chairs. "My little sister said the only boy she'd ever introduce to Sea Saw was the one she'd marry."

The whole room broke out in hoots and whistles. Brock felt his face turning even more colors as Laurel shooed her brother's ideas away with one hand and dragged Brock away with the other. When they got outside and closed the door, Brock laughed. "Did you really?"

"I know we kissed, but I'm not asking you to marry me." She slapped him lightly on the arm. "Don't get any ideas, but yes, I always said that. I love my Sea Saw. Wait till you see him. You'll know why."

She held Brock's hand and led him all the way to the barn, and he didn't try to break away. Instead, he tightened the grip between them. Her fingers were long and strong and cool. He thought his might be a little sweaty, but she didn't seem to mind. The big barn doors were open, but there was no sign of their parents. They walked in and as Brock's eyes adjusted he realized there were more than a dozen horses in spacious wooden stalls. Fresh hay mixed with the smell of horse droppings.

"It doesn't smell too bad." Brock sniffed the air; it was rich and earthy.

"There's hope for you yet." Laurel stopped in front of one of the stalls, lifted the latch and led him inside before closing it. Standing on the straw-covered floor was an animal so black and sleek and strong-looking that Brock took in a sharp breath.

Sea Saw looked down at him with a big glassy eye, then walked over to Laurel and nudged her shoulder with his nose.

She wrapped both arms around his head and cooed as she stroked the ridge of hair between his eyes and nose. "There's my boy. Good Sea Saw."

Then she stepped back and took Brock's hand, guiding it toward the horse's face. "Sea Saw, meet Brock. He's the boy I told you about, the boy who kissed me."

Brock shook his head. He wanted to tell her that it was *she* who kissed *him*, but something told him to keep his mouth shut and pat the horse, so he did.

When they heard the sound of voices entering the barn, they both froze. Laurel grinned and held a finger up to her lips. "Shh."

Brock heard his father's voice, and then Laurel's mother answer back.

Laurel giggled, but muted it with a fist. "Let's listen. You want to?"

Part of him did. He wanted to listen and see if his master plan was unfolding. But part of him didn't. He knew it wasn't right to spy on people.

It was too late anyway. The parents had led their horses past Sea Saw's stall. They'd gone quiet, and it would have been too uncomfortable at this point to pop out of Sea Saw's stall and say "hi," so Brock nodded that he'd be quiet too.

"Shh." Laurel nodded and winked.

Laurel's mom burst out suddenly and loudly, with passion. "I just don't understand . . . Why?"

Brock's heart froze.

It was unmistakable, beneath the sound of her words.

Laurel's mom was sobbing.

64

Brock could imagine the look on his father's face by the tone of his voice. He could see the dull eyes and the flat mouth, that blank look.

"I can't explain it. I'm sorry."

"If you need time . . ." Laurel's mom seemed to almost be pleading.

"That's not it."

Brock's stomach plummeted. He couldn't even look at Laurel. He sensed she wanted the same thing he did, for their parents to become a couple.

"But, we've . . . you've . . ." Laurel's mom's voice turned a bit angry.

"We're friends, Kim. Our kids are friends. I thought I was clear."

"I thought you were playing hard to get." Her mom barked

out a quick laugh. "I am such a fool."

"You're not." Brock's dad's voice softened a bit. "And I'm sorry I can't explain. Maybe one day I can."

It got quiet. Sea Saw grunted and shifted hooves, scratching the straw. Brock tried to quiet his breathing.

"Leave!" Laurel's mother's shout made Brock and Laurel both flinch. "Just leave here! I don't want to see you. Don't come back. Go!"

Brock could imagine that his father nodded his head without expression.

"I'm sorry," his father mumbled.

Brock heard the scuff of his father's feet as he turned and left the barn. Laurel's mom let loose an agonized groan, then she ran out the opposite way.

Brock couldn't do anything other than look at Laurel and, by the expression on her face, he knew that everything was ruined.

65

Laurel looked as stunned as Brock.

Neither of them spoke. She led him silently out of the barn, not by the hand, but by some invisible tether that tugged at him. The sun settled like a red ball into the trees across the river, the sky above bruised and bleeding. Thick dark clouds promised something ugly. A fitful wind began to whip at their faces and hair. They circled the house, coming at the terrace from the opposite direction to find Brock's dad standing above them. He had his hands braced against the railing, facing the weather, and leaning into it like the prow of a ship.

"Time to go, Brock," he called out as they approached.

"Yes, sir." Brock snuck a look at Laurel.

Her face was tight and her eyes moist. She shook her head at him. She didn't know what to say and he rewarded her with the same blank mask his father wore.

"Thanks for everything," he said.

"My pleasure." The formal sound of her voice cut him.

His father turned and Brock followed him through the house, thinking how comfortable they both were to just walk right on through like they owned the place. Out the front door they went, Laurel closing it behind them as they climbed into their car. Brock waited until they were out on the highway before he spoke.

"What's wrong?" he asked.

His father glanced over as if in surprise. "What do you mean? Nothing."

Brock shook his head violently. "Not nothing, Dad. You left without saying good-bye to Laurel's mom?"

His father heaved a sigh. "Laurel's mom and I . . . it can't go any further, Brock. We had a misunderstanding."

Rain, fat as gumdrops, began to plop down on the windshield.

"Why? What kind of misunderstanding?" Brock asked, panicked and desperate for a miracle.

His father rubbed his beard. "It's a grown-up thing."

That was it. That was all his father planned on giving him. They silently wound along the highway for the next few minutes, then into town. They passed the school and Brock could see the football field where they practiced.

"No!" Brock startled himself with the shout.

His father turned to look at him, his eyes flickering, voice soft. "Excuse me?"

Brock slammed his hand against the glove box, then clutched his head in both hands. Rain began to patter against the glass. "Why? Why? I thought things were going to be *normal* here. That's what you said!"

His father set his jaw, flipped on the windshield wipers, and kept his eyes on the road. "Is normal moving into a castle and living like someone you're not? Having a guy in a silly hat drive your boat? I'm not a horse. Neither are you."

"What's *that* got to do with it?" Brock tugged his own ears.

His dad's fingers went white on the wheel. "Kim is a wonderful person, but she's rich beyond belief. She gets whatever she wants, boats, houses, cars . . . million-dollar horses. But you can't buy everything you want, Brock. You can't buy love."

"She wasn't trying to *buy* you. She's nice. That's all. They all are, and they're on the inside of this place and we're *out*. You? You don't care. You walk around like a zombie. You don't *love* anybody."

"Hey!" His father's mask broke. He jammed on the brakes and pulled over to the side of the road beside Bank Park. "I love *you*. That's who I love. You know that! You've seen what I do for you. Don't you *ever* say that!"

Tears sprang from Brock's eyes. "I'm not talking about *me*. I know you love *me*. I love you too, but we're not the only people in the world, Dad. That's not normal. You said things would be *normal*."

"You have no idea, Brock. You're a kid!" His father looked so ferocious, so angry, that Brock had to get out. He flung open his door and just ran. Rain quickly soaked him. He ran through the park with its empty benches and gazebo, gloomy and dead without people or light. He ran toward the pier, remembering when they'd pulled into Three B's with Laurel's family, happy, a part of something.

It made Brock sick. He heard his father shout his name, but he kept going, out onto the pier. The river slipped by, dark and unending. Brock stopped at the edge, rain spattering him now, and thought about just throwing himself in.

He knew he wouldn't do that. Still, it hurt. It hurt bad, all of it. Once again, running away to a new place didn't seem so terrible. It hurt to be the new kid, but it didn't hurt like this.

He felt his father's hands on his shoulders.

"You're right," his father said.

Brock turned to see what that kind of face his father had on. It wasn't a mask. It was hurt too, real, and twitching beneath the eyes and cheeks.

"I owe you an explanation," his father said. "I understand what you were thinking, where you thought all this was going. I get that. It cannot be, but you do deserve to know why."

His father's eyes glowed in the lights from the bridge. Rain danced on the river. Hair plastered his father's new face, a face Brock knew wasn't really him. Brock touched his own nose because it wasn't real either.

"Why?" Brock asked.

"Because I can't be what Kim wants me to be," his father said.

"But *why*?"

A gust of rain swept over them. "Because of your mother, Brock. Because of *your* mother."

Rain and tears dripped down Brock's face. "Mom's dead, Dad."

"I know that." His father bit into his lower lip. "And I thought maybe I could start over, but I can't. It won't work. Kim is wonderful. But everything she did, everything she said, I only thought of your mother. That's not fair to Kim."

"But Mom's gone, Dad. I don't like it either, but she's gone."

His father clenched his hands into fists. "No. Not to me. She's never gone.

"Listen to me. We were together in everything, she and I, like pieces of the same machine. We worked together, fighting the bad guys, protecting this country. But we were best friends, too. We'd go to movies in New York, or walk along the river in Paris under the moon, or eat ice cream on a beach in Israel. And we loved each other so much. We had *you*."

"But . . ." Brock understood, but still he wanted to move forward.

His father's eyes pleaded with him. "Look, it's like a soldier who loses his legs. His legs are gone, but he still *feels* them. They itch and they hurt and it's like they're really *there*. *That's* how it is, Brock."

His father waved his arms and looked all around them, confused and angry. "She's still *here*."

His father's face trembled and he blinked and turned, no longer upright, no longer a concrete post or a bronze statue. He walked slowly off the pier, under the weight of the world.

Brock followed him back to the car and got in. They rode back across the bridge to the Flatlands, both of them soaked to the bone.

The next day, Brock went to school like everything was normal, even though it wasn't. When the bell rang and science class ended, Laurel left the room, but stood waiting for him in the hall with her hands full of books and folders.

"Hi." He stopped and leaned against the wall of lockers.

"Hey," she said. "Still friends, right?"

"Yeah, sure." He sounded as upbeat as he could, but he could tell everything was different. He wasn't big on texting, but they usually sent one or two back and forth at night. Last night, there was nothing.

"Okay." She forced a smile and they bumped fists with no real enthusiasm.

"See you at the game tonight?" Brock raised his eyebrows. It wasn't like the whole town didn't go to the varsity games.

"Well, my dad's coming in from Dallas, so I'll probably

sit with him and my mom."

"Your dad?" Brock couldn't help his look of disgust. "That's awful soon, don't you think?"

Laurel's face flashed with anger. "What's that mean?"

"Nothing." Brock dropped his expression. "Just that I thought your mom . . ."

"My mom what?" Laurel snarled. "My dad's been begging to come back for a year and he has every right to see my brother play, unless someone made you Lord of the Universe and I just missed the memo."

"No, I, uh . . . ," Brock sputtered.

She tilted her head, spun, and walked away.

When Brock turned, he saw Mak standing there.

Mak put a big paw on Brock's shoulder. "What'd I tell you about all that kissy stuff? You gotta focus, dude. We gotta get you on that first team."

Brock shrugged him off and headed for math. "Like that's gonna happen, anyway," he mumbled.

Mak fell in alongside him. "It could. It's a funny game. Funny-shaped ball. Never know which way it'll bounce. You know . . ."

"Don't tell me." Brock held up a hand. "That's what your dad says."

Mak knit his eyebrows together. "How'd you know?"

Brock snorted. "I just lost my inside edge, Mak. First team ain't gonna happen for me this year. We're two and zero, and I'm at the bottom of the barrel without a ladder in sight. My ladder just stomped off."

"Hey, Laurel Lehman and her mom aren't the only people

who can help you make first team." Mak put his arm up, blocking Brock's path into their math class.

"The bell's gonna ring." Brock was annoyed, but he stood still. "Okay, what friends do I have?"

"Dude, seriously?" Mak looked hurt. "You got *me*."

"Mak, I love you like the brother I never had, but you're from the Flatlands too. Your mom's not president of the Mom's Club and your dad's not a former NFL player. The Koletskys aren't going to be able to put any pressure on Van Kuffler to change either. No offense, but we're both from the wrong side of the river."

Mak shook his head and lowered his voice. "I'm not talking about getting Coach to change his mind. I'm talking about changing it for him."

Brock narrowed his eyes. "For him?"

"Uh-huh."

"And how is that done?" Brock asked, unable to help sounding annoyed.

"Have you heard Coach Delaney yelling all week about Isaac Subich?"

Brock scratched his neck. "Uh, I guess."

"Sure, they make Ethan Kinney wear a number seventy-seven jersey in practice, pretending he's Subich, so the offense can get used to looking for where Subich lines up so they can run away from him, right?"

"Oh, yeah," Brock said. "That."

"Yeah, that. Kid is an animal. They rattle his cage and let him out on Saturdays to play middle school football. I've seen him. He already shaves. He's six feet tall and he's got six quarterback sacks in the first two games. He knocked the Roseville quarterback out for the year with broken ribs."

"Okay, but what's that got to do with *me*? I'm not even gonna get on the field to have to worry about this gorilla."

"You might get *on* the field if someone else gets carried *off*," Mak said.

"So, maybe Wally gets hurt," Brock said. "You said that would happen against Moravia. He took plenty of shots, but he was fine."

Mak shook his head. "He didn't take any free running shots from his blind side, though, not from Isaac Subich."

"Wait a minute." Brock's eyes widened. "Are you saying what I think you're saying?"

Before Mak could answer, the bell rang.

68

Mr. Jenson, their math teacher, groused at them to sit down and stop holding everyone else up. All through Mr. Jenson's explanation of how to compute the area of circles and trapezoids, Brock had to wonder if he was right about what Mak intended to do about Wally. Finally, they got their homework assignment and the bell rang. Brock sat closer to the door, so he waited for Mak in the hall and they walked toward gym class together.

Brock took hold of Mak's thick arm. "Mak, you can't do that. I appreciate you wanting to help me, but that's just not right."

"Do what?"

"Let this Subich kid crush Wally."

Mak frowned. "Well, I'm not talking about just *letting* him crush Wally, but people miss blocks. Stuff happens."

"Not on purpose, though." Brock knew he was arguing against his own best interests, but he couldn't help it. "Not to get someone *hurt*."

"No. Not on purpose." Mak smiled. "I promise. That, I wouldn't do, even to Wally. But it *is* football. People get hurt. My dad says football's not a contact sport. Dancing is a contact sport. Football is a *collision* sport.

"On the other hand," Mak continued, "if something *did* happen, well, I don't want you complaining about it. My dad would call that looking a gift horse in the mouth, and that you do not want to do."

Mak shook free and started down the hall, waving a hand back at Brock as he galloped away whinnying like a horse until his laughter exploded off the lockers.

Brock's head seemed to shake on its own as he followed his best friend to gym class. They didn't talk about it after that, because every time Brock opened his mouth, Mak would cut him off.

"No." Mak held his hand up in Brock's face like a stop sign. "Stop worrying. I told you, I'm not going to do anything wrong, but Subich is a killer and I'm not perfect, and, hey, my dad says all's fair in love and war, and, buddy . . . this is war."

On Friday night, Brock's dad asked him if he wanted to go to the varsity game against Bradley West.

Brock didn't lift his face from the book he was reading. "Nah."

His father laughed. "What? Seriously?"

Brock sat on the couch. His father bent over and, without looking down, unlaced his work boots on the front doormat.

"What about a movie?" Brock asked.

"Brock, you've talked about nothing but football since we got here. Football and Taylor . . . oh." His father scowled and peeled off his boots before rising up and walking toward Brock. "I get it. Sorry, buddy."

"It's not Taylor. I'm still rooting for Taylor, and the team." Brock was thinking about Laurel's dad, the former NFL player, but he didn't want to tell his dad that. If it was over, it was over.

No sense making things ugly.

"Just need a break?"

"Yeah," Brock said. "A break."

"Okay, a movie," his dad said. "I'll make us something and we'll go."

After dinner, they loaded into the car. They could see the glow of the stadium lights on the hill above town as they headed in the opposite direction for the county mall. They ate popcorn and watched an action flick about spies who infiltrated al-Qaeda to stop them from releasing a biological weapon in New York City. On their way through the mall parking lot, they could see that the stadium lights still glowed.

"I wonder if they won." Brock's dad unlocked the car door and they got in.

Brock was thinking about the movie instead of the football game. "How much of that stuff was real?"

His father started the car. "What stuff?"

"When they tracked that guy down like that? I mean, he had a new face, like us. Can they get you with your voice too? You said the government monitors all the cell phones and knows where everyone is."

"Well, they *can* know where everyone is. Everyone who uses a cell phone. They don't *know* where everyone is because there's just too much information."

"Can they get your voice like that, though?" Brock couldn't help thinking again about Boudantsev, even though he didn't want to.

His father squinted one eye and tilted his head at the road. "I never saw it, but . . . I'll say maybe. Technology changes every day. Everything's digital. They'd have to gather a massive amount of digital information, I mean, massive, then filter it. That doesn't even speak to the legal aspect of it."

"What legal aspect?" Brock asked.

"We do have privacy rights." His father flashed him a smile. "Under the Constitution. Remember that thing from history class? 'We the people'? They'd have to get a court involved."

"But they could, right? I mean, you were in the government and you were doing things you weren't supposed to do."

"I did what I was told, Brock," his father said. "I trusted the people I worked for."

"Was that a mistake?"

His father clamped his lower lip between his teeth before speaking. "Most people are good, Brock. Sometimes you get a bad one. If you live your life always worried about that one bad one, you never trust the good, and that's no way to live. But this isn't about the government, is it?"

Brock shook his head, and he asked, "Are you worried about Boudantsev coming back?"

His father sighed. "No. I'm not."

"Okay," Brock said after a pause. "Thanks."

"You want to get an ice cream?" his father asked.

They were driving through town and his father pulled over on Main Street at the ice cream shop. An older man with thin white hair and a mustache sat in a chair behind the counter, reading a paperback. He looked up, surprised to see them. "Game over already?"

"No. We just got an early start tomorrow," Brock's dad said. "I'll have butter pecan on a sugar cone."

"You look like a football player yourself." The old man nodded at Brock as he scooped up the butter pecan and handed it over the counter.

"I am." Brock pointed to the glass case. "Can I have black raspberry? A triple."

"Play for the freshman team?"

"Seventh-grade," Brock said.

The man handed Brock his cone. "Big boy, you are. Good luck tomorrow."

Brock's dad paid. Out on the sidewalk, they heard a roar from the hilltop stadium, then the tinny sound of the band.

"Sounds good for the Crab Nation." Brock's dad licked his cone and got back into the car.

Brock listened as the cheering continued, his hand frozen on the door handle. He closed his eyes for a moment before getting into the car and wondered if it would ever be for him. He opened his eyes as the cheers faded and looked in the backseat of his father's car, where a pair of work gloves stained with dirt and grease rested, and realized—in this town anyway—how stacked the odds were against him.

The next morning a gloomy gray light seeped into Brock's bedroom window. He blinked at the bright red numbers on the clock and fumbled to turn off the alarm. The chill and the patter of rain against the window made the nest of covers difficult to leave, especially for a football game. They ate breakfast, mostly in silence, and his dad dropped him off at the school to change into his uniform with the rest of the team. Bradley West Middle School was a long bus ride away, curving along the river and through the steeply wooded hills. They drove through the town in the rain, and it reminded Brock of the Flatlands. Old factories stared blindly with glassless windows and crumbling seams. The middle school field sat on a terrace of land behind the school, a crouching red brick building with a flat roof. Brock got off with the team and marched down onto the grass field with its mostly muddy center. The rain continued to fall steadily through warm-ups.

Coach Hewitt called them all in to listen to the referee's talk about sportsmanship. Coach Hewitt stood like a boulder, his hat floppy and dripping. The ref looked up at the sky before giving his speech and asking for the team captains to meet in the mud for a coin toss. Except for the devoted parents hunched over in bright red, yellow, and blue rain gear, the stands were mostly empty. Mak had that crazed look he got whenever he was getting ready to smack people.

Brock grabbed his arm to make one final plea. "Do not let Subich through."

"What's the matter? Too wet for you today? Don't you want to get in there and get your hands cold?" Mak screwed up his face.

"I want it." Brock gritted his teeth. "I just don't want it the wrong way."

"Relax." Mak hawked up some snot from his throat and spit it through his mask into the mud. "I'm not letting that goober off the line of scrimmage. He'll be lucky if he walks out of here."

"Good." Brock felt like junk. He *wanted* Subich to knock Wally out of the game so he'd have a chance to play; he just didn't want to be the one who caused it to happen.

"Okay already!" Mak snapped then turned away, snarling to himself.

Brock watched the coin toss—which they lost—and held his hand up for their three wins cheer before wiping water from a spot on the bench with his hand and plunking himself down. The kickoff went sideways in the rain, and Bradley West recovered it on the fifty. Their offense jogged out and began to thrash Calhoun's defense, grinding away with their running back picking up five or six yards a play until they put it into the end zone.

Coach Hewitt barked and snarled and howled at his defense as they jogged to the sideline. Calenzo fielded the kickoff and ran it twenty yards before being pounded into the mud. Brock stood and slipped up alongside Coach Van Kuffler to hear what was going on. The offense jogged out, Wally Van Kuffler leading the pack. Brock's eyes were on Mak. The Bradley West player opposite him—wearing number 77—stood taller than Mak and nearly as thick, but without the stomach. It was Isaac Subich.

Brock knew from listening that the first play was a sweep away from Subich. On the snap, Mak fired into the big defensive lineman and the two of them smashed each other back and forth. Neither of them appeared to care about the rest of the play going on around them. Calenzo got stuffed at the line.

The next play was a run up the middle. Mak and Subich went at it again, but this time Subich slipped free toward the middle of the line, grabbed hold of Calenzo, and stuffed him into the mud.

"Koletsky!" Coach Delaney screamed. "You gotta stay on your block!"

Mak slapped his own helmet repeatedly as he returned to the huddle.

The next play was a pass, no secret on third down with nine yards to go. Brock tensed up as Mak jogged to the line and set up in a two-point stance. Wally took the snap on a quick count.

Subich fired out for Mak. Mak braced his feet for the impact and punched his arms out to deliver a blow of his own.

All he hit was air.

Subich tilted his body sideways and swam his arm over Mak's left shoulder pad. With fury, Subich launched himself at Wally—who stood like a statue, ready to throw, with his back to the big defensive lineman. Everyone on the Calhoun sideline winced. The crack of helmet on helmet sounded like a gunshot. Subich jumped up out of the mud and pumped his fist in the air with a war cry. The thin crowd jumped to its feet, home team cheering, visitors gasping.

Wally Van Kuffler lay planted in the mud . . . and he didn't move.

71

The ref tossed a yellow flag in the general direction of Subich for unsportsmanlike conduct. The Bradley West star player stopped what he was doing to give the flag a sad look, while his own coach screamed at him from the sideline. The penalty would give Calhoun a first down, but the damage was done.

The Calhoun trainer and a doctor from Bradley West helped Wally stagger off the field along with his uncle, Coach Van Kuffler. They got him to the bench where his eyes rolled in his head. His mother came out of the stands to fuss. Calhoun's three coaches conferred near the sideline. Brock broke into the coaches' huddle, buckling up his chin strap.

"What's the play, Coach?"

Van Kuffler's eyes narrowed and he grabbed Brock's face mask, pulling him close. "You think I don't know you two planned this?"

"Coach!" Coach Hewitt slapped Van Kuffler's hand away.

"That flathead Koletsky!" Van Kuffler glared at Coach Hewitt and his arms flew wildly through the air and spit spewed from his mouth. "You heard Coach Delaney. Koletsky wasn't holding his block the last play! He did this! He whiffed on purpose so his Flatty friend could get in the game and now my neph—my starting quarterback's seeing stars!"

"Subich hit him, Coach, not Koletsky. Stop this! Brock's our backup quarterback. Give him the play and let's get some points on the board." Coach Hewitt folded his arms and stared hard at Coach Van Kuffler.

Brock watched the rage worm its way across the surface of Coach Van Kuffler's face. Van Kuffler looked at Brock and spoke through his teeth. "One mistake . . . *just one*, and your little game is over. Trips Right 27 Counter-trap."

Brock nodded and took off for the huddle, his heart jackhammering in his chest.

Brock called the play.

The offense jogged to the line. He saw Subich, hunkering down in his stance across from Mak, and knew the counterplay would allow Subich to run free upfield so that Calhoun's pulling guard from the right could blindside Subich, sending him into a daze of his own. The fifteen-yard penalty put the ball right up into the middle of the mucky part of the field. It was pure mud and Brock's feet sloshed in his shoes, their laces bubbling in the slop.

He barked out the cadence, took the snap, and did a reverse pivot, faking a toss to Calenzo. Calenzo took a jab step right, then cut back left. Brock ran toward him and stuck the ball right in his gut. Calenzo grabbed it, slipped in the mud, and fumbled the ball. Subich came free upfield, saw the ball, scooped it up, and ran into the end zone as Mak chased hopelessly after him.

All Brock could do was stand and stare, frozen in shock by the sudden change of events.

His ears rang with Van Kuffler's screaming.

Brock turned and jogged toward the sideline. Coach Hewitt had his head in his hands as if trying to keep it from flying off his neck. Coach Delaney threw his clipboard into the mud. His teammates' shoulders sagged under the weight of dripping pads and spirits.

"That's it!" Van Kuffler kept screaming. "That's it! He's done!"

Coach Hewitt finally secured his head. He looked at Brock sadly. "Wentzel!"

Wentzel appeared, chin strap already buckled. He leaned close to Brock. "You're pathetic. You know that?"

Brock couldn't respond, even though he didn't believe it was true. He knew he'd gotten the ball into Calenzo's hands. After that, it was up to Calenzo, but that's not how it was playing out, and he knew any explanation would be viewed as an excuse. He made his way toward the bench without even trying. Now, more than ever, he knew he needed Laurel's mom—or someone like her—to fight on his behalf. He needed someone who mattered to get into the coaches' faces and keep them from blaming Brock for something that clearly wasn't his fault.

When he felt a hand turn him around, he braced himself for more screaming.

It was Mak, with a drop of blood seeping from his nose. Wet strings of hair hung limp from beneath the helmet's padding. Sadness swam in his droopy eyes through the metal grill of his mask. "Hey, buddy. That wasn't your fault. I don't care what they say."

"You didn't let Subich crush Wally on purpose, did you, Mak?"

Mak shook his head. "No, I told you I wouldn't. I *missed*, and I am gonna smash Subich now."

The Bradley West fans cheered as their team kicked the extra point.

Brock sighed. "Well, no one will listen to you, either, I guess. But you're still first team."

"Yeah. Well." Mak looked down at his feet and Brock could see a blurry and distorted reflection of himself in the glossy wet helmet. "I better go."

Brock sat down, and he watched Mak push his way through the gang of players toward the field where he joined the other Calhoun first teamers, which now included Wentzel.

Wentzel didn't do much better than Brock. Although there were no fumbles or interceptions until the fourth quarter, the offense didn't move the ball either. When Mak finally started to contain Subich, the Bradley West coaches simply flipped him to the other side where he continued to terrorize Calhoun's offense. Subich had a couple of clean shots on Wentzel, but nothing that sent him into la-la land quite like Wally Van Kuffler, who'd been hustled away by his mom to go get X-rays.

In the end, Calhoun lost 27–0, an embarrassment of historical proportions. Still, as much as the offense—and Wentzel—struggled, they never again looked Brock's way. He had no idea what would happen next, and he sat silently like the rest of the team on their long, wet, bumpy bus ride home.

263

Brock's father waited for him in their car outside the school. Brock could see his father's shape through the rain-smeared windows. The car spewed smoke from its tailpipe, which rose up in the face of the steady rain. The wipers squeaked as Brock opened the passenger door and slipped in. His father offered a silent smile, then put the car into gear and took off.

They stopped for the light in the center of town. When it turned green, his father got underway again before he spoke. "Tough deal."

Brock shook his head and gently pounded a fist against the window.

"That Wentzel kid looked really bad," his father said.

Brock snorted. "Not that it matters."

"It might. You never know."

"I know, Dad. That rat Van Kuffler wouldn't put me in if I

was the last person on earth."

"They might have an open competition," his father said. "Coach Hewitt's not going to want to lose the rest of the games like that."

The car tires hummed across the bridge.

"Maybe Wally will get better."

"I think with all the worry about concussions, he'll be out for at least a week, maybe more. Hey, this could be when you make your move." His father looked over at him. "What? Why are you shaking your head?"

"We're on the outside, Dad. If I grew up on this side of the river and you were a lawyer, I'd get a chance. Or if you were still with Laurel's mom . . ."

"Oh, right, then you'd be football royalty and they'd put you in and everyone would live happily ever after. All I had to do was pretend to love someone, and that's easy, right?" His father twisted his lips in doubt. "Sometimes in life things don't just slide into place, you have to fight for them. And sometimes that lets you know how much you really wanted something. You persevere, never quit."

Brock didn't even bother responding. At home, he took a hot shower, then went downstairs and sat on the couch as far away from his father as he could to read. Rain pattered against the window and Brock—like his father—got lost in his book. Later, they ate a quiet dinner and watched a movie before turning in.

"Maybe we'll take a drive tomorrow and a hike." His father stood in the doorway to Brock's tiny bedroom. "Guy at work said Burr Oak State Park is supposed to be pretty nice. Take a swim? Pack a couple sandwiches."

Brock sat propped up in his bed, and he didn't raise his eyes from the book. "Maybe."

"Suit yourself." His father sighed and turned out the light.

Brock heard the sounds of his father getting ready for bed before the house went silent. His eyes lost their focus on the page in front of him and he thought about everything that had happened, all his ruined plans.

"Couldn't get much worse." He spoke quietly to himself as he reached up and turned off the lamp on his nightstand.

The steady rasp of rain on the roof and exhaustion carried him off to sleep.

Time passed before the squeak of the narrow stairs outside his bedroom pulled him back. Frozen, he listened and heard it again, softly, almost too soft to hear through the rain. He blinked and tried to clear his head of sleep, wondering if he'd heard anything at all. Without moving his body, Brock slowly raised his head.

A shadow yawned across the opening between his bedroom door and its frame. He felt a jolt of panic, blinked, and the shadow was gone. His eyes stayed wide and his ears strained for a sound while his mind raced around the image of Boudantsev. A tiny groan escaped his throat.

His legs and arms felt like water balloons, heavy and sloshing and lifeless.

Then he heard another creak, and the hinge on his father's bedroom door opening. He recalled in that split second all the times his father had told him that it was him they wanted, not Brock, and that they would kill him.

Brock slipped out of bed, still hoping his mind was playing tricks. He peeked out his doorway into the little hall. His father's bedroom door was open. Brock fished through his mind, trying to remember the sounds of his father getting ready for bed. He was almost certain he'd heard the final click of the knob as his father had closed the door.

He took a step and his feet immediately felt the chill of water. He realized that whoever it was, they'd tracked in the rain. Brock moved to the open door of his father's bedroom and gasped. Only the faintest light bled in through the curtains from the pole light down on the street.

Standing over the bed, an inky shadow extended its hands toward his father's face.

74

Something deep within Brock—a groan, maybe a roar—gurgled in his throat, then he leaped across the bedroom. He knocked the intruder sideways. The lamp beside the bed crashed. Brock was flipped through the air. He thumped his head against the floor, saw stars, and heard ringing in his ears.

He sensed, more than saw, his father fly out of the bed, snatch the intruder in midair, and whip him to the floor with a bang. Brock scrambled away, backing like a crab into the corner by the window and pulling his feet free from the fallen intruder. As the intruder rose from the floor, Brock's dad struck him in the side of the head and spun around behind him like a spider, arms and legs wrapping up the intruder like a caught fly.

With one arm around the intruder's neck and the other pinning both arms to his side, Brock's dad shook him, then clamped down on the choke hold even tighter. "Stop! Don't move."

The intruder went limp. "Let me go."

Brock gasped at the sound of the voice. There was no heavy Russian accent. It sounded like . . .

His father backed against the light switch and flipped it up and on with his elbow. "Brock, take off the mask. Brock!"

Brock jumped up, broken from his trance. He reached carefully for the edge of the mask, peeled it off the intruder's head, and found himself frozen in place by two dark eyes.

Brock's stomach plunged. "Oh my God."

Brock knew the face, not from real life, but from a picture.

In the box Brock's father took with him wherever it was they had moved—the one he kept hidden in his sweater drawer—just beneath the newspaper article about the death of his mother, was a photo. Ocean, grassy dunes, and wind in that picture surrounded his parents, a younger-looking father and a woman with the same liquid-brown eyes as Brock and the nose he used to have—long, narrow, and upturned. She was a beautiful woman with a tangle of dark hair swept from a forehead lined with worry.

Brock had seen her face many times in his sleep. His mother would come to him in his dreams. It wasn't unusual. Still, he realized that those images were more of a *feeling*, like a picture out of focus.

This, the face of the person whose neck was wrapped in his

father's strong arm, wasn't fuzzy at all. It wasn't the face from the photo. But the eyes . . .

"Dad, stop. It's her." Words spilled from his mouth like a broken bag of jelly beans.

"It's Mom."

76

"Audrey." Brock's father choked on the name.

At first Brock thought his father had hurt her, but he realized as she reached for both their faces at the same time that she was softly crying because of *them*. She pulled them both to her so that Brock could feel his father's skull against the side of his head and his mother's collarbone in his face. She held them both and they wrapped their arms around her too. They were a bundle of limbs and elbows and fingers hooked like claws holding tight.

Finally, they broke their hold and sat down on the edge of his father's bed, his mother between them, explaining.

"I wanted to wake you gently," she said to his father. "I came as soon as I could. I didn't know our son was a guard dog."

Brock let her laugh wash over him. Part of him wanted to close his eyes and just listen to the sound of her. The sight of her was almost too overwhelming, a yellow bulldozer in your living room, big and permanent and impossible all at once.

"I'm sorry," Brock said.

"Me too." She smiled though, and rubbed the back of her head.

"I can't . . . I can't believe this . . . You're . . . You're here." When Brock's father finally stopped sighing and smiling and holding her by the cheeks, he asked her, "What happened?"

She hunched her shoulders and bowed her head, hands clasped. "They took me . . . to Cuba, to a cell in a police station in the middle of nowhere. After a few years I got very sick, a fever. The police chief's wife took care of me. I almost died, but I didn't, and we became friends. She was the one who helped me get away."

She sighed. "That was five years ago. I snuck back in on a boat to Miami, but I never even tried to find you. I was afraid they *let* me go, so they could follow me to *you*. I knew they wanted those bank accounts—people will do a lot for a hundred million dollars."

"A hundred million?" Brock looked at his dad.

His father nodded. "Boudantsev stole it from several European banks and I—we—took it from him, thinking we'd give it back until we realized something was wrong. There were bad guys on both sides who wanted the money for themselves."

"I knew they'd kill to get that money and, even more," she said, looking at Brock's dad, "they wanted to make sure you could never talk. There's only one way they could do that. Kill you. I wanted so bad to find you, but I couldn't take that chance. Do you understand?"

She looked up with tears in her eyes. "I wasn't ever going to let them. . . . So I got a job as a teacher in Fredericksburg, Texas, and I hid. But then you accessed our safe-deposit box. I had paid the bank manager a lot of money to call me if anyone ever did, and when you went into it, there was a dust I put there that let me track you."

"Dust?" Brock wrinkled his face.

"Nanotechnology." Her frown suggested the world was a better place without such things. "You can't see it or feel it or smell it, but it gets in your skin and stays there. Anyway, I knew what was coming, with those arrests and deportations I read about in the newspaper. I waited for all that to happen before I started after you. But when I got here I realized they weren't gone, not all of them, and they *were* following me."

"Boudantsev," Brock said.

His mother narrowed her eyes without looking at him. "Yes. Him. He was still after the money, and he's known all along that your father was the only one who could get it."

"I saw him, Boudantsev." Brock nodded, both relieved that he wasn't losing his mind and frightened at the same time that he'd been so close to the man who struck fear into his parents' hearts.

Brock's mother nodded too. "I thought I lost him, and I still don't know how he followed me. When I saw him here, I just kept going to lead him away. I don't know how many of the others he was still in touch with. I don't know if they're sending more. I have to believe they will, don't you, John?"

Brock realized by the tone of her voice that John must be his father's real name.

"I do," his father said. "They'll always send more, but if we leave the money alone, maybe we'll be all right. I take it Boudantsev himself isn't coming back?"

She chewed on her lower lip. "I let him follow me to Cleveland and I took a boat across the lake into Canada. That's where he is, in Canadian waters anyway, about two hundred feet deep. That's where I . . . left him. He had one other with him. He's at the bottom of the lake too. If there's anyone else, they're not in the States, or they weren't yet."

A light went on in Brock's head. "The Audi at the park. Was that you?"

"That was careless." His mother's voice got quiet. "I shouldn't have followed you like that, but I wanted to just *watch* you. You're my son. We were trying to get out of the game, and that's when they found out about the money and all the information we had. When you were born, we both swore we'd protect you, no matter what. For me, that meant being alone for the past five years. But, you know what? You were worth the wait."

She touched Brock's cheek.

"So we're safe?" Brock's father asked.

"Yes." Brock's mother stiffened. "You have a new life, John. Both of you. And I know you thought I was dead. I want you to be honest; is there a place for me here?" Her tone wasn't mean or angry, but the question made Brock think she must have known about Laurel's mom, must have seen them together when she was watching them.

His father brushed a strand of hair from her face. "There's never been a place for anyone else. Isn't that right, Brock?"

275

"Do you like the name, Brock?" She touched his cheek with the backs of her fingers.

"I chose it," Brock said.

"You deserve to choose it." She rubbed his head. "I think a boy needs a mother. Better late than never, right?"

Brock let her pull his head into her shoulder.

"Yes," he said. "Much better."

77

The story they would tell the few people they knew in Calhoun was that Brock's parents were never married. They had separated when he was young and his mother had gone to South America. Recently, they had reconnected on the internet and . . . here she was. Brock had told enough stories during his life so that it was easy. He knew from experience that the key was to keep things short and simple and not to talk too much.

The next day they all went to Burr Oak State Park. Sun shone down on them, warming the air enough for Brock to wade into the water. His parents acted like they'd never been apart over the last ten years. They were affectionate toward each other, but they weren't mushy, so Brock felt really comfortable hanging out with them on a blanket all day, reading, hiking around, and tossing Frisbees and a football.

For dinner, they stopped at a Cracker Barrel off the highway.

Brock ate fried chicken with mashed potatoes and gravy and drank lemonade. His mother watched him the whole time he ate, her eyes occasionally welling up with tears that made him study his food.

When he'd finished and wiped his mouth on a napkin he said, "Dad says he was the cook."

His parents looked at each other and laughed.

"That's one thing you *didn't* miss," his mom said. "Trust me on that. No, your dad's the cook, if either of us is."

"What does that mean?" His dad broke into a grin and tickled her.

She screeched.

"Guys." Brock looked around, but no one was paying attention, and his dad didn't stop acting like a kid until their waitress coughed and asked if they'd like dessert.

On the car ride home, Brock sat in the back with his head against the window. He didn't know how he felt about it all. He was glad his mother was back, but as much as he wanted to *feel* something, he honestly didn't. It was like a flashlight in the dark; he could *see* it, he knew it was there, but he couldn't *feel* it. It had no warmth. He looked at his father's eyes in the rearview mirror, thinking of the way his father could sometimes be so cold and distant, and wondering if that was the way he was doomed to be too. Who didn't get excited about his mom?

They were driving through town, his parents chattering back and forth about all kinds of things, when his dad pulled over into an empty spot along Main Street.

"How about ice cream?" His father looked at his mother. "Maple walnut?"

"Of course," she said. "And your butter pecan?"

"Of course."

Brock sighed and got out. His mother smiled and hugged him to her, kissing the top of his head. "Did I tell you that I taught fifth grade? Well, I'd always watch the boys around me and wonder all the time which ones you were like. And now, to see you and you're so grown-up. My baby."

Brock tried not to struggle to get free, but her bones felt like iron angles against his face and chest and she smelled like the kind of coconut soap Brock didn't like because his fourth-grade teacher in Petaluma, California, had used that kind of soap, and she'd been a witch.

It seemed like she sensed his hesitation because as they walked, she held his father's hand, but allowed Brock to walk on the other side and avoid holding her other hand.

As they headed down the sidewalk toward the ice cream parlor, her face glistened with happiness. Just as his father reached for the handle, the door to the ice-cream shop jingled open.

Brock and his parents stood face-to-face with Laurel, Taylor, Gracie, and Laurel's mom.

Laurel looked beautiful. Her hair was pulled back so that it dropped from behind her head in a thick hay-colored tail. She wore a pink summer dress that made her skin look smooth and golden as toffee. Her pale-blue eyes were icy crystals circling wide round pits that made Brock think of black holes in space, matter so dense their gravity sucked everything in.

Brock's eyes went from Laurel, to her mom, to his own dad. His father wore a blank stare that told nothing.

It was Laurel's mom who spoke first. "Hello, Peter. Brock . . ."

Laurel's mom turned her eyes on Brock's mom and extended a hand. "Hi. I'm Kim Dahlman."

Brock watched his mom's face turn instantly into a blank screen. She took Kim's hand. "Audrey Fallon. I'm Brock's mom."

Laurel's mom's jaw went slack, then she recovered and forced a smile. "Brock goes to school with Laurel, my daughter. Say hello, Laurel."

Laurel did as she was told, then flicked her eyes at Brock with disapproval. Brock could only shrug.

"And my son, Taylor. He's our football player. He's been helping Brock learn the Calhoun offense. Are you a football fan?" Laurel's mom cocked her head.

"No, but it's very nice to meet you all. Thank you for being so kind to Brock."

Brock's parents both stared until Laurel and her family gathered themselves up, filed out of the ice cream parlor, and marched down the sidewalk in the opposite direction.

"Who was *that*?" Brock's mom asked.

His dad ordered ice cream over the counter and only answered when both the young girls behind the glass were hard at their scooping. "Long story. Let's save it for later."

"We can." His mother accepted her cone. "She's very pretty."

"Later." His father paid.

They took a stroll through Bank Park, walking along the river and circling back around the gazebo. Brock tried to stay out of the conversation. It was a bunch of remembering on his parents' part. He had no recollection of any of it, and besides, he was distracted by the look Laurel had given him. It kept popping up in his mind. As he walked—and maybe it was the affection his parents had for each other—he realized that Laurel meant more to him than an opportunity to be on the first team.

He missed her and the idea of her being there, rooting for

him, caring about him . . . liking him.

Now, in a state of almost total confusion about everything, Brock felt an ache in his chest and knew that it was a longing to somehow get her back, at least as a friend, despite everything else.

When they returned to the house, it was already getting dark. Mak's bicycle stood on its stand at the edge of their driveway. In the dying day, Brock could make out Mak's bulky shape sitting on their front steps with his face supported by two hands braced against his knees. When they pulled up alongside the bike, Mak stood and stretched like a bear emerging from hibernation. Brock wondered if his friend was sore from the game. He tensed a bit, knowing he would have to introduce his mother, but one look at his father's blank face inspired him.

Brock let his own face fall. They got out and Mak met them on the broken concrete walk between the house and the driveway.

"Hey, Mak. This is my mom."

Mak's frown grew confused, but he held out a thick hand to Brock's mom. "Hello, Mrs. . . ."

"They're not married," Brock said, "but she's my mom."

"Wow." Mak shook her hand anyway.

"Please, call me Audrey." Brock's mom smiled.

"Mak." His father nodded a friendly hello, but his empty stare kept Mak from asking questions. "It's pretty late."

Without further explanation, Brock's parents carried the things from their picnic inside.

When the door closed, Mak turned to Brock. "You wanna tell me—"

"Who we playing this week?" Brock asked.

"Who we . . . Okay, I get the icy stares. I'm good. Hey, that's kinda why I'm here anyway, who we're playing, I mean. I know you don't text half the time and I wanted you to hear this from me."

Brock narrowed his eyes. "Hear what?"

"Look, you know I'm on your side, right?" Mak said.

"My side of what?" Brock asked.

"Everything." Mak's hands flew up in the air before they fell with a slap to his legs. "So I want to say that I kind of get it. I don't think you should feel that bad."

"Mak, you better stop and tell me."

"Good news first?" Mak asked. "Or do you want the bad news?"

Brock stared at him for a moment, trying to read his eyes. "Good news first."

Mak nodded. "Wally Van Kuffler is out for four weeks with that concussion."

Brock's heart soared. This might be his chance. But, if it was his chance, why did Mak wear a frown? "So what's the bad news?"

Mak puckered his lips. "You know who Asa Pagano is?"

Brock knew he knew the name; it was an unusual one, but he couldn't place it.

"Sixth-grader?" Mak cocked his head. "Quarterback?"

Brock had a sinking feeling. Part of him said it shouldn't matter, not football, not school, not Laurel, none of it. He had his *mom* back. How could he care about anything else?

But he did.

His missing mom was like a wet match. He kept striking it, but nothing happened. Not even a spark. Not even close. Brock searched his soul for the gaping hole that left him so empty. He had to be empty, didn't he? A boy who worried about football when the mother he thought was dead turned up in the night, and she was *wonderful*.

"What about Asa Pagano?" he asked to fill the silence.

"He's not bad, and he's big for his age, like us." Mak nudged him. "He has to pass some kind of physical or something, but I thought you should know, so when that dork Van Kuffler throws it in your face, you're ready."

"They're bringing him up?"

"He's got good numbers, Brock, and the sixth-grade team is crushing everyone." Mak fumbled with his fingers. "It's not certain yet, but his dad's the treasurer of the booster club and the word is he's kind of pushing it. Hey, you're still gonna be the future of Calhoun. You and me. Bonnie and Clyde."

"Bonnie and Clyde were bank robbers."

"Yeah, but heck, they were tough guys, though." Mak gave him a thumbs-up. "Bad hombres."

"Bonnie was a girl."

Mak crunched his eyebrows. "No."

"Yup."

"Batman and Robin? I mean . . ." Mak glanced at the yellow light leaking from behind the curtains of the big front window. "I know you don't want to talk about it, but is your mom . . . is your dad . . . are they, like, together?"

"They are."

Mak's face really fell. "What about Laurel's mom?"

286

"Nope." Brock clamped his lips and shook his head.

"Her brother? Is Taylor still gonna help you out? Teaching you the offense?"

"I have no idea, Mak. Why would he?"

"I know the romance angle dried up, but you didn't ditch Laurel did you?" Mak asked.

"No, I didn't ditch her."

"'Cause then maybe there's still a chance. I mean, he's a good guy, Taylor, and you didn't ditch her. Right?"

Brock huffed. "I said I didn't."

"So, hypothetically, you could be schooled up by next year no matter what Van Kuffler does. You got all spring and summer, next year."

"I'm gonna play baseball next year."

"But football too? I told you, this is a football town, buddy. You gotta play."

"It's not doing me much good right now. Is it?"

"Well, but you gotta try." Mak put a paw on his arm. "It's all new for you. You're gonna be first team, I know it."

"What is first team, Mak?"

Mak blinked. "What do you mean?"

"What is it?"

"You know. You're the starter. You're tops. People respect you."

"Who? People like Wentzel?"

Mak shrugged. "Everybody. I'll let you get inside. I just . . . I was trying to help. My dad says you're only as good as you think you are, and I didn't want you to think you aren't . . ."

"Hey, Mak." Brock spoke quietly.

"Yeah?" Mak was quiet too.

"I'll see you tomorrow, okay?"

Mak brightened. "Want me to pick you up on my way?"

"Sure."

"Well, that's good." Mak put his hands on the bike's handles and kicked up the stand before he looked at Brock. "My dad says sometimes things seem better in the morning."

Brock doubted it. "Yeah. Maybe they will."

Mak took off, pedaling steady, but wobbling ever so slightly until the shadows of the Flatlands swallowed him whole.

The next day Brock's mom planned on setting out to find a job of her own. The three of them had a quiet breakfast, and when his mom hugged him, Brock did his best not to shy away.

When they separated, she took him by the shoulders. "It's okay, Brock. It'll take time, I know, but we've got time. Lots."

Brock's face flushed and he avoided those dark-brown eyes of hers, fearing he might cry and not even know why. "Thanks."

Brock rushed out of the house just in time to see Mak chugging up the street.

In school, Laurel acted like Brock didn't exist. He waited for her outside her English class, but when she almost bumped into him, her eyes never wavered. She looked right past him and kept on going. Brock clenched his teeth and fumed through the rest of the school day, determined to ignore her as well.

When the final bell rang, Brock marched toward the locker

room to change for football.

The idea that Coach Van Kuffler was about to spring Asa Pagano on him only added fuel to the fire in his gut. Without thinking, he turned down the hall that led to the main entrance. He saw Laurel's blond ponytail bobbing down the steps and he caught up to her in the crowd.

"I have to talk to you." Brock grabbed her elbow.

Laurel yanked free and screwed up her face into a nasty snarl. "You don't touch me."

"Laurel, please." He hated the begging sound of his voice and could feel the eyes of everyone on him.

"Don't 'please' me. Why would I talk to *you*?"

"We're friends."

"Ha! You don't know what a friend is."

"I had nothing to do with any of this. Won't you just *talk*?"

"No, Brock, and if you don't let go of me, I'll scream. I'll call a teacher and you'll wish you never came here."

Brock let his hand fall. "I already wish that."

"Good." She gave him one last sneer, then hurried off into the crowd.

Brock hustled to the locker room and threw on his gear. He tried not to look at Asa Pagano, but it was like trying to ignore an elephant in the room. Asa stood just a few inches shorter than Brock, but his bare chest was packed with muscles you didn't normally see on a sixth-grader.

Mak gave Brock a sad puppy-dog look before strapping on his helmet, banging his head into the locker with a growl, and heading out onto the field. Brock followed and jogged over to where the quarterbacks were. He went through the motions of warming up, throwing to Xaviar, while Asa and Wentzel worked together under the toothy chipmunk grin of Coach Van Kuffler. When the ball Xaviar threw back to Brock went wild, Brock jogged over by the fence to scoop it up. That's when he saw Coach Hewitt standing on the side of the bleachers talking to not only Coach Spada, but to Laurel's mom as well. Her hair was pulled up into a pile on top of her head and she wore a baggy Calhoun Football sweatshirt and faded jeans.

Brock's stomach somersaulted. He already knew he wasn't going to be first team, or even second team, but he had no idea what other horror was being planned for him. He knew it was something though, without a doubt. He wondered if Laurel had complained to her mother about Brock grabbing her arm. Would she really destroy him over that?

His worst fears were confirmed when Laurel's mom pointed at him and all three of them looked his way.

"Brock!" Coach Hewitt shouted.

Brock clutched his football and jogged toward the three of them, butterflies in his stomach.

Coach Hewitt cupped his hands to shout again. "Coach Van Kuffler!"

Brock's heart huffed like a panting dog. Van Kuffler scowled and trudged toward them, forcing a smile onto his face that looked like someone getting ready for a dentist's drill.

"Coach?" Van Kuffler faked admiration for his head coach before nodding politely to Coach Spada and Laurel's mom.

"Coach Spada wants a word with you and me." Coach Hewitt turned to the varsity head coach.

Coach Spada gave Laurel's mom a grim look then pointed at Brock. "You'll start him this week, Coach. If it doesn't go well, you can use Asa next week. Keep Wentzel as your backup."

Coach Van Kuffler's mouth opened nearly as wide as Brock's eyes. "Coach, all due respect, Brock doesn't know the offense. The chances he's had, well . . . things haven't gone well."

"Because *you've* done nothing to help him!" Laurel's mom put her hands on her hips. Her face twisted up and trembled with rage. "That's enough of that, Frank. You'll give him the game plan and Taylor will teach it to him."

"Me?" Brock couldn't believe what he was hearing.

Van Kuffler blinked and addressed Coach Spada. "Coach? Is this how we do things?"

"I'm sick of this nonsense, Frank." Coach Spada snarled. "You took what I told you to do and threw it out the window. We've got *Groton* Friday night. They run a 46 Defense and they run it well, but what am *I* doing? I'm here with *you,* talking about things I already told you to do. *No*, this isn't how we do things, Frank. So you either hear me and get this right, or it's over. Do I have to explain 'over'?"

Coach Spada turned to Coach Hewitt. "Buzz, I want a copy of the game plan. Taylor will make sure the new kid knows it and you'll run those plays and *only* those plays against Groton. I want the starters in there with him, and I want good play calling. I can't be there to babysit, but I trust you'll get this done."

"Don't worry, Coach Spada." Laurel's mom smiled wickedly. "I'll be there, and I'm a great babysitter."

Coach Spada puckered his lips, then huffed. "If the kid looks good, he'll stay with the first team for the rest of the season. If he chokes, he's all yours. But he gets a chance."

Coach Spada turned to Laurel's mom. "*One* chance. We all

on the same page?"

The adults nodded together. Coach Spada narrowed his eyes at Brock. "And you understand?"

Brock nodded violently.

Coach Spada extended a hand. "Good. Good luck, kid."

Coach Spada marched off. Laurel's mom turned to follow him, then stopped, spun around, and leaned close to Coach Van Kuffler so she could whisper. "You messed with the wrong mother, Frank."

Coach Van Kuffler stuttered, then finally got out his words. "You're not his mother."

"No." Laurel's mom gave Brock a strange look. "But I'm his friend."

"Dude, how did it happen?" Mak's eyes bugged out of his head. "Did Coach Spada actually pee on Van Kuffler's leg? Because that's what a couple of the guys were saying."

"Nobody peed on anybody, Mak. That's crazy." Brock tried not to giggle at the image. He got on his bike and started pedaling. Mak followed him, catching up and riding without hands so he could gesture as he went.

"But you're *first team*! Buddy, it's a miracle."

"I am for Groton. I gotta perform."

"You *will*. I know it! Man, was it great to see Van Kuffler choking like that during practice, giving you the plays and no more junk. Hey, where you going?"

Brock had taken a turn away from the center of town. "Out to Laurel's. You can come."

"Dude, you're just riding out there? What are you gonna say?"

Brock shrugged without letting go of his handle bars. "I don't know. Thanks, I guess."

"Just text her, dude. You ride out there, she might not like it. Maybe her mom did all that on her own."

"Maybe she did. Then I'll thank *her*. I need to know, right?"

"I don't know about that." Mak puffed as they pumped up a long slope.

"I do." Brock said nothing more, but kept on riding, turning off the highway and in between the stone gates.

"I don't think you can just ride down in here." Mak followed despite his protests.

"Stop whining." Brock thought of Laurel's mom saying they were friends. He set his jaw because he didn't think Laurel shared her mom's kind feelings. "I guess maybe it's Taylor. I mean, I know he liked me. I know he thinks I can play."

They pulled up to the front entrance and parked their bikes. Brock marched up the steps. Mak followed. Brock looked back. Mak had stopped halfway up. Brock shook his head and rang the bell. Heavy chimes rang from deep inside the house. It wasn't Laurel who appeared when the door swung open, but her mom.

"Brock. Hi."

"Hi, Ms. Dahlman. I hope we're not disturbing you. Um, this is Mak Koletsky."

"Hello, Mak." She nodded at Mak and he hustled up the steps and shook her hand.

"I'm first team left tackle." Mak puffed up his chest. "I got his blind side."

"But Brock's a lefty," she said.

Mak deflated. "Yeah, well, technically, but we're best friends, so I got his back on the field and off."

"I bet you do." She smiled at Mak and turned to Brock. "Taylor won't be home for another hour, Brock."

"I came to see Laurel . . . and you."

"Me?"

"Yes. Why did you do it?"

She bit her lower lip and swung the door wide. "Come in."

They followed her into the massive kitchen. She motioned them to the wooden table tucked into a bay window looking out over the river. Brock had heard it referred to as the break-fast nook.

Laurel's mom put an opened box of bakery donuts on the table in front of them.

"Milk?" she said.

"Yes, ma'am!" Mak already had his hands on a powdered jelly, and when he took a bite some of the insides dribbled from the corner of his mouth.

"Sure." Brock reached in and took a glazed, his mouth watering.

Laurel's mom filled two pint glasses with cold milk, set them down, and took a seat across from them. "Laurel doesn't like to hear this, and I'd appreciate it if you didn't talk with her about it."

"I don't think she'll talk to me about anything," Brock said.

She smiled sadly. "She will. Give her time. She's worried about me since her father and I got divorced, and what happened with me and *your* father was a huge disappointment. Sooner or later, though, she'll realize it had nothing to do with you."

Brock nodded. "So why are you helping me like this?" Brock asked.

She looked past them, out at the river. "Your father . . . he's a very unusual person. I'm used to fending people off, not the other way around."

She looked at Brock now and he saw she was sad. "Then, I saw your mom and I understood. And I respect him."

She smiled. "I've taught my kids—and I believe this with all my heart—that we need to do kind things for people just for the sake of being kind. It's important. My kids know I was upset by what happened with your dad. My helping you is a great example for them. Kindness. It's so important."

Brock still wasn't sure.

"All this?" She waved her hands and looked around. "It was my father's. He taught me before anything else that none of this does you a bit of good unless you're kind. It's how we live, Brock. And I like you. You're a great kid. Taylor likes you too, a lot, and he raves about the kind of player you could be."

Laurel's mom patted his arm. "And Laurel likes you too. Maybe most of all. You see? What I said to the coaches is true, we *are* friends."

Brock swallowed and nodded his head.

She kept looking at him and he looked back and saw that her eyes were exactly like Laurel's. "This is a tough town, it always has been, but not tougher than me, and I'm happy to help."

"Thank you again." Brock wanted to say so much more, but it was all he could muster.

"There is something you need to do, though." She put a hand on Brock's shoulder.

"Talk to Laurel?" Brock said.

She chuckled and shook her head, then leaned toward him. "Don't worry about Laurel. No. What you *need* to do is go out there on Saturday and light up that scoreboard."

The next week flew by. He and Laurel started talking again. It was just "Hi" at first, then "What's up?" but that turned into complete sentences with smiles to go along with them. By the end of the week, they were back to being friends. Brock wasn't sure if they'd be more—maybe they would—but they *were* friends again, and that sure felt good. Before Brock knew, it was game day.

Since Groton was Calhoun's biggest rival, the seventh-grade team—along with the youth-league teams and the eighth-grade team—got to play on the varsity field. Calhoun's sixth-grade youth team won 34–28, and Asa Pagano had four touchdown passes. Brock jogged onto the field with the seventh-grade team, which benefited from fans who stuck around from the morning youth games as well as some early arrivals for the eighth-grade team. The stands were nearly full, but half wore Groton purple.

An army of clouds marched across the sky. The sun shone down, flashing bright between them. A chill wind licked at the nervous sweat on Brock's upper lip. Cut grass mingled with the smell of hot dogs, Italian sausage, and peppers creeping across the field from the concession stand grill. The toast and peanut butter from breakfast climbed the walls of Brock's stomach and he fought the urge to throw it up.

After pregame stretching and agilities, Mak slapped him on the back, hard. "Hey, hey, buddy. This is it. This is what it's all about. Look at them."

Brock stared over at the purple-and-white players and remembered the story of a Minnesota Vikings defense so ferocious they were called Purple People Eaters.

"What are you thinking?" Mak shook him and peered through the bars in his face mask.

"Just . . . let's crush them, right?" Brock knew it didn't come out quite right.

"Well, you're a quarterback. You don't have to crush anyone, but *I* will." Mak looked at the visiting team and snarled. "Stomp their guts all over this field."

"Yeah." Brock slapped him five. "Get 'em, Mak."

"Oh, I will. You just throw the ball, buddy. Throw the ball like you can." With a thumbs-up, Mak jogged over to where the other linemen were.

Brock threw the ball. He warmed up with Wentzel and their receivers under the stern eye of Coach Van Kuffler. Wentzel's passes had an annoying wobble, but he was hitting his receivers. As he had all week, Van Kuffler said almost nothing to Brock, and Brock could only assume that their little truce would end after today. He felt pretty certain that whatever happened in the next two hours would determine which one of them would go and who would stay.

Brock wondered what the fallout would be for him quitting in the middle of the season. Would they let him even try out for the eighth-grade team next year? Brock slapped his own helmet. This was no way to be thinking.

"I can *do* this." The words sounded flat, so he said them again, slapping his helmet more forcefully.

Coach Hewitt blew his whistle and they all gathered around him on the sideline.

"You see that crowd?" Coach Hewitt's eyebrows jumped and he pointed a thick finger at the stands. "This is what Calhoun football is all about. This is why we're here. *Pride.* We are Calhoun, and today, you guys are gonna smash it right down Groton's throats. Bring it in, pride on three . . . One, two, three . . ."

"PRIDE."

Just that one shout tired Brock out. His limbs trembled. He knew it wasn't good. He looked up into the stands. His parents sat high up in the back row. They waved down at him. He raised a limp hand and dropped it. He wished his teammates would stop slapping his back. It wasn't helping.

They took off their helmets for the national anthem. When the song ended, Brock caught some motion in the corner of his eye. He looked toward the fence behind the bench. Someone was waving at him.

Brock blinked and bit hard into his mouthpiece.

He raised a hand; this time it wasn't so limp. He felt a sudden charge of energy at the sight of Laurel, her brother, and her mom. Laurel most of all.

"Go, Brock!" she shouted. Her hair glistened and her mother put a hand on her back.

Brock flushed with pride. With a nod, he jammed the helmet back on his head and turned toward the field. The butterflies still fluttered in his stomach, but his limbs seemed suddenly alive and strong.

Taylor appeared beside Brock. "Hey."

"Hey," Brock said, blushing and even more excited because he knew—after the past week of evening whiteboard sessions—that Taylor was his football guardian angel.

Taylor patted Brock's helmet, then walked over to the coaches. "Hey, guys. Coach Spada let me out of video early so

I could help signal in the plays."

"Great," Coach Delaney said.

"Nice." Coach Hewitt looked down at his game notes.

Coach Van Kuffler looked like his head might explode. "We're good here. I don't need any help."

"Yeah, but . . . you know Coach Spada. I kinda gotta do what he says." Taylor wore a false smile.

"What he says, or what your mommy says?" Coach Van Kuffler's voice turned nasty.

"Frank. Enough." Coach Hewitt's jaw jutted out at Van Kuffler like a warning sign.

"Whatever." Coach Van Kuffler threw his hands in the air. "You think this kid's got what it takes? Let's see. I think he's a choker."

The three coaches and Taylor turned to Brock. Brock clenched his teeth and gave the offensive coordinator a nasty stare. Van Kuffler snorted and shook his head and looked at the field.

Calhoun won the coin toss. Brock was relieved that he'd get to go right out on the field without having to wait for their defense to get the ball back. Brady Calenzo fielded the kickoff and ran the ball back to the thirty. Brock looked up at Coach Van Kuffler. Coach Hewitt stood beside him, waiting and scowling.

"Trips Left 34 Dive." Coach Van Kuffler's voice was flat and he didn't even look at Coach Hewitt.

"Don't forget to reverse pivot before you hand off," Taylor said.

Van Kuffler sneered. "You wanna go out there and hold his hand?"

Taylor never stopped smiling. "You wanna win, right, Coach?"

Van Kuffler's face trembled.

Brock, Mak, and the rest of the first team offense jogged onto the field. Brock called the play in the huddle, went to the line, and remembered to pivot. Calenzo got stuffed for no gain. The Purple People Eaters (Brock couldn't get that out of his mind) celebrated with howls and high fives.

Brock looked to the sideline. Coach Van Kuffler signaled in a run fake with a short pass to the tight end. He called it and went to the line. The Purple People Eaters growled with hunger. Brock faked the handoff, pulled up to throw, but a defender jumped up in front of the receiver. Brock pulled the ball down and took off. He made three yards before being sandwiched between a linebacker and a defensive end who had apparently been stuffed with concrete.

Brock's head rang.

He shook it to clear the cobwebs and looked to the sideline. Coach Van Kuffler was already halfway through the signal. Brock didn't know the formation, just the play. He held up both hands as the play clock ticked down toward zero. Taylor saved the day by repeating the signal. Brock knelt and called the play.

"Spread Right Alaska 99 first sound, ready . . ."

The offense broke the huddle. Brock went to the line. He had no time to check the defense over, but knew what he wanted to do. He could feel the uncertainty in the players around him. Even Mak hadn't looked him in the eye as he'd called the play. He would go deep, to the outside nine route where Xaviar Archangel, his fastest receiver, would streak toward the end zone along with the other three wide receivers.

Brock flicked his hands and barked. The center snapped the ball to him. The defense came hard and fast, squeezing the pocket like a fist. Xaviar slipped past the coverage, but needed time to get open. Brock hung in, stepped up, and rifled the ball downfield.

Someone smashed Brock from behind. He banged forward, colliding with his center, a barrel-chested monster who caved in on top of him. From the ground, Brock heard the fans cheer. But he didn't know which fans.

The pile of bodies trembled with excitement as the players jumped up and broke away from the stack. Brock struggled to his feet, looking all around. The daze cleared from his head. Behind him, he saw a purple defender holding the football high above his head in the end zone. Brock had no idea how, but Groton had intercepted his long pass and ran it back for a touchdown.

Brock hung his head and jogged to the sideline.

Coach Van Kuffler was gesturing wildly to Coach Hewitt while Coach Delaney tried to keep things calm. Brock steered clear of the three men. Taylor found him on the bench and slapped his shoulder.

"Hey." Taylor spoke in an urgent whisper. "Head up. That's it. Don't you quit on yourself now. Picks happen. Peyton Manning throws picks. Life of a Q."

"Not on the first series he ever played on the first team I bet he didn't." Brock slapped his leg and pounded the bench with a fist.

"Especially in the first series of the first game." Taylor laughed. "Ask Brett Favre. He threw six picks in his first NFL start. Set a record! *He* didn't do too bad."

Brock looked up. "Six picks?"

"You can throw four more and *still* be better than Favre."

Brock had to laugh.

"That's it." Taylor slapped his shoulder again. "Shrug it off. Come on. Get up. The other good thing about a pick-six is that you get to go right back on the field after the kickoff. You don't have to wait to redeem yourself. Come on."

Brock followed Taylor back to the sideline.

Coach Van Kuffler was screaming. Most of it Brock couldn't understand, but one thing everyone heard was "That woman!" which Van Kuffler repeated over and over again, pointing to where Laurel's mom stood by the fence.

"Oh, boy. Now he did it." Taylor was looking back past the bench. He turned away, rolled his eyes, and threw his hands up in the air.

Brock looked and saw that Laurel's mom had let herself inside the fence and was marching toward the coaches.

"What's she gonna do?" Brock asked.

"What *isn't* she gonna do?" Taylor rubbed his hand down over his face.

Brock edged closer, eager to hear. He was slightly disappointed. When Laurel's mom spoke it was soft and pleasant.

"Coach Van Kuffler? If you point at me again, if you shout about 'that woman' again, I promise this will not only be the last game you ever *coach* in the town of Calhoun, it'll be the last *job* you ever have in Calhoun. Now, let these boys play, whether you like them or not."

Taylor leaned into the ear hole of Brock's helmet. "Van Kuffler actually got off kind of easy."

But Laurel's mom stopped suddenly and turned, speaking so everyone could hear. "By the way, who calls a Spread Right Alaska 99 against a team that plays cover four on third and long? Just stupid. Really, Coach Hewitt, shouldn't *you* be calling the plays? Just a thought."

She continued on, leaving all three coaches' mouths wide open. When she reached the fence, the other parents in the stands broke out in polite applause, backing her for whatever she said to get Van Kuffler to shut his big mouth.

Brock looked at Coach Van Kuffler's red face. His hands held the play sheet like a squirrel holds a nut, but he wasn't looking at Brock. His face was twisted and oozing hate. His eyes were distant, like he was looking at the clouds.

"Frank?" Coach Hewitt spoke softly and reached for the play sheet. "Maybe I should. Then no one can say . . ."

Coach Van Kuffler's face came to life. He snarled at Coach Hewitt and snatched the play sheet back. "*I'll* call this game. *I'm* the offensive coordinator! But you're gonna give me a quarterback I can work with, Buzz, not this *new kid*."

Coach Hewitt shook his head like a shaggy dog. He stiff-armed Coach Van Kuffler and snatched the play sheet from his hands. "No, Frank. Brock's the quarterback. Look, I can call the plays."

"Oh, really?" Van Kuffler wore a mean smile. "Maybe I should just go sit down and watch you and this kid kill our season. How about that?"

Coach Hewitt sighed. "Fine, Frank. Do that. Have a seat."

"Are you serious?" Van Kuffler screwed his face up tight. "You do this to me and I'm *finished*. Got that? I'm done coaching, Buzz."

Coach Hewitt sighed. "Yeah, I guess you are finished, Frank. And, I gotta say, it already feels so good to have you gone."

Van Kuffler whipped around and stormed through the bench area, then straight through the opening in the middle of the bleachers, heading for the parking lot.

Coach Hewitt turned to Taylor. "Taylor, give me a hand here, will you? I think you know this offense better than Coach Spada."

Taylor smiled and nodded. "Happy to help, Coach."

Coach Hewitt turned to Brock. "Okay, kid, this is it."

The sight of Taylor Owen Lehman signaling in the plays cooled the blood running through Brock's veins. It didn't slow the blood, but Brock took a deep breath and felt the peace of knowing someone important was on his side. The signals came quick and correct. The plays made sense, and even Brock could see the pattern emerging where the offense would try one thing and keep doing it until the defense stopped it, then attack another area of the field left unguarded by the defense's focus on the prior plays.

It all worked. Brock moved the offense up and down the field. He threw two touchdown passes, pumping his fist and jumping up and down after each one. Taylor almost knocked him over both times when he returned to the sideline. Brady Calenzo ran two more in. The problem was that Groton's offense was even better and, with forty-seven seconds left to go in the game, Groton scored on a long pass to take a two-touchdown lead.

On the Calhoun sideline, heads hung low.

Those same hung heads all turned when Mak bellowed like a stuck bull, pounding his chest and wagging his head from side to side. When everyone was looking at him, Mak whipped off his helmet and glared around at them.

"We will NOT lose this game!" Mak's eyes blazed out at them from his sweat-drenched face. "Do you hear me? We will NOT lose! Now everybody pick his head up and let's go GET IT!"

Coach Hewitt stepped up. "Mak is right! Pick your heads up! We go score a quick touchdown, get an onside kick, and this is OURS! Bring it in! Calhoun pride! Pride on three . . . One, two, three . . ."

"PRIDE!"

Brock felt it too. Electric energy ran through them all. Brady Calenzo ran the kickoff back to the fifty. Calhoun fans cheered, gaining some life and hope.

Coach Hewitt grabbed Brock's face mask and pulled him close. "I want it right *now*. Spread Left Double 79. Pump fake right to draw off the safety, then look for Archangel on the left. We need this, Brock!"

Brock could only nod his head.

Taylor slapped his shoulder pad. "Just like the backyard. Throwing at a target, buddy. You got the arm. You can do this."

Brock dashed out onto the field with his teammates, called the play, broke the huddle, and jogged to the line. The butterflies were back. They'd been gone for the past two quarters of the game, but here they were again.

He took the snap, dropped back, pump-faked right, then reset his feet and fired downfield.

Xaviar Archangel reached out, stretching, but never stopped running. He caught the ball and ran into the end zone.

Calhoun's sideline and fans went crazy.

Brock's teammates swarmed him, but the celebration was short-lived. They kicked the extra point, a wobbly side-winding thing. It struck the goalpost, bounced up into the air, and fell just inside the upright.

The team gathered around Coach Hewitt. "Okay. Onside kick. We've never done it, but we've practiced it. Eli?"

Everyone turned their attention to Eli Cash, their kicker, who was a redhead with pale skin and freckles. Eli nodded his head, but grabbed his stomach and gagged before a jet of puke shot from his face mask like somebody had broken a water balloon.

Coach Hewitt looked down at his sneakers and the orange

spots of vomit, then back up at Eli. "Better?"

Eli nodded that he was.

"Can you do this?"

Eli gagged a little, then nodded again.

"Well . . ." Coach Hewitt scratched his head and looked at Coach Delaney, who shrugged. "We got nothing else. Give it your best, guys. Let's go!"

The kickoff team bolted out onto the field and set up in onside kick formation, overloading the ten players besides Eli into a clump next to the Calhoun sideline.

"Get some topspin on it!" Coach Delaney shouted at Eli.

Eli raised his hand, took two steps, and puked again.

The crowd groaned.

The ref jogged toward Eli, but Eli waved him off and held his hand up again to start the sequence of the onside kick. This time he took five steps and kicked it. The ball skittered toward the sideline before its tip suddenly caught the turf sending it twenty feet in the air.

A Groton player got directly under it and prepared to make the catch, hang on, and end the game.

The Calhoun players swarmed toward him like killer bees.

89

Instead of falling on the ball, the Groton player clutched it tight and tried to run. It wasn't smart, but Brock could see the panic in the kid's eyes. Brady Colenza hit the ball with his shoulder and the Groton kid exploded. Arms, legs, and the ball flew up into the air. Players from both teams piled onto the spot where the ball hit the ground. The refs blew their whistles and peeled players off the pile, one by one. When there were just three left—two Groton players and Eli Cash—the head referee got down on his hands and knees and looked into the tangle of limbs, jumped up, and chopped his hand toward the Groton end zone, signaling a Calhoun first down. Eli popped up with the ball held high.

The Calhoun sideline went wild again, as did the Calhoun fans, but Brock felt a fog of calm. Even Mak, screaming into Brock's face with his red cheeks ready to burst, didn't get Brock flustered. He looked at the scoreboard. The clock read thirty-three seconds. Coach Hewitt and Taylor sandwiched him.

"Thirty-three seconds," Coach Hewitt said.

"Four plays, maybe five if we get a first down," Taylor replied.

"What do you think?" Coach Hewitt asked. "All at once, or work it down the field?"

Taylor looked at Brock and bit his lip. "He's never run a two-minute drill in his life, but with his arm, he can almost reach the end zone. I'd take four long shots. He'll hit one of them. I know it. Then, gosh, Brady can run it in, or we throw a play-action pass. We've got one time-out, so we can stop the clock."

Even though he was calm, Taylor's confident tone alarmed Brock. He didn't feel that kind of unwavering confidence, but he didn't have time to think about it much at all. The offense was charging onto the field, led by Mak who leaped like a ballet dancer, spinning as he jumped and slapping everyone's helmet, urging their finest effort.

Brock listened to the play and ran in. His voice quavered in the huddle, but no one seemed to notice. The look on his teammates' faces said his arm was what kept them in the game. He could see they believed his arm could also win it. They broke the huddle with a loud clap and jogged to the line. Brock took the snap from five yards deep, but before he could even look downfield, a defender appeared from nowhere and hit him square in the face. Brock saw stars on the hit and another burst when he struck the ground.

Mak was beside him quickly, shoving the defender off and

raising Brock to his feet. "It wasn't me, buddy. They sent *two* guys off the edge."

"Two?" Brock thought that wasn't possible. His head was foggy, but shouts from the sideline drew his attention toward Coach Hewitt and Taylor. They both waved their arms frantically. They were pointing, but pointing everywhere, at the scoreboard, at the defense, at him, at their wrists. Brock walked toward them.

They waved him back, still shouting. Brock had no idea what was going on.

Brock knew he was missing something, and he knew it was costing them the game.

Coach Hewitt threw his hands up in the air, then made them into a T and directed his shouting at the referee. The ref blew his whistle and made an X with his arms that signaled a time-out, stopping the clock. Coach Hewitt motioned for Brock to now come to the sideline, along with the rest of the offense. Brock jogged over, knowing that he'd done something very wrong, but unable to sort it out. His head was swimming in a fog and time slowed to a crawl until he saw a face in the crowd, shining out at him like the sun.

Next to Laurel's mom against the fence stood Brock's dad, and next to him was Brock's mom. She wore a look so full of intensity and so full of love that he *felt* it. While everyone in the crowd wanted him to win, he somehow knew *she* didn't care. She only cared about *him*, and he realized he had a *mom*, and that this was *home*, a place they'd all live in *together*, whether he won the game or didn't, whether he was first team or not.

Brock beamed at her. She smiled back, gave him a thumbs-up, and blew him a kiss that knocked him back into reality. Time sped up again and he realized the coaches were talking at him.

"The *clock*." Coach Hewitt shook his head.

Taylor pointed at the scoreboard. "When you get sacked, the clock keeps running. We wanted you to run the next play and save our time-out."

Brock looked and saw that now the clock read eight seconds. He thought of the Groton player who mindlessly ran the ball on the onside kick instead of just falling on it, and Brock slapped his own helmet. "Stupid."

"Hey." Taylor shook his head. "Don't do that. It's over. You've never done this before. We're okay. We've got two plays left if we do it right, if the receiver can get out of bounds. Focus on that."

"Mak said two guys came. One of them hit me." Brock rubbed the back of his neck and found Mak among the rest of his teammates crowded around the coaches. "What did you mean?"

Coach Delaney appeared with a whiteboard and knelt down with it to show him a series of Xs and Os. He used a marker to circle one of the Xs, then drew a line with an arrow from that X straight to the quarterback. "They're playing a Man-3 Prevent, but they blitzed the safety off the slot. They left the slot uncovered underneath. I'm sure they'll do it again, but not with the same guy."

"Which one?" Brock asked.

"He has to see it," Coach Hewitt said, glancing at Taylor.

Taylor bit his lip and gripped his forehead, thinking, before he looked at Brock. "You said you're a pitcher, right?"

"That's baseball." Brock was really confused now.

"Yeah, but when you look at the batter, what else do you have to see?" Taylor asked.

"Well, if there's a runner on first, I gotta see him too in case he steals."

"Right!" Taylor slapped Brock's shoulder pad, then knelt beside Coach Delaney, taking the marker and looking up at him. "That's what this is. You look downfield at the free safety, deep in the middle, but you've got to *see* the whole field. They're gonna send one of these four guys."

Taylor quickly circled the four defensive backs opposite the offense's four wide receivers spread across the line. "You don't know which one, but whichever one they send, that's where you gotta throw it. The receiver will be wide open. Let's hope it's Xaviar."

"So what's the play?" Brock asked.

"Spread Right Alaska 99 Peel." Taylor looked at Coach Hewitt, who nodded in agreement, then around at the receivers. "You guys, if the man covering you blitzes Brock, you gotta stop and turn and look for the ball, that's the peel. Brock'll hit you. The rest of you gotta run downfield as fast as you can to draw off the 3 Deep Zone. Don't stop until you hit the back of the end zone, and keep your eyes open because you never know. Linemen, when Brock throws the ball, you get downfield and block. This'll only work once. Whoever catches the ball, get to the sideline if you don't have an opening for the end zone. If you can't score, you have to get out of bounds to stop the clock so we'll have the chance to run another play."

"Let's go, Coach!" The ref barged into their crowd, tapping his watch.

Taylor grabbed Brock's face mask and tilted it so that Brock's eyes were aimed at his. "The one thing you *can't* do is hold the ball."

Brock didn't even know what he meant and his face twisted with confusion.

Taylor huffed impatiently. "The clock. Eight seconds. You gotta throw the ball quick. If you do, we can get off another play. If you hold it, you'll burn up all the time and the game will be over. You can do this, Brock. Now go!"

Taylor shoved him toward the field and slapped him on the back. Brock jogged out with his teammates. They got in the huddle, and Brock called the Spread Left Alaska 99 Peel. He wanted to remind the receivers to run to the end zone. He wanted to tell them that whoever's man came on the blitz to be sure to peel off the route and stop. But he was too busy going over it in his own mind and nothing came out of his mouth.

Brock staggered toward the line of scrimmage. His teammates got set in their positions all along the line. The defense was just what Coach Delaney had drawn for him on the board. Four linemen to rush the passer, four defensive backs pressed up tight on the wide receivers in man-to-man coverage, and a 3 Deep Zone behind them. He took a gulp of air and started the cadence, directing his eyes down the middle of the field at the free safety, but trying to *see* the whole field, knowing one of the front four defensive backs would come full speed at him, unblocked.

He took the snap and dropped back. The defensive back came free, this time from the right instead of the left, Brock's blind side, but because of Taylor's warning, he saw it. Brock flipped his hips to the right and snapped his arm back to throw. The defender was nearly at him, head down, a blazing bullet, but the receiver didn't stop and turn for the ball. He forgot to peel!

If Brock was sacked, the game was over.

Taylor's words flashed in his mind: "You can't hold the ball."

He couldn't hold it, but he couldn't throw it. It was like everything else in Calhoun since the day he arrived. Nothing fit quite right. Nothing worked the way it was supposed to.

He froze.

And the defender smashed into him.

Brock didn't exactly fly through the air, but he was propelled backward so fast his feet lost contact with the ground. If Mak wasn't there, wrestling with the defensive end like a dancing bear, he would have crashed to the turf.

But Mak was there, and Brock rebounded off him and pumped his legs. The defender hit him so hard and so fast that he hadn't been able to wrap his arms around Brock's body. Brock sprang loose from his tackler and took off to his right before he saw the defensive end break free in front of him. Brock spun back, running to his left, and around Mak, who now had his man planted in the turf. The open space let him dash nearly ten yards ahead before he stopped short of the line of scrimmage to keep his pass legal.

Brock knew precious seconds had ticked off the clock and he heard Taylor's words again, but something else told him not to throw it. Something told him this was his last chance, and he had to make it good. He knew Xaviar was in the left slot, and he saw him way down the field just left of the middle, nearing the end zone. The free safety had positioned himself halfway between Xaviar and the slot receiver on the right, both of them running full speed and straight.

In that moment, Brock thought about baseball again. When you wanted to move a leading runner back on the base, you faked like you were going to throw. That's how you moved people in sports, with a fake. Brock faked a throw to the receiver on the right. The free safety fell for it, darting that way and separating himself from Xaviar.

Brock reset his feet and fired the ball with all his might. Xaviar saw it, and kept running. The ball flew up and away, arcing down toward the end zone, spinning in a blur, and dropping fast. Xaviar stretched out his arms.

Brock clenched his teeth.

92

The ball stuck.

Xaviar pulled it in, cradling it, hugging it, loving it, before he held it over his head and spun around, jumping up and down. Whistles blew. The crowd went wild. The Calhoun players went wild.

Brock fell to his knees and looked up at the sky just as Mak and some teammates bowled him over, slapping his helmet while others reached through the pile of bodies to touch him. As they laughed and hooted and cheered, Brock struggled to his feet. Mak hugged him, laughing and crying at the same time and spun him around, yelling something Brock couldn't understand through the mouthpiece Mak had forgotten to remove. Mak kept spinning until Brock was dizzy, but he couldn't miss the people closest to him against the fence.

Laurel and her mom, and next to them Brock's own mom

and dad. Taylor stood with them now, inside the fence. Brock grinned and waved at them all before struggling to free himself from Mak.

"Put me down, Mak. Mak! What are you saying? I can't even understand you."

Mak put him down and pulled the mouthpiece free from his lips, yanking it like a bath drain, spit flying everywhere. He huffed and grinned and his eyes twinkled in the red dough of his face. "First team! That's what I was saying, bro. You and me. Forever. First team!"

Turn the page to check out
the first three chapters of

KID OWNER,

a brand-new football book from Tim Green!

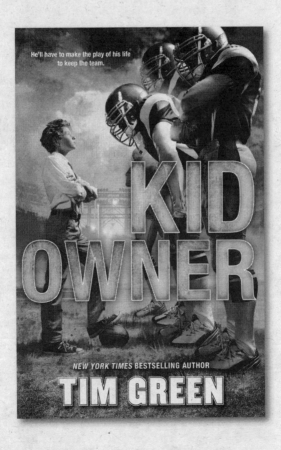

PRESENT . . .

It's not easy to be different.

They say everything is bigger in Texas, and for the most part I'd agree. Everything around me is as big as my state: our home, the truck my mom drives, the football program in our town, even my best friend—all big. That's why being known as the little guy is tough. I'm scrappy, though, and I play football like so many other kids, whether they're really made for it or not. At the end of practice the day my life took a wicked turn, the big Texas sky opened up so that we ran our sprints through a cascade of water falling from above. In August, even the rain can't deliver you from the heat, so when I got home I needed a shower pretty badly. I dried off and had dinner with my mom. Afterward, I sat in my favorite chair in the living room with *The Chocolate War*, a book our English teacher had given us for summer reading to prepare for our first assignment as seventh graders.

I was pretty well into the book and liking it when I heard the tune of my mom's phone ringing in the kitchen, where she sat at her computer, and I sensed the distress in her voice after she answered it. I let the book fall into my lap as I listened in with no idea what had happened, only knowing that whatever it was, it wasn't good. I heard her say thank you and good-bye and then her footsteps coming my way. I put my nose back into my book until she cleared her throat.

"Hi," I said, looking up. "What's going on?"

She crossed the room, weaving in and out of the dark wood and leather furniture, and took my hand. The sun had gone down, leaving a pitch-black sky. Lightning flashed in the big picture window and a rumble of thunder shook the house before she spoke. "Ryan, your father passed away."

I blinked up at her, speechless.

"I—I just thought you should know." She squeezed my hand and walked away without another word.

I didn't know what to do, or say, so I looked down at my book again and read a couple sentences before realizing I had no idea what they had said. I let the book drop again into my lap, thinking about the power of words. Two words, actually: *father* and *football*.

YEARS EARLIER . . .

These two harmless words were never spoken in my house while I was growing up.

They were the F-words. That's what my mother called them.

The father thing I understood. Everyone had one except me, so even *I* didn't like to talk about that. I remember a few years ago, when I was really little, we had to draw a picture of our family in kindergarten. I'd drawn Julian off to the side so people might *think* he was my father. He and his wife, Teresa, work for us and live in our guesthouse. When my mom had seen the red Texas Rangers hat on the stick figure of a man, she'd known it was Julian, but my teacher and classmates thought it was my dad. I couldn't have really drawn my father because I'd never met him, never seen a picture of him, and knew nothing about him.

By the time I was eight years old, though, the idea of my dad had grown into something much bigger than a stick figure. I knew he was out there, somewhere. And I felt I would someday meet him, so I wanted to be worthy. My plan was to become the most important and awesome kind of person there was: an NFL football player. And I'd planned on being a quarterback. I was small—I knew that. But there were other small NFL quarterbacks, and their lack of size only made them that much more special. My father would be amazed.

I'd dreamed of one day inviting him to a Ben Sauer Middle School game. Maybe we'd be playing Eiland, our toughest rival. After a glorious win, he would wait for me outside the locker room along with the families of my teammates. I'd come out, totally exhausted from several touchdown runs. My father would see me and his eyes would grow wet. He would ache for the times he missed with me growing up. He would wish with all his heart that the two of us could now become even closer, to make up for lost time.

I would smile warmly and keep my cool, because I didn't really know the man. I grew up keeping an emotional distance from the thought of my dad mostly because I suspected he had done something wrong to my mom. Why else would he have run off? Why else would my mom avoid talking about him altogether? Why else would *father* be an F-word?

Football being an F-word was another story. I didn't get that one.

In Texas, football is a religion, but it wasn't in my house. My mom didn't like it, and that's putting it mildly.

"Too much violence," she'd say.

I mean, I was small and fast like my mom, so I understood why she pushed me to play soccer, but why couldn't we *talk* about football? *Football* being the other F-word didn't keep me from being a closet Dallas Cowboys fan, though. I'd sneak away and watch their games at other people's houses. I'd watch reruns of local sports shows featuring Cowboys players and coaches on my iPad. I even hid a box of playing cards in the garage inside a spare tire under a tarp in a far corner.

I was okay keeping my love of the game a secret because my mother and I had made a deal. If I played soccer for three years and really tried, she'd let me play football when I was older.

"How old?" I'd asked.

"Third grade." She threw that number out there probably because it seemed so far away at the time. I know it did to me.

I took those words and planted them in my heart. And they grew fast and big like the seeds of a tree. So by the time I was eight, they were as large as the monster oaks in our front yard. I never considered my mom might not know they were there.

Who in Texas *didn't* dream of being a football player?

I don't mean to knock soccer. I loved the game, and I was pretty good. But when I was at school, I couldn't get through lunch without hearing about football. So, it was lunch that killed soccer for me.

Every fall in elementary school, week after week, all the guys in my neighborhood would sit at the lunch table and talk about the Highland Knights youth football game coming up on Sunday morning. They'd be playing Carrollton or Grand Prairie or North Haven Park, and they made every week sound like it was going to be as important and monumental as World War III.

The only other kid who'd played soccer with me was Melvin Patterson. At first, we'd try to talk about our games, cramming our mouths with ham and cheese sandwiches, slurping our milk through straws. But it was never as exciting. Even our rivals sounded lame: the Innwood Spitfires or the Royal Creek Robins. So we'd sit with our heads bent low over Premier League football trading cards, uttering names like Yaya, Suárez, Messi, and Rooney, but all the while secretly listening to talk of trap blocks, go routes, reverses, and safety blitzes.

Then, in the beginning of August, during the summer between second and third grade, the day finally came: sign-ups for Premier Youth Football League, the finest football in Texas. The chatter about PYFL between my future teammates had begun months before, at the end of second grade.

It became clear to me that I'd have to cut Melvin loose and save myself. Melvin's dad would never let him play football.

That summer I'd started asking my mom to invite the guys from my class over for swimming. I may know kids with an even bigger house than ours, but I'd never heard anyone say we don't have the best pool. We have this waterworks thing in the shallow end with sprayers and hoses and a big plastic alligator that spits water. There are these gears you can crank around to change which spouts spurted, dribbled, or sprayed in crazy zigzag liquid ropes. And in the deep end is a fifteen-foot curlicue slide along with a high dive.

That summer, I'd drop hints about maybe playing football. By the time all the moms had started buying new shoes and lunch boxes, I had myself slated as a key player for the Highland Knights.

All the kids and I pretty much knew the entire roster and who would likely play where. Mr. Simpkin, Jason Simpkin's dad, who used to play for SMU, was our coach.

One night, when all the guys were having a sleepover at Jason's house, his father was in the backyard tossing a football around with us. Kids were racing each other to show their coach how fast they'd become. Jason's dad watched with interest and when I'd suggested that I race Jason—who had beaten everyone else—his father had smiled at the joke and said, "Sure. Let me see you and Jason go at it."

Jason was a cobra, lean and strong with poison in his mouth and eyes dead as glass. He had looked at me and snorted, and the gang all stopped and stared. No one challenged Jason Simpkin and won.

We crouched low and took off together.

Mr. Simpkin had nodded wisely and chuckled after I beat Jason to the swing set by two strides. "Well, you're small, but with that kind of speed, I could see you making a heck of a third-down slot receiver."

I grinned. Talk about heaven. I lay awake that entire night, staring up at the fluttering roof of the camp tent in Jason's backyard beyond the pool, dreaming of third-down plays where I'd streak into the open and make a spectacular grab. Thinking if my dad could've seen me, he'd have been so proud.

I didn't keep my mom up to speed on any of this. I probably should have told her that I was going to hang up the soccer cleats forever. But *football* was an F-word.

So I'd waited until sign-ups were being held at Williamson Elementary before I told my mom about my dream, and that we needed to go down there with my birth certificate and a check for $795.

I had planned to tell her in the car ride home from day camp at the country club, but the knot in my stomach said to wait. Then, during dinner, when Teresa was serving veal cutlets—one of my mother's favorites—as soon as we'd said grace, my mother cleared her throat and asked, "Is everything okay, Ryan?"

That had flustered me. My mom is a pretty woman, but she has these eyes that can burn into you like the desert sun through a bug glass, and that's scary. I nodded and mumbled that I was fine and quickly cut loose a hunk of veal, stuffing it into my mouth. Every swallowed bite was an opportunity to bring up football, but my tongue stayed tied.

Finally, Teresa cleared the dishes and my mom took a deep breath and a sip of iced tea and asked me what I had planned for the evening.

And then, it was go time. Sign-ups only went until 7:30, and it was already 6:53.

"Mom . . ." Her look—just a simple smile—terrified me, because I knew how quickly it could change, like a summer thunderstorm blowing up out of the desert.

"Now are you going to tell me what's wrong?" Her smile went sideways and she took another sip from her glass before tilting her head to wait.

"We have to go to my school." My words were barely a whisper.

She scowled. "Why? What's wrong?"

"For sign-ups." I still couldn't *say* football.

"Sign-ups?"

I stood up from my place. "We have to go now, Mom. It only goes until 7:30. And you need to bring a check."

"A check for what? Hey, mister." Her stern tone stopped me cold. "What's going on?"

"And my birth certificate." My eyes started to well up and I sniffed and looked at my sneakers. "Football sign-ups, Mom. Everyone's doing it. The Highland Knights. I'm gonna play this year. Remember our deal?"

I looked up at her with as much confidence as I could muster, knowing that the deal she'd cut with me three years ago might be something she'd forgotten completely. That's how adults are—they never remember the details like that.

"Football?" She'd practically snorted the word. "Ryan, what are you talking about? You're a soccer player. We've talked about this. Football isn't part of who we are. End of discussion."

I'm a pretty good kid. I know it's me saying it about myself, but other people—teachers, parents—think so, too.

And I don't get into trouble. That's because I stay inside the lines—almost always. But I have a flaw: sometimes, I blow my stack. I flat-out lose it. I can't tell you why, but sometimes it's a little thing that triggers it while big things just float on by and I stay cool. And sometimes, *ba-boom.*

And when my mom called me a soccer player, I lost it and grabbed my water glass and slammed it so hard onto the kitchen table that it shattered. I barely noticed the shards of glass on my hand when I screamed, *"I hate when you do this! You said I could! Don't lie!"*

My mother is small but tough, and she was up out of her chair in a blink. She had me off my feet, lifting me by the collar and marching me down the hall and up the stairs before tossing me onto my bed. She stopped at the door on her way out to point a finger. "You don't call your mother a *liar*. Who do you think you are, young man!"

She turned and slammed the door before I could speak, partly from surprise, but mostly from having been choked by the collar-carry.

"LIAR!" I screamed in defiance.

The word hung in the air like an exploded bomb of silence. From all the way downstairs in the kitchen I could hear the tinkle of glass as Teresa swept up the broken pieces. Then the rumble

10

of my mother's footsteps filled the hallway, coming closer by the instant, so that when the door flew open and smashed into the wall, I was ready for it.

"Who do you think you *are*? You're acting so disrespectful!"

"You *said* third grade! I played that hot-poop sport for *three years* because you said I *had* to. You said if I played soccer and I still wanted to play football that I *could*. *That's* what *you said!*"

"This is coming out of nowhere, Ryan! You don't just drop something like this on me! Maybe, *maybe*, if you'd talked to me about this earlier, I could have *considered it*! Not now, though, mister. *NO WAY! NO HOW!* You are *not* playing football!" She slammed the door shut again. It was meant to be final.

I jumped up off my bed, fired my Lionel Messi bobblehead at the door, smashing it and putting a divot in the wood to punctuate what I was about to say.

"THEN LET ME GO LIVE WITH MY FATHER!"

ALSO FROM
TIM GREEN

BE SURE TO CATCH ALL OF THE BASEBALL GREAT NOVELS

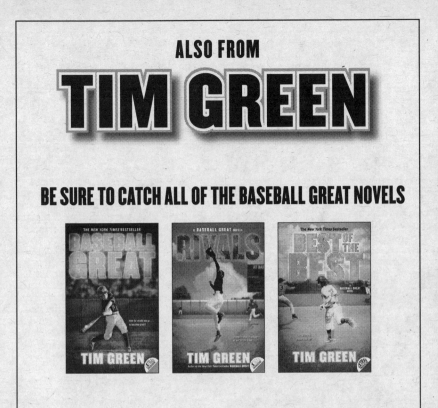

PLUS TIM GREEN'S OTHER HOME-RUN HITS

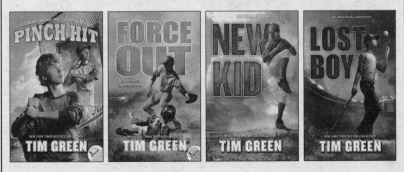

HARPER
An Imprint of HarperCollinsPublishers

www.timgreenbooks.com